OFFICER'S NURSE

An utterly spellbinding uplifting historical saga

MERRYN ALLINGHAM

Daisy Driscoll Sagas Book 2

Originally published as *The Nurse's War*

JOFFE BOOKS

Revised edition 2024
Joffe Books, London
www.joffebooks.com

First published in Great Britain by MIRA Books
in 2015 as *The Nurse's War*

This paperback edition was first published
in Great Britain in 2024

Cover art by Jarmila Takač
Cover figure by Richard Jenkins Photography

ISBN: 978-1-83526-473-7

The past is the present, isn't it? It's the future too.

Eugene O'Neill, *Long Day's Journey into Night.*

CHAPTER ONE

London, early April 1941

The footsteps were growing louder. Or, at least, more distinct in the darkness. Very gradually the sounds of night had fallen away and Daisy had become conscious of the man's step. She was in no doubt that it *was* a man. He had an uneven tread, as though he were limping. No, not limping, she thought, but walking uncertainly, as though he feared to give himself away. She had no idea how long he'd been following her, since it wasn't until she was passing Middle Street that she'd become aware of him.

It had been a long and exhausting day and she was almost asleep on her feet. The night shift had come on duty at six as usual, but the wards were full to capacity and she had volunteered to stay on. It had meant returning to the Nurses' Home alone, through the black pall that nightly covered the city.

At first, the blackout had come as a severe shock. In an instant the familiar had been transformed into the frighteningly unfamiliar. But after a while, like most people, Daisy had adapted. Now, with only the slightest trace of moon to light her way, she was confident enough to walk almost blind through murky streets and around dim corners. Until, that is, she'd heard the footsteps. They were there still: left, shuffle, right, shuffle. She felt her shoulders grow tight at the sound and scolded herself for her timidity. They were in the middle of a war and she was falling into panic over a man's footfall. After all, he'd made no attempt to overtake her; in all likelihood he was an innocent, lost in a maze of unrecognisable streets and trying only to battle his way home.

For several minutes she was comforted. But then a thought struck, unbidden and unwelcome. For a stranger to lose his way in these streets would be extremely unusual. The only men she ever encountered at this time of night were there for a purpose. Patrolling wardens with their constant refrain of *Put out that light,* members of the Home Guard who would flash her a greeting with their torches when they caught sight of the nurse's uniform. This man was alone and, surely, it wasn't her imagination that he walked stealthily. Whatever his intentions, she doubted they were benign. The blackout had brought its own troubles and not everyone was doing their bit for King and country.

Out of the darkness a freshness filled the evening air, the freshness of new grass. She must be approaching Charterhouse Square and sent up a prayer of thanks. She was nearly home. In her eagerness to reach safety, she quickened her pace again. The clouds momentarily cleared and, through the trees, she glimpsed the outline of the Nurses' Home, its pointed gables floating against the night sky and its large oak door standing sturdily on guard, a portcullis resisting all invaders.

She was crossing the square now, fumbling in her bag; she must have her key ready for the minute she reached the door. But the man had increased his pace, too, and Daisy was having almost to run to stay ahead. She fled across the grass, ducking between branches, brushing her way past newly budding leaves. By the time she reached the road on the far side, her heartbeat was drumming in her ears and her breath coming short. Speeding across the last few yards of pavement, she slowed herself as she reached the iron railings, then quickly up the whitewashed steps, the key clenched in a hand that she couldn't quite keep steady.

The moon had once more disappeared behind a blanket of cloud and she was forced to feel for the lock. Let me get it right, let me get it right, her mind repeated frantically. The key slotted into the lock and she felt the breath escaping from her body in a sigh of relief. Then, without warning, a hand emerged from the blackness and wrestled the key from her hand. It fell uselessly to the ground but, when she opened her mouth to scream for help, another hand clamped itself to her mouth and stifled the cry.

'Daisy. It's me.' The words hissed through the air.

Her attacker had said her name. But how? And whose was the voice?

'You're perfectly safe, but you mustn't scream. If I take my hand away, promise you won't.'

It could not be. It could not. She was hallucinating. He was dead. She'd seen with her own eyes his fall into the swollen river. He was dead, he was dead.

'Promise you won't make a sound,' the man repeated. 'Nod your head.'

It had to be his voice or it was that of his ghost. And Daisy didn't believe in ghosts. Dumbly she gave a nod and the hands released their hold. She stood not daring to move, her limbs immobile, but her chest rising and falling in rapid motion. The figure beside her was searching for something. Then, the sound of a match being struck, and a small, solitary light flared for an instant. It was sufficient.

She had not been hallucinating. The face had changed — the skin was weathered, the face bones gaunt, but it was him. It was Gerald. He had not died in that Indian river. For a moment, she was overcome with a sudden nausea as the old guilt broke free of its moorings.

Somehow she managed to find her voice, hoarse and hardly recognisable. 'Is it really you? I don't understand.' How ridiculous that sounded. The understatement of all time.

The memory was so vivid that every one of her senses added a layer to the image. She could still hear the shouts of her captors, feel the hot rain soaking her dress, see the raging waters closing on her husband's head. How then could he be here? At one violent stroke, the past she had tamed had broken its bonds and was showering her with its fragments. She began to shake uncontrollably and was forced to lean against the massive oak door for support.

'It's me all right.'

'But how . . . ?' The question was dredged out of her.

'I escaped, that's how. Pure luck.'

'But how?'

'My shirt snagged on one of those damned festival floats — would you believe? But it stopped me from going under. I was pulled down the river for miles — you know how fierce the water was. Then the float got pushed into the bank and lodged there.'

'And you weren't injured?'

'A broken arm, that's all, and it mended pretty quickly. People came from the village to see what had drifted their way and found me instead of the goddess they'd expected. They looked after me until I was fit to leave.'

Standing silently, she tried to absorb his words. 'You had an astonishing escape.'

How trite she sounded, but in the face of such extraordinary fortune, what more was there to say? Except there was more. The shock was slowly receding and the questions had begun.

'Once you were well, though, once your arm had mended, why didn't you go back to Jasirapur?' Why didn't you face the crime you committed, her inner voice accused. 'And the — the incident — happened well over a year ago. Where have you been since then? And how did you find me?'

The moon was still in hiding and she couldn't see his face, but she could imagine the irritated expression it wore. Her questions had always annoyed him. He left most of them dangling in the air, choosing only to answer the last.

'I used my head, Daisy, that's how. I didn't know if you were in London, but I thought it was likely. Thought it worth looking for you here.'

What he really meant, she thought, was that he hadn't known whether she was alive or dead, but that was something he wasn't going to say.

'If you'd returned to London,' he continued smoothly, 'it was possible you'd gone back to Bridges to work. So, I called at their perfume counter. You weren't there, but I had another piece of good fortune. One of the girls you used to work with had seen you. Quite recently, too. Her sister had been a patient in St Barts for a while and, when this girl visited, she was sure she'd seen you there. She said you were wearing a nurse's uniform. So . . . I've been hanging around the hospital for days, hoping to catch you. But no sign. I thought my luck must have run out at last. When I saw you leave tonight, I'd almost given up.'

'I'm not always at St Barts. Sometimes I have to travel to Hill End. It's in the countryside, near St Albans. Patients are evacuated there as soon as they're stable enough.' She felt stupid — why was she bothering to explain? 'But what girl at Bridges? And where are you living?'

A chilly breeze had sprung out of nowhere, snaking around the corners of the square, and whipping up the edges of her cape. Across the grassed space, the leaves rustled angrily. For an instant, she felt a shadow pass across her vision and blinked in surprise. It made her shiver slightly. She was sure that Gerald had seen it, too, for he shifted uneasily from foot to foot, and his voice when he spoke held the barely contained impatience she had come to know so well.

'We can't talk now, but I need your help. We must meet — soon — but somewhere else.' He reached out and gripped her by the arm. It was such a fierce tug that she let out a small cry of pain.

He stepped back and his tone was conciliatory. 'I'm sorry. I didn't mean to hurt but I have to see you. Here—' and he pushed a piece of paper into her hand. 'Send your message to this address. It's a corner shop, one of those that sells just about everything. They've agreed to hold post for me.'

Even in her confused state, Daisy found herself pondering why he couldn't simply give her his address. It would be difficult for her to get to the shop, as nursing staff were allowed only a short break during their working day. But she was given no chance to refuse.

'Don't let me down, Daisy. Remember, you're still my wife,' he said.

It was almost a threat, at best emotional blackmail, and from a man who had wronged her dreadfully. She should tell him to go away and never return, leave her to whatever peace she'd found. But old loyalties were not so easily subdued.

'I'm not sure that I can help.' At the very least, she must dampen his hopes.

'You've got to. I've no one else. My parents are dead. The house they were living in is a pile of rubble, like most of the East End.'

Had what happened in India robbed him of his memory? Where was the story he'd been at pains to impress on her, that his parents had died years ago in the Somerset manor house that was their family home? Years ago, not now, not in wartime, and not in a miserable tenement in the poorest part of the city. But she wouldn't remind him of the lies he'd told. It was too complicated.

'I don't know how I can help,' she repeated. 'I've no money. I'm a nurse in training and my pay is barely sufficient to buy essentials. I live board free, here in the Nurses' Home.'

But he wasn't listening. His own tale, his own needs, were too urgent. He grabbed hold of her arm again. 'I'm a deserter, Daisy, that's what it's come down to. Do you understand what that means? I could be picked up at any time and locked up for years. Do you want to see me go to prison? I have to get away — to a neutral country where they can't touch me. I have to have papers and you're my only hope. Send me a message tomorrow with a time and meeting place.'

He turned to go and she was left standing helplessly on the threshold. At the bottom of the flight of steps, he turned to face her again. 'By the way, I'm not Gerald Mortimer any more — for obvious reasons. Send your message to Jack Minns. That's who I've become.'

And who you always were, she thought. But he had gone, stealing noiselessly into the soft thickness of the night. Bending down, she moved her hand over the stone step trying to locate the dropped key. At last, her fingers fastened around it and, with a shaking hand, she managed to slot the key back into the lock and let herself in.

CHAPTER TWO

The room Daisy occupied was small and bare, containing nothing more than a narrow bed, a chest of drawers and a desk which had also to serve as a dressing table. But it was her room and hers alone, and she was fortunate to have it — most of the student nurses were forced to share. The Home was always a noisy and boisterous place, reverberating with laughter, with chatter, with music from radios played too loudly. Tonight, someone at the end of the corridor was banging on the bathroom door in an effort to gain entrance, someone else was calling to her friend, asking to borrow a hairbrush, a girl two doors down was pleading for quiet to study. Daisy cherished the privacy of her room and, this evening, it was beyond the price of rubies.

The day had been disastrous. The buses had been late leaving for Hill End and thrown everything out of kilter, with patients still in beds they should have left hours before. And, then, a sudden influx of people suffering severe influenza had made the last few hours chaotic. Barts had been designated a casualty clearing station and most of the medical staff had been transferred to the country hospital. Daisy had felt honoured to be one of the small number who'd remained in London to deal with casualties and any medical emergencies. But honoured or not, it was gruelling work. For most of last year, London had endured constant bombing and she had seen some terrible injuries. Whole legs smashed, backs full of broken glass, crushed hands and feet. Injuries that required dedicated nursing alongside the unremitting duties of every student: making beds, emptying bedpans, sluicing foul linen, rolling bandages for the dressings trolley. It was a relentless round of physical labour. And tonight, just when she'd barely been able to keep herself upright from fatigue, this blow had fallen on her. An unbelievable blow.

Throwing her respirator into the corner of the room, she fell on the bed still fully dressed. She was tempted to sleep in her uniform, except she couldn't see how she was ever to sleep that night. Supper had been missed, but she hardly cared. A plate of stodgy carbohydrate was the last thing on her mind. She lay looking up at the ceiling, her eyes painfully sore, tracing every crack in the plaster, every smudge in the whitewash, round and round, up and down. Shock and disbelief rippled through her in great, unfettered waves. Guilt, too, swelled and foamed in their midst. There had always been guilt. Gerald had wronged her, but he had also given his life to save her.

Except that he hadn't. He had lived, and now he was on her doorstep asking for help. She was his wife, he'd said, and she had to aid him. That angered Daisy. She had been no wife in any sense of the word. Gerald had made sure of that. He hadn't wanted to marry, had accused her of forcing his hand, and she'd been made aware of his resentment almost every one of the days she had spent with him in India. The bungalow they'd shared had become a prison. Now, it suited him to remember there had been a marriage and that she owed him loyalty. But, even if she agreed and was willing to help, how on earth was she to do that? He hadn't listened, but Daisy had told the truth when she'd said that she had no money and no contacts. Nobody who could miraculously produce papers that would get him to another country.

She fixed her eyes on the ceiling, following again the cracks as they traced a snaking path from one side of the room to the other. Her mind was roaming to a dangerous place, to the one man who might know how to pull strings. But she would not think of Grayson. She had trained herself not to. She wasn't sure he could help or that he'd be willing to, and she certainly wasn't going to ask. Gerald was a deserter and Grayson would take a very dim view of that. In any case, her friendship with him was over, decidedly over. Six months ago, he'd taken his dismissal — almost gratefully, she'd thought — and moved on to a new love. No doubt he was already halfway to being married himself.

She uncurled the piece of paper Gerald had pushed into her hand. The address he'd written was a street she knew well, one deep in the East End and near her own birthplace. Near Gerald's birthplace, too, though he had never admitted it. Until tonight when he'd spoken of his parents. But that was a slip of the tongue, she was sure, brought on by the stress of the moment, and it wouldn't be repeated.

Clambering wearily off the bed, she removed her uniform, piece by piece. However distressed she felt, she had to get some sleep. The alarm was set for six o'clock and tomorrow would be another exhausting day. It was her turn again to accompany a group of patients to St Albans. From early in the morning, the converted ambulances would be waiting in convoy outside, ready to convey to safety those casualties well enough to travel. St Barts had received several direct hits and, though no one had yet been killed, the blasts had been severe enough to blow several nurses across their wards. In comparison, Hill House seemed a sanctuary.

* * *

Daisy had been asleep barely an hour when a hammering on the door woke her. The Home Sister, Mrs Phillips, was making her way along the corridor, shouting at the nurses to come down immediately. Through the blur of sleep, she heard the unmistakable sound of the siren and in the near distance the drone of planes and the roar of guns massing in unison. Another night raid, another night spent on mattresses in the basement. Daisy wondered why they'd ever complained about the phoney war. Until last May they'd been waiting for bombs that never came. If only that had continued.

Initially, there'd been a flurry of planning. A million burial forms had been issued, the Zoo had killed its venomous snakes, and London had been emptied of its children. And then the wait for something to happen. At the time, it had seemed endless but, when it was finally over, Daisy wondered why they'd wished for anything else. Fifty-seven nights of continuous bombing had reduced London to a state of siege. Then, out of the blue, the bombs had ceased. People had begun to relax. They'd lost their tired and haunted look, lost their red rimmed eyes which told of fear and sleepless nights. But it hadn't lasted and, a few weeks' ago, the bombardment had started anew and nerves were once more becoming stretched.

She staggered to her feet, wondering how big the raid was likely to be and whether or not she might make it back to bed that night. She had reached the door when a loud thump on the other side made her jump back.

'You clumsy idiot!'

It was the voice of Lydia Penrose and Daisy had a very good idea of the victim. She opened the door a fraction and saw Lydia picking herself up from the floor, her face an ugly red. A briefcase had disgorged its contents and books and papers lay scattered on the landing.

'I didn't push you,' Willa Jenkins was assuring her colleague. 'I think you must have caught your foot in the carpet. It's worn into a hole back there. Look.' And she pointed behind her to the staircase both girls had just run down.

'So you're saying it's me that's clumsy!' Lydia barred the way aggressively, standing with hands on jutting hips. 'That's pretty good coming from someone who breaks everything in sight. You can't have earned a penny since you've been here with all the stuff you've had to pay for.'

Willa stood her ground. 'I may have broken a syringe or two, but I didn't push you.'

'A syringe or two!' Lydia snorted. 'The factory can't keep up with you Jenkins, and I distinctly felt your fat little hands in the small of my back.'

For once Willa was proving obstinate. She shook her head, refusing to take the blame.

'I'm not arguing with rubbish like you,' Lydia flung at her. 'You can pick up everything you made me drop.'

When the girl made no move to comply, her tormentor came right up to her and shouted in her face, 'NOW!'

Even then, Willa didn't immediately do as she'd been ordered — Daisy could see her trying to summon the courage to resist. She knew that feeling. How many times in the orphanage had she tried to fight back and failed? And it was the same for Willa. The girl's shoulders sagged and she knelt down on the landing and obediently began to heave books and papers into the briefcase.

'Do it neatly,' Lydia almost screeched. 'In the right order. In the order I had them.'

'I don't know what that was,' the girl said miserably.

She was still picking up books when Sister Phillips' head appeared over the bannister. 'Get a move on nurses, the raid is almost on us. And that means you, too, Driscoll,' she scolded, catching sight of Daisy in the doorway.

'I'm coming, Sister.'

Mrs Phillips was not a woman you disobeyed lightly. She did her job dourly and any nurse who stepped out of line knew she would face a sarcasm that could wither. But tonight Daisy was willing to risk it.

When the senior nurse had disappeared down the stairs, followed by her two acolytes, she crept back into her room and shut the door behind her. Tonight, she could not bear to be in the company of her fellows, to share the basement's windowless prison, to lie and listen to the sniffs, the coughs, the fidgeting limbs of a score of bodies, while she longed for forgetfulness. She would stay above ground and hope to sleep once the bombers had passed.

That wasn't yet. The sound of approaching aircraft was growing louder. A mad cacophony of guns and bombs burst through the night and assailed the dark, empty streets. With care, Daisy lifted the corner of the blackout curtain and squinted through the small square she'd uncovered. She saw immediately that it was another big raid. The sky was laced with light: the beams of searchlight batteries, the stars from bursting shells. A rainbow of colours — green, red, yellow, white — tumbled one over another in endless profusion. Coloured tracers like giant strings of beads winged their way through the sky in search of planes which had no right to be there. Planes which brought death and destruction.

Whichever way she looked, from east to west, the night was aglow. Flashes from hundreds of incendiary bombs split the darkness and on the horizon dozens of fires burnt, as though they were giant open air furnaces. All around Charterhouse Square, the stone of old buildings was lit with a white glare. Wearily, Daisy let the curtain fall and climbed into bed. She would stay here and take her chances.

* * *

It was not until early afternoon that she climbed aboard one of the specially adapted Green Line buses travelling to Hill End. Last night's raid had wreaked enormous destruction and casualties had been pouring into the hospital from the moment she'd walked on to the ward at seven that morning. As civil defence teams continued to dig people from the rubble, a trickle became a stream and very quickly, a river. Medical staff had been working through the night and Daisy and her new shift were met by nurses and doctors near to collapse. Their official handover was brief; time was short and, above the jangle of ambulance bells and the sobs of hurt and shocked people, they could barely hear each other speak.

She was set to work immediately, bathing newly admitted casualties, a lengthy business since the wounded were covered from head to foot in brick dust and blood. The nurses worked tirelessly and at great speed, their aprons bloodstained, their young faces marked by weariness. There was no time to eat. A snatched slice of bread and dripping and a large mug of tea was all Daisy managed before the ward sister called her over.

'You should go, Driscoll. The escort party is waiting and we can spare you now. The ward is running well.' Sister Elton gave the glimmer of a smile. It was the nearest she would ever get to giving praise.

Daisy made her way down the two flights of stairs to the street. Her head was aching and her legs hardly felt her own, but there was no possibility of rest. There was always more work to do. A nurse helping to load patients into one of the makeshift ambulances, scrambled down to greet her.

'Where did you get to last night?' As she spoke, the girl tried unsuccessfully to tuck the straggling ends of her bright red hair into the starched cap.

'I'm sorry I missed you, Connie, but I worked on. Sister needed extra help and by the time I got back, I was too tired even to speak and went straight to bed. I didn't even make it to the basement.'

Connie Telford was her closest friend. Their rooms were next door to each other and, in the last few months, they'd often been rostered to work on the same ward. It was rare for them to miss an evening cocoa together, but Daisy had been too shocked last night to go in search of her friend and certainly in no mood to exchange confidences.

'I can't see us getting this lot settled before midnight.' Her friend gestured to the line of buses waiting to leave. 'Looks like we'll be drinking our cocoa in the small hours.'

Daisy smiled a little wanly. If only cocoa was her sole concern. Today had been so hectic that even the reappearance of Gerald in her life had been pushed from her mind. But now he'd returned and was looming large. Tonight, she would have to sleep at Hill End and would not return to London until the following morning. There would be no opportunity to send the message he'd demanded.

Perhaps if she didn't respond, he would go away and leave her in peace. If only he would. She could see he was in a dreadful predicament, but meeting him was pointless. All it would achieve was to bring back the terror and grief of those last days in Jasirapur. It already had, she thought angrily.

He demanded loyalty as his right, yet he'd explained nothing. How had he reached England, how travelled those thousands of miles alone and without money or support? His rescue by the villagers Daisy could just about understand, but even that was extraordinary — the power of the water had been immense. Had she not faced it herself, standing on that riverbank, ready for the blow that would send her to her death? It was Grayson who had arrived to rescue her, but too late to save her husband.

Yet, somehow Gerald *had* survived. Survived to be a deserter. He hadn't returned to his regiment in Jasirapur, hadn't confessed his wrongdoing. Instead, he'd gone into hiding. But he would be discovered sooner or later, that was certain, so why did he not give himself up and face just punishment? Running and hiding could only be done for so long. And it was cowardly. She, and everyone she knew, was working tirelessly for their country, fighting for its very existence. Should she really be helping a man — husband or not — to abandon his homeland and make a bolt to safety?

CHAPTER THREE

Today, the journey to Hill End seemed longer than ever and, once they'd arrived, there were hours of work ahead of them. For the rest of the day, while her hands bandaged, soothed, gave medicine and spooned food, Daisy's mind was elsewhere, circling the same questions but unable to find a solution. By ten o'clock that evening, the ward was calm and the night staff could be left to manage alone. The ward sister who had accompanied them from Barts shooed her nurses off to bed. At least, there was no Mrs Phillips here to monitor the food they were eating or check that bedroom lights were out by ten thirty.

Daisy usually enjoyed the break from the inflexible rules at St Barts. The challenge of nursing in London was a constant source of adrenaline that could buoy her on the most fatiguing of days but, at times, its iron conventions made her yearn for a less rigid regime. No chattering, no sitting on beds, no eating — not even a single precious sweet offered by a patient. And one's uniform had always to be immaculate: dress uncreased, pinafore starched, and without a single lock of hair escaping the small cap. It was no wonder that Connie was in perpetual trouble, fighting a losing battle with her tumble of long, red waves.

She came bustling up at that moment — their shift had finally come to an end — and grabbed Daisy's hand, dragging her into the sitting room used by the permanent staff at Hill End. A few nurses were lolling in one or two of the shabby chairs dotted around the room, or flicking idly through a pile of dog-eared magazines while they carried on a desultory conversation. Her friend steered her into the quietest corner.

'Now, Driscoll, what's up?' Hazy green eyes, wide with curiosity, fixed her to the spot.

'Nothing, nothing at all.' Daisy did her best to look unconcerned.

'That's rubbish. Something is definitely wrong. I've been watching you since we got here and you're not yourself. Now, tell me what's happened.'

Daisy reached up and unpinned her cap, shaking out the dark waves as though to free herself of constraint. She stabbed a hat pin through the starched white material. 'I can't,' she said at length. 'It's too complicated.'

'Don't I know that? Everything to do with you is complicated. Whereas me, I'm an open book.'

Connie's grin elicited a smile. Daisy could never feel downhearted when she was with her. The girl was chock-full of cheerful common sense and practical to her fingertips. She'd had to be, of course. As the eldest sibling in a crowded Dorset cottage, she'd borne the brunt of her mother's frequent pregnancies and her father's forbidding temper. Her sweet nature, though, had gone unvalued and, despite a large family, she appeared to be as lonely as Daisy. It was telling that she'd chosen not to train in Dorchester, but to move miles away to the big city. It was probably that solitariness, Daisy mused, that had drawn them together in the first place. But by now, they'd become the firmest of friends, confidantes in the daily struggle of nursing through a war.

'It's complicated because it doesn't just concern me,' Daisy said awkwardly.

'So who else? Who else does it concern? Who else do you know?'

Connie wasn't giving up, it seemed, and she longed to confide in her. It would be good to share the burden, but it would also be grossly unfair. Gerald had committed a crime and she must be careful not implicate Connie by confessing the trouble she was in.

She felt her hand squeezed and her friend's voice, low and encouraging. 'You know that whatever you tell me, I can keep my mouth shut. Who is worrying you so badly?'

Perhaps, if she said only a little? She'd already told Connie more than she'd ever thought possible, months ago abandoning her ingrained reserve to confide that she had once been married. Connie was the only one she'd ever told about Gerald.

She took a deep breath and met her friend's eyes. 'It's my husband.'

The girl's mouth fell open and it was a while before she could speak. 'But he's dead.'

'That's the problem. It turns out that he isn't. And he's managed to trace me — it doesn't matter how — but he followed me back to the Home last night. I think I'm still in shock.'

'But how *can* it be him?' Connie was floundering. 'You saw him drown.' The phrase was blunt and to the point. And it was true, she had seen him drown, or so she'd always believed.

'He didn't die. His clothes were caught up on one of the floats. You remember? — we were at a festival called Teej and there were all these stupendous floats carrying huge gods and goddesses launched into the river. I guess most of them were smashed to pieces when the monsoon broke — the river turned into this raging torrent — but there was enough left of one, apparently, for Gerald to catch hold of and survive. He was rescued further downstream.'

'And then?' Her companion edged forward.

'I have no idea. How he got to England is a mystery.'

Connie gave a soft whoop. 'That's quite a story. Romantic, too. Your husband has travelled thousands of miles to claim his wife! You told me things were bad between you before he died, but maybe this is a turning point.'

'Unlikely. He's come back because he has nowhere else to go. And he's come to me only because he needs help. But there's no way I can give it — and he won't believe me.'

Her friend wrinkled her forehead, the freckles almost joining each other in puzzlement. 'What kind of help does he want?'

She took some time to answer, weighing up how much she should say, how much she dare tell even a close friend. It would not make a good hearing and it might make a dangerous one. But Connie was right when she said she could keep her mouth shut. It was a quality that was necessary, Daisy guessed, living amid a large, raucous family.

'I've never said anything before,' she said slowly, 'but Gerald was involved in some wicked doings in India. He plunged into the river after trying to rescue me from a dangerous gang.' She saw Connie's bewildered expression. 'I told you it was complicated.'

'A dangerous gang? What on earth did you get yourself involved in?'

'I made a discovery that I shouldn't have. Something that could have hung every member of the gang. And they knew I knew, so I had to die.'

'My God, Daisy!'

'Gerald found the place they were holding me. He put up a fight and that messed up their plans — it gave the police sufficient time to get to me.'

'It might not be exactly romantic but—'

'He wasn't innocent,' Daisy said quickly. 'It was his association with the gang that put me in danger.' She wasn't going to mention the 'accidents' that Gerald had been happy to agree, accidents that had been meant to frighten her away but hadn't. 'In the end, he did the decent thing, I know.' She tried to sound grateful. 'And he paid a price for it. Not death, as it's turned out, but as good as, I guess.'

Connie's mind had not left the past. 'What happened to the gang?'

'They went to prison and they're still there, still believing that Gerald drowned. His regiment never knew the truth either. They assumed he'd died trying to rescue me — the army had no idea of the real situation, of what he'd done — and they still don't. Gerald never went back to Jasirapur once his injuries were mended. If he had, he'd have faced a court martial, after which the Indian Army would have turned him over to the civilian courts. Anish warned me he could face criminal charges as well as military disgrace.'

'I'm sorry for all these questions, but who is Anish?'

'It doesn't matter.' Daisy couldn't bring herself to talk about the man who had masterminded her downfall, yet for whom she was still grieving. 'The point is that Gerald is a deserter who wants my help, and I don't know what to do.'

Connie shook her head. 'You can't turn him in, that's for sure. Whatever he's done, he's still your husband. Could you persuade him to give himself up?'

'I doubt it. Gerald is someone who first and foremost looks after his own interests. In this case, it's making sure he keeps out of prison. He wants to leave England and travel to somewhere he'll be safe.'

'And he thinks you can help him do that?' Her friend had the ghost of a smile on her lips.

'Exactly. It's stupid. There's no way I can. I've no money and I know nobody who could get the papers he needs.'

Connie was thoughtful. 'But if you could get those papers, it would mean you'd lose him from your life once and for all. I know you think you've put the whole Indian thing behind you, Daisy, but it's clear that you haven't. Until tonight, I didn't know how awful it had been for you, though I knew something pretty bad had happened. You never talk about the past. Whenever I've touched on India or your husband, you've brushed it off as though your time there wasn't worth mentioning. It's obvious, though, that it still looms large.'

It did and Daisy couldn't deny it: the frightening months she'd spent in Jasirapur when she'd suffered one so-called accident after another, only to discover that it was her husband behind them, and then to find that her dear friend, Anish, was the ultimate puppet master! The grief at losing him, the guilt at not grieving for Gerald, had been too much, and she had shut her mind fast. The past could be locked up in a box and the key thrown away. That's how she'd thought of her time in India. It was the reason she'd been unable to be more than a poor friend to Grayson. He was too involved in the whole business, a constant reminder of what she had to forget.

'What about Grayson Harte?' her companion asked out of the blue. It was almost as though Connie had read her mind. 'Isn't he in the Secret Intelligence Service? Surely, he could manufacture false papers. That's what they do, isn't it?'

'No.' Her response was unequivocal.

'What do you mean "no" — I think it's a brilliant idea.'

'I don't see Grayson any more. You know that.'

'But you could. You know where he works. What's to stop you visiting him?'

'So, I just turn up at his Baker Street office and say, *Sorry, Grayson, that I wasn't able to return your feelings, but actually you can do me a favour. Gerald didn't die after all, can you believe that? He's back in England and living in London. He's a deserter, of course, and I need your help to get him out of the country.*'

'Okay, I understand. I know it won't be easy.'

'Not easy! It's impossible. And I refuse even to think about it.' She uncurled herself from the lumpy chair and walked to the door, unable to stifle the first of many yawns. 'I'm so tired, Connie, I don't think I can even find my way to bed.'

'You will,' her friend promised, 'and you'll sleep and sleep. And tomorrow you might feel quite differently.'

CHAPTER FOUR

But Daisy didn't feel differently, when back in London again, she walked through the darkened streets the next evening. This time she was careful to leave the hospital with other nurses who had come off duty at the same time. After the encounter with Gerald, she was taking no chances, but the only footsteps she heard were those of her small party and she reached Charterhouse Square without incident. At the huge oak door, she waited patiently while the girl in the lead fished around in her bag for a key. Tonight, the darkness seemed more impenetrable than ever, not even a glimpse of moon or stars. Several seconds of fumbling produced the key and Daisy mounted the steps behind her companions.

Half turning at the doorway, she glimpsed for an instant a shadow passing between the square's trees. Or so she thought. She couldn't be entirely sure, but her eyes had slowly grown accustomed to the intense gloom and what she'd seen was definitely a form that was blacker than the rest. And it was a form that was moving. Could it be the figure of a man and that figure, Gerald? She'd had no time to send the note he'd insisted on, so had he come to check on her, to harangue her on where her duty lay? It was more than likely.

Daisy walked into the tiled entrance hall and stood still, aware of her pulse having gone into overdrive. She was becoming stupidly panicked and she must stop herself from seeing things that were probably not there. Given the heightened state in which she'd been living these last two days, it was unsurprising her mind was in complete disarray. Fear of bombing raids was one that everyone shared. So, too, fatigue from the unremitting labour of nursing during a war. But this was a fear peculiar to her alone: alarm at finding her husband alive, and not just alive, but close by and demanding her aid.

She passed the staff pigeonholes with hardly a glance. There were never letters for her. Tonight, though, something white glared balefully from the scratched wooden box. An envelope addressed to her. She recognised the writing straight away. It *had* been Gerald lurking in the trees, watching for her, waiting to accost her. But why hadn't he done so? Instead, he'd pushed the missive through the letterbox and someone had picked it up and put it in her pigeonhole.

She took the envelope and held it up to the dim light — a bare bulb dangled from the ceiling. Now that she looked closely, she saw the letter had not been hand delivered at all, but had come through the mail. It was postmarked 10 a.m. It had come in the morning post and been waiting for her all day. So, the shadow she'd seen . . . it couldn't have been Gerald. But if it wasn't, who was it?

Daisy's heart again began to beat far too rapidly, sounding heavy in her ears. She tried to calm herself by visualising what she'd seen. It must have been imagination, she told herself, but the more she thought of it, the more certain she became that there had been a figure. Fixing her mind doggedly on the blurred image, she was reminded of another shadow she'd glimpsed recently, one that had passed like a ripple through those self-same trees the night before last, when Gerald had stopped her on the front steps. Had someone been watching them then? Was someone watching her now? Or was that someone looking for Gerald, looking perhaps to find and hand over a deserter? She shook her head. It was better to think it merely the wind in the trees.

Gerald's note was brief and to the point. She hadn't named a meeting place, he wrote accusingly, so he would: *Hyde Park, the eastern edge of the Serpentine. Tomorrow at two o'clock*. Didn't he realise that she was a working woman, a nurse who had barely a day to herself every month? She felt exasperation riding tandem with misgiving. Meeting him was the last thing she wanted, but she would have to go or she would have him knocking on the Home door, or even worse, accosting her in the ward. Whether or not she could take her free time would depend on what was happening on the ward. She would have to petition Sister Elton first thing in the morning and hope for permission, calculating that she could just about make it to the park and be back on the ward within two hours. That was the most she could count on. But what she was to say to Gerald, Daisy had no idea.

* * *

She still had no idea the following afternoon when she walked into Hyde Park. Speakers' Corner was unusually crowded for a weekday, despite the lack of an orator and soap box. A rare burst of spring sunshine must have tempted the mill of people. Daisy wound her way through the crowd as quickly as she could, negotiating a host of children and their nannies and a small group of women on their lunch break enjoying a cigarette. The military post on her left was quiet and soldiers stood chatting to members of the Home Guard. A heavy anti-aircraft battery had been set up nearby, along with a number of rocket projectors. She'd been told they fired six foot shells packed with metal debris — broken bike chains, old razor blades — just about anything that could be loosed skywards and disrupt the flight of bombers swooping up river from the docks to the West End.

Today, though, there was so little activity you could almost forget the guns' incongruous presence in this beautiful, green space. The false sense of tranquillity was increased by dozens of barrage balloons which floated serenely thousands of feet above her head. They were supposed to force enemy aircraft to a height where aiming their bombs would be difficult, but the 'blimps' as they'd been nicknamed, had so far proved ineffective. Their silvery presence, though, added a dreamlike quality to the scene.

Reaching the path leading to the Serpentine, she felt inside her cape for the watch pinned to her bib. She wasn't at all sure that she would make Gerald's deadline, though so far luck had favoured her. She hadn't had to ask for time off. Sister Elton had noticed how pale her nurse was looking and insisted, during the rushed morning tea break, that Daisy take several hours away from the ward once lunch had been served and the medicine trolley had done its rounds. Then, as she'd left the hospital, one of the few doctors who ran a car, had offered her a lift as far as Oxford Street. Connie was on a short break, too, and off to sit in the cathedral gardens at St Paul's. She saw Daisy getting into the car and pulled her mouth down as if to say, *I told you so*. It was her friend's running joke that Dr Lawson had a particular fondness for Daisy.

If he had, she certainly wasn't going to play on it. Work filled her entire life and that was fine. She was simply grateful for the lift. Even so, she was having to walk fast, winding her way on and off the path and around the trenches that had changed the face of all the London parks. By the time she reached the lake, she was breathless. Once more she flicked her watch face upwards. A minute to two. She'd made it, but not before Gerald. He was marching up and down beside the still water, his shoulders hunched and a frown darkening his face.

'I thought you weren't coming,' was his greeting. 'You didn't contact me — you said you would.'

'I couldn't.' She forced herself to remain calm despite his blustering. 'I've been out of London for several days and it was last night before I collected your note.'

'Now you are here, we shouldn't waste time.'

Daisy was taken aback by his abrasiveness, but why should she be? It was something she had grown used to in the few months they'd spent together. Now, though, she wasn't the same girl who had travelled to India to marry him, a naive innocent who'd foolishly believed herself loved. Her emotions had been put through fire, and she'd emerged with a new, tempered edge. If they were going to talk, she wanted some answers.

'Shall we sit down?'

She gestured to one of the deckchairs lined up around the lake. In the first few months of the war, the chairs had been whisked from sight, but popular protest had succeeded in getting them reinstated. He didn't immediately sit but instead scanned the park for some minutes, turning his head in a complete circle. Then, seemingly reassured, he slumped heavily into the nearest seat and swivelled to face her.

'Well? What's the plan?'

'I have some questions.'

He screwed up his face in an expression of deep frustration. 'While you're asking questions, I'm falling into ever greater danger. You don't seem to appreciate that.'

'If I'm to help, I need to know what's happened since the last time I saw you.'

That was mendacious. No matter how much he told her, she was unlikely to be able to help. But she deserved to know how this ghost husband had come back to her from the dead, and she was willing to wait while he found the words. He was staring straight ahead, his face fixed and giving no sign that he was willing to talk. From the corner of her eye she noticed a small boy arrive on the other side of the lake. He was cradling a boat in his arms and bouncing excitedly up and down beside his mother. He was about to sail a new toy, she thought, and that was a big event in this time of austerity.

'I've already told you all you need to know,' Gerald said at last, his tone grudging. 'I was saved from drowning, broke an arm and a few ribs, was patched up by a local wise woman and sent on my way.'

'And the villagers never asked where you'd come from?'

'I made up a story.' Of course, he would have. 'I said I was a businessman — said my name was Jack Minns and I was trading in rapeseed. There's plenty of that around Jasirapur, and they didn't question my account.'

She considered how credible that might sound. Gerald had not been in uniform, she remembered. He would not have had any form of identity on him. His story would be the only one in town.

'But how did they think you'd ended up in the river?'

'That was easy to explain. The celebrations got a bit boisterous. They always do, don't they? And somehow I tripped and fell, and my friends weren't able to reach me because the river was flowing too fiercely.'

'Surely, then, they would have sent to Jasirapur for someone to come and collect you.'

He shook his head. She noticed a crafty smile playing around his lips. 'I told them the friends I'd been with were also traders and by now they would have moved on, travelling north-westwards. That was the direction I intended going, towards the Persian border. Once I was on my feet again, I said, I'd start out and join them. And I did. Not join them, of course, because they didn't exist, but I travelled north-west to the border.'

'Without money?'

'There are ways. The villagers sent me off with a few rupees and India is full of temples.'

'You begged your way to the border!'

'More or less.'

'And after that, when you got to Persia?'

'I scrounged whatever I could, then when I reached Turkey, took whatever job I could get. Anything that would feed me. Once I had sufficient money, I travelled on to the next place. It was bloody awful, I can tell you. The things I had to do . . . but once I reached France, life improved. I travelled up the country as far as Rouen and got taken on as a waiter in a local bistro. The tips were good and I actually enjoyed the life — not waiting, of course. Being at everyone's beck and call didn't suit me at all. But the idea of running a restaurant, that really appealed and still does. When I get to the States, that's what I'll do. It's America I want to go to.'

She had been listening to him in disbelief. How much credence should she give to this account of his travels? Could she really imagine the arrogant, young cavalry officer she'd known begging at temples or scavenging food bins or waiting on tables? Or was that as much a fantasy as his plan to open a restaurant in America without money and without papers?

Daisy said none of this. Instead, she asked, 'If you liked the life in France so much, why didn't you stay?'

'Ever heard of Hitler? That's why, Daisy. The Jerries were about to invade and it wasn't safe. I'd picked up a bit of French here and there, but any German soldier with the slightest ear would know I was English. If they found me, I'd have been interned immediately. I reckoned I might as well languish in prison here as there.'

He saw her surprised expression. 'Not that I've any intention of languishing anywhere, but I needed to get to England pretty damn quick.'

'And you did.'

'I met a chap at the restaurant. He used to eat there pretty regularly. He was English, but had been living in Rouen for years. For a while, he'd been holding his breath over the political situation, but once the Germans invaded Poland, we both knew the game was up. France as well as Britain declared war two days later and it was only a matter of time before the Germans arrived. The bloke decided to make a bolt for it back to England. Fortunately, he owned a car and I travelled with him.'

'I see.'

She didn't really. She couldn't understand how Gerald had managed to get past border controls without a passport or any form of identification. But in wartime everything was in flux and he must have looked and sounded the English gentleman. She imagined he'd told them some sad story and got them to believe it.

'So, where are you living?'

Her question was deliberately bland. When he'd appeared on her doorstep the night before last, he had let slip that he'd looked for his parents in the East End, but he was not about to confess the layers of mistruth he'd been spinning ever since she'd known him. And now his mother and father were gone, wiped out by a German bomb, there seemed little point in raking up old lies.

'The East End,' he said awkwardly. 'Whitechapel.'

She remembered the address he'd given her, a shop in Gower's Walk. She knew the road and it struck her that it was only a stone's throw from Spitalfields, where they'd both been born. He misinterpreted her silence and said defensively, 'I've hardly any money and it was the cheapest lodging I could find.'

Daisy was still thinking. She had a very small sum saved. Should she offer it to him, or was that ridiculous? It was nowhere near enough to purchase a berth on a ship to New York. And that was without reckoning on those all-important papers. Even more important in America, she imagined, since the country was not at war and would police its borders rigorously.

'Is the interrogation officially over?'

He smiled across at her and for an instant she glimpsed the old Gerald, the man with whom she had fallen so deeply in love. Or thought she had. His fair hair gleamed bright in the spring sunshine and, though his cheeks were emaciated and his frame thin, he could almost be the same handsome man.

'I'm sorry if it sounded like an interrogation. I didn't mean it to be. But so much has happened to both of us since . . .'

She saw a quick flush mount to his face. 'I presume Grayson Harte rode to your rescue.' So far he'd said nothing about that terrible night, but that was not surprising.

'You know what happened?'

'The tale spread like wildfire. Tales always do in India. The village was naturally desperate to hear the gossip from upriver and seized on anyone who'd been in Jasirapur. But the story they got was only half a one. I gathered from their talk that the gang had been apprehended and put in jail awaiting trial, but I heard nothing about you. I had no idea if Harte and his minions turned up in time.'

'As you see, they did.'

There was a cold silence as they sat staring across the lake, small ripples now disturbing its surface. A stiff breeze had begun to blow and the little red painted boat was bobbing precariously away on the waves. The small boy started to cry.

Gerald shifted irritably in his seat. 'So — what's your plan?' he repeated.

CHAPTER FIVE

'I don't have one,' Daisy said calmly.

Apparently, India was to be a closed subject between them, and they'd said all they were going to say about the terrifying event they had shared.

'What do you mean, you don't have one?'

'I told you, Gerald, I have no idea how I can help you.'

'Jack,' he interrupted her.

'Jack,' she repeated, though the sound of the name stuck on her tongue. 'I've very little money, but you're welcome to what I have. I doubt, though, it will get you much further than Southampton. And, as for the papers, how am I to get them?'

'You're a nurse. You have patients.'

'What has that to do with anything?'

'Patients are always grateful to their nurses and some of them must have influence. Surely you can use that.'

'I work at St Barts — in the City.'

'A City man then. Perfect.'

'The City men, as you call them, go home to the suburbs at night. They have transport and money to escape the raids. It's the East End that suffers — you must know that — you're living there. Its people are our patients, people from small terraced houses, from crowded tenements, people with very little and even less when the bombers have finished. They're grateful certainly, but influential, no.'

'You've changed, you know. You've become a hard woman.'

'Because I can't help you? You're being foolish.' She looked away from him. 'If I have changed,' she said slowly, 'it can only be a good thing. At least for me. It means that for the first time in my life, I'm strong enough to defend myself.'

He had the grace to look uncomfortable, but it didn't stop him from harassing her.

'Grayson Harte was never a District Officer in India, was he? I knew from the first he was an imposter. I told you so, didn't I?'

She said nothing, wondering why he should alight on Grayson's name out of the blue. She wasn't left in ignorance long.

'I've been thinking.' He stretched his legs full length and relaxed back into the canvas. 'The District Officer role was just a blind. Harte was in Secret Intelligence, wasn't he? Most of those beggars are working in London now, I'll be bound. Harte may have had to stay in India for the gang's trial, but he can't be there still. He's almost certainly here, close by, and if we're talking influence, who better than an SIS officer to help me?'

She swallowed hard. It was exactly what Connie had said, but she hadn't wanted to listen to her and she didn't want to listen to Gerald either. Contriving a meeting with Grayson was the last thing she'd expected to do, and the last thing she wanted.

'Nothing to say? Harte always had a soft spot for you. Sweet on you, I thought. And he was the one who proved your white knight in the end, wasn't he?'

There was a new bitterness to his voice. Even now, Daisy thought guiltily, even now that she had Gerald beside her, flesh and blood and alive, she hadn't thanked him for his final act of heroism in trying to save her life. She should do it, but she couldn't. She couldn't bring herself to utter the words. Her sense of betrayal was just too great.

'Who better to get me my papers?' he taunted.

'I don't see Grayson.'

'Now, I find that remarkable.' He gave a supercilious smirk. 'I thought he'd be a regular at the Nurses' Home.' She could have hit him, but instead clenched her fists tightly. He looked down at her hands and the smirk grew. 'What's the matter? Didn't it work out between you? That's sad. But comfort yourself with the thought that it wouldn't have worked out anyway. You have a husband alive and Grayson is far too much of a gentleman to steal another man's wife.'

'I don't see him,' she repeated heavily.

'But you could. If you chose.' He leant over and took her hand. His touch was far gentler than she expected. Rhythmically, he stroked her forearm. She would have said it was a loving touch if she hadn't known better. 'And you could choose, Daisy.'

'I haven't seen Grayson Harte for months. We've gone our own ways.'

'I'm sure you know where he works. though.' She didn't answer and he took her silence as confirmation. 'You could pay him a visit. Call on him for old times' sake. Don't mince your words — tell him your husband has reappeared and is an embarrassment, an embarrassment you'd like to get rid of. I'm sure he'll find a way of obliging.'

'I can't turn up out of nowhere and demand papers for you. He'll want to know why you're here, how you got here. He'll know you've deserted. What if he decides to turn you in?'

'Dear Daisy, he won't. Because if he did, you would be implicated. You would be the wife of a deserter. Think how your nursing colleagues would react to that little piece of news, think what the hospital might do. About your job, for instance.'

'You're threatening my job?'

'Not threatening, merely pointing out the salient facts — as a friend, of course. You really would be best to keep my unfortunate situation as quiet as possible, and Mr Harte will appreciate how necessary that is. He's a master of discretion, I'm sure.'

Daisy was caught. She could feel the underlying menace in every one of his words. If he didn't get papers, didn't get money and a way out of England, he wouldn't go quietly. If he were taken into custody, he would shout his story to the sky, and it would spread like a fungus, inching its diseased path into every crevice of her life. Including her workplace. And the job she loved would be in ashes, another dream destroyed.

'If I go to him and he refuses to help — even if he doesn't inform the authorities you're in London — will you leave me alone?'

'He can't refuse.' Gerald's tone was adamant. 'He has to help. My situation is desperate. Spies are his *forte*, aren't they, and I'm surrounded by them. I have to get out now.'

Her eyes widened. 'Surrounded by spies?'

'Yes, spies. I'm almost certain of it.' She recalled the anxious scanning of the park before he'd consented to sit down. It seemed he believed what he was saying. 'There's something odd about the two men who rent the room below me. For a start, they're both Indians. Well, one is Indian, the other's Anglo. I met the Indian chap on the landing one day and he said he was a soldier. I saw his cap — it had the badge of the Pioneer Corps pinned to it — and I reckon he was telling the truth. But why isn't he with his regiment? And if he's left the army, why hasn't he returned to India? There has to be something going on, some reason they're hanging around. They're watching me, I'm sure. They must know I've deserted.'

'How can they know?' The claim seemed utterly absurd and she wondered if Gerald's ordeal had affected his mind as well as his body.

'If they don't actually know, they suspect. Think about it. I'm an able-bodied man of twenty-eight, yet I'm not with any of the Services and I'm not engaged in essential war work.'

'And are they? They might be deserters, too.'

He shook his head. 'Deserters from what? The character from the Pioneers has a limp, so he's unfit to fight. I know his unit was brought over from the Punjab to work on demolition. Clearing derelict buildings, that sort of thing. Some of them were skilled engineers. They'd need to be, using dynamite. He might have been one of them and suffered an accident. But that doesn't explain why he hasn't been put on a boat back to India. He's not British and he shouldn't be here.'

'And the other man, the Anglo-Indian?'

'Yes, what about him? What the hell is *he* doing in this country?' Gerald's voice rose and she could see panic bubbling beneath the surface. 'Why hasn't he been interned with everyone else, I ask you? Every foreigner, anyone who might assist the enemy, even the poor blighters who've escaped from Hitler, has been banged up.'

'But why should these men be a threat to you?' She hoped a quiet voice would calm him.

'They are. I know they are.'

She had never known her husband so agitated, not even in the dark days of mischief in India. His voice had risen even higher and Daisy saw the woman who had just rescued her child's boat, look up, perplexed by the sound.

'They sent me a white feather. How about that? It was under my door this morning. You know what that says.'

'Cowardice?' She hardly dare say the word.

'Precisely. They're calling me a coward. The next step will be to denounce me to the authorities.'

'But how do you know they were the ones who posted it? It could have been anyone in the neighbourhood.'

'I can't be entirely sure, but who else would it be? They've been watching me closely and they know my movements, know I don't have a job. *And* that I've a connection with India. They speak to each other in Hindi and I accidentally let on I understood some of what they were saying. That must have made them even more suspicious.'

She shook her head. Gerald was imagining a persecution she was certain didn't exist. He had built a ridiculous story around two innocent men, interpreting their looks and actions in the worst possible way. It was because he was strung tight by the fear of discovery, Daisy could see, and if he didn't get away soon, he was going to do something very stupid. She had no alternative, she thought wretchedly. She would have to try to get help, even if it meant searching out Grayson and braving a face-to-face meeting with him.

'I'll go to Baker Street. That's where Mr Harte works. I'll try to see him.' There was only a slight quiver to her voice.

'When?' The question was urgent. Her promise had not been sufficient to calm him.

'As soon as I have time off.'

'Soon?'

'Yes, soon.' She looked at her watch. 'I must go now. If I have any luck, I'll send a message to the address you gave me.'

'You've got to have luck.' And his tone allowed for no other outcome.

CHAPTER SIX

The meeting had been unsatisfactory. Gerald wasn't sure he could depend on her to go to Grayson Harte. He'd said she had changed and he'd been right. Not to look at. She was still as pretty, prettier if anything. She'd filled out since he'd last seen her, become more womanly. The dark eyes, the darker hair, the skin that in an English climate had regained its smooth creaminess — not quite peach, not quite olive, but soft and clear — still drew him. Was it any wonder he'd lost his head all those months ago in London?

It had been a thoroughly boring leave, he remembered, and then he'd gone to buy perfume for the woman he'd decided to love, and there she'd been. Beautiful Daisy. He'd meant only to enjoy a few days with her, but the days had stretched into several weeks and when he'd left to go back to India, he'd felt real regret. Although not that much regret, he supposed. He'd been looking forward to rejoining his regiment, getting back to the pleasures of life as a cavalry officer. Looking forward, too, to seeing Jocelyn Forester. He'd set his sights on winning the colonel's daughter and was sure in time that she would reciprocate. The perfume was the first step in his campaign.

But then those pleading letters from Daisy. A baby was coming; she had to marry. And what had that been all about?

A miscarriage on board ship, no baby, and a marriage he hadn't wanted. He'd been angry and he hadn't treated her well. He didn't like to think of those days. He'd betrayed her, he knew, betrayed her for money, that's what it came down to. He'd allowed Anish to talk him into a pit of evil. Just for money, just to pay the debts which terrified him. He'd had no idea that Daisy would prove so difficult, so obdurate, so intent on involving herself in what didn't concern her. Until, eventually, she'd faced death. Even now he couldn't believe that Anish had sanctioned such a thing. It was too awful to think about. He'd done his best to save her, but it had been Harte, the perfect District Officer, who'd finally been her rescuer.

No, he didn't like to think of those days. Daisy had been a gentle girl when he met her, vulnerable and soft. Now, though, she seemed to have grown a shell, and he could only hope that he'd managed to pierce it today. He wasn't entirely convinced she would do as she'd promised. Something had happened between her and Grayson Harte that made her reluctant to meet the man. She'd better, though, he thought belligerently. He'd hated having to confess the mess he was in, having to abase himself by begging for help, but he'd had no choice. No choice either about holding a threat over her head. He could congratulate himself on that, at least. He'd hit on the right thing — her job — he'd seen that immediately. The threat of having to leave nursing would make her do what he asked, whether she wanted to or not. It would get him the papers, if anything would.

Trudging his way back through the West End and into the City, his feet were aching and sore. There had been a big raid two nights ago and the roads were still badly damaged. He'd hardly seen a bus on his way to Hyde Park, but even if one had turned up, he couldn't afford the fare. He could barely afford to eat, and the small sum he'd saved from working in France was dwindling by the day. Look at his shoes — the soles almost falling off, the backs broken down. Dear God, what had he come to? A proud officer in a crack regiment of the Indian Army and now this, hiding away in a dingy, rat-infested room, and dependent on others for his salvation.

But then he'd always been dependent, hadn't he? His whole career had rested on a father who'd sacrificed everything for his only son. An ungrateful son. And that was something else he didn't want to think about. When he'd returned to England, Spitalfields was the first place he'd gone to. He'd had some wild idea that somehow he could reconcile himself with the parents he'd abandoned, the prodigal son returned, that kind of thing. An unspoken thought, too, that maybe his father could get him out of his predicament as he had so many others in the past, though what a poverty- stricken old man could do, he didn't know. But when he'd rounded the corner of the street — the address had been at the top of the letter his father had sent, begging for money his son couldn't spare — he'd been appalled. There was nothing, literally nothing. A whole street had disappeared.

After two years of war, he thought, London smelt of death and destruction. Everywhere shattered windows, roofs caved in, water pipes, gas pipes, all fractured, telephone wires waving in the breeze. The people he passed were every bit as shabby as their city since new clothes were a rarity. Shabbier still in the East End where, for a pittance, he'd managed to rent a room. Street after street of mean little houses with open doors and broken windows; filthy alleys in which ragged children played, their pale, pinched faces speaking of years of deprivation before ever the German bombers arrived. And everywhere stank — of waste, of unwashed bodies, of stale beer.

He was walking through the City now, past one ruined church after another, their steeples scorched and discoloured by fire. There was something heroic in their tragic silhouettes, he thought, heroic yet futile. They belonged to a past that no longer had meaning. It was the New World that promised, the New World that offered a future. In front of the Royal Exchange, an enormous hole in the road had still not been completely filled after the Bank station had been hit in January. So huge was it that the Royal Engineers had had to build a bridge across for people to get from one side of the street to the other.

The East End had fared even worse, of course. Whole terraces mown down and streets almost entirely rubble. Grotesquely, the building on the corner of Leman Street, he noticed, still had a side wall intact and a framed view of a Cornish landscape hanging from the picture hook. He crunched his way along the pavement, littered with shards of glass and cracked roofing tiles. The breeze had begun to blow strongly again and pillows of white dust swirled around him. For a moment, he had to stand still, his eyes closed against it.

Turning into Ellen Street, he saw the lodging house ahead, black roof and sightless windows, hovering against the clear blue sky. It loomed discordantly over the dribble of smaller houses, as though it had risen from the pages of a Nordic fairy tale and found itself out of time and out of place. Several of the surrounding properties had been hit on successive nights and had crumbled at one blow. That didn't surprise him, knowing how shoddily they were built, but at least the debris was light enough for more survivors to be pulled free. Alive, but dispossessed. The house adjoining his had had its front cut away as though it were a doll's house. Skyed high in the air was a dented bath and a lavatory, with a sad little roll of toilet paper still attached to the door. A staircase led to an upper floor that no longer existed. But the house where he lodged had survived all attacks — so far.

He trod up the stairs as delicately as he could. The ground floor of the house was occupied by an old woman, ninety if she were a day, half mad he was sure. He glimpsed her sometimes through her open door crooning quietly to a cat or slumped in a fireside chair, staring blankly at the bare wall in front of her. Sometimes she would stir herself to fling random curses at whoever was unlucky enough to catch her glance, but she rarely noticed his comings and goings, being so deaf that a bomb could have fallen outside her window and she'd not have flinched. It was when he approached the first floor that he steeled himself to tread more softly still. He tried to shut his mind to the ill will he imagined lay beyond that door.

His years in the army had given him a nose for danger and he was sure the men who lived there were up to no good. It wasn't just that they'd ended their conversation the minute they realised he understood Hindi, nor the sheer absurdity of finding two Indians living in the middle of the East End in the middle of a war. It was the nagging matter of why they were there. The Indian might be a soldier as he claimed, and the man's cap badge seemed to prove it, but why wasn't he with his regiment or returned to India? And what was the Anglo doing here? You couldn't trust Anglo-Indians, they were neither one thing nor the other, neither British nor Indian. It was why they so often had a chip on their shoulder. Did this one? Did the man mean to expose him as a deserter, imagining perhaps that he'd be paid for the information?

He was sure it was this man who'd pushed the white feather beneath his door, and that was a warning if ever there was. The sooner he was out of Ellen Street, the better. If Daisy did as she promised and tackled Grayson Harte in the next few days, he might have the papers he needed within the fortnight. Harte could do it if he wished, and he would wish. The man had liked Daisy just a little too much.

And his wife had liked him back, despite the doubts he'd tried to sow in her mind all those months ago when Harte had played at being a District Officer. Gerald had no compunction in throwing them together again. 'Wife' was just a word now, not that it had ever been much else. For a split second, he felt remorse at what he'd done to the young girl he'd met at Bridges. But not for long. There was no point in looking back. And he had no qualms in using Grayson's feelings for Daisy. Not if it would get him what he wanted.

He put one foot on the stairway leading to his attic. It creaked badly and he froze where he stood on the landing. He tried to breathe very quietly. Were the men on the other side of the door listening? Edging closer so that his ear was almost touching the blistered wood, he heard angry footsteps pacing the bare boards. And two voices — both men were at home. Gerald was sure that one of them, at least, had been following him recently. Several times, he'd half sensed a figure at the periphery of his vision and wondered if it was his neighbour. When you said it aloud, it sounded ridiculous, yet . . .

The men were talking loudly, animatedly. Their voices came to him in blurts of noise. He'd heard them argue before, but today there was a new harshness, a new agitation. They were speaking Hindi for certain and the heat of their disagreement was leaving them careless. He caught words here and there, 'car', 'hotel', 'Chandan' — was that a name? — disconnected words that made no sense. But he dared not linger and very carefully he placed his shoe on the first step, bracing himself for another agonising creak. Thankfully, the wood remained silent and on the balls of his feet, he tiptoed up the remaining stairs.

The two small rooms he rented were airless, worse than airless, for the smell of thick dirt was overwhelming and so intense it seemed alive. He could hardly breathe the atmosphere and had to force himself to swallow it in great slabs. The two small windows were glued shut and muslin curtains, elephant grey in colour, drooped undisturbed against grimy panes. Several more flies had buzzed their last since he'd left that morning and now lay shrivelled on the uncovered floor. The room was as dark as it was airless, and through the gloom only the dim outlines of a few pieces of broken furniture were visible.

Flinging himself down on to the iron bedstead, he pushed aside a tousled heap of clothes. For a long time he lay there, sprawled across the questionable mattress and trying not to think. His eyes travelled around the brown papered walls, blotchy and peeling from the damp, and upwards to the pitted ceiling, tracing as he had done so many times these past few weeks, the cracks that disfigured it. He no longer saw its ugliness but, instead, had created a map of his own devising. This was him, here on the left, in the centre of that large, brown stain. The mass of small, thin lines stretching westwards were the waves of the ocean he would soon be crossing, and there on the other side of the ceiling, a solid splurge of colour — old paint, he thought, working its way to the surface — was surely the New World beckoning him to its shore. He laid there, looking upwards, for as long as his eyes would stay open.

CHAPTER SEVEN

'Are you going then?'

Connie punctuated each of her words with a particularly vicious scrub. The urine testing had been done for the day and now they were in the sluice room, grinding their way through the cleaning of bedpans. It was a messy undertaking, mops and Lysol everywhere.

'I have to. I promised.' Daisy's voice trailed miserably beneath the thunder of water. She didn't want to seek out Grayson, didn't want to see his slow smile and lose herself in those deep blue eyes.

She felt Willa Jenkins looking at them from the opposite line of sinks. 'Take care, Willa,' she called across at the girl, 'there's another heap of pans just behind you.'

It had amazed them when Willa had managed against all the odds to pass her probation on the third attempt. She was slow at her work, constantly getting things wrong, and very clumsy. Broken china, smashed thermometers, bent syringes, followed her wherever she went. Daisy had often come to her rescue, helping to hide the wreckage before Sister caught a glimpse.

Their fellow nurses had gradually lost patience with such an awkward colleague and were not above joining in a communal teasing that at times verged on unkindness. The girl was an outsider like herself, Daisy thought, but unlike her hadn't learned to blend in, to stay unobtrusive. She'd done what she could to protect Willa, remembering her own isolation as a servant and the scourging meted out by the shop girls at Bridges, but it wasn't always easy to intervene, and she was aware of how very unhappy the girl must be. Lately, too, she'd become even more withdrawn, ever since the news had circulated that her brother had been killed on his last training flight. Willa's interest in their conversation today was the first she'd shown for weeks and, at any other time, Daisy would have tried hard to include her. But this was such a very personal matter.

Connie was still speaking, her voice lowered. 'Cheer up, Daisy. It's a good thing, surely. Get the papers Gerald wants and you're a free woman. Once he's in America, he won't come back. You can file for a divorce or an annulment or whatever it is.'

Daisy's mind stuttered at the thought. 'There's a host of things to sort out before I get there. That's the stuff you deal with at the very end of a marriage.'

Or when you've come to terms with the end, she thought, and wasn't sure that she had. When her husband had accosted her outside the Nurses' Home, he'd simply been a figure in the dark. He'd sounded like Gerald and, in the brief flare of the match, he'd even looked like Gerald, but somehow his resurgence had seemed a fantasy, a mythical phoenix, risen from the ashes. Today, though, in the sunlight of a London park, she'd had to accept that he really had come back to life and was not going away.

Connie stopped scrubbing and fixed her with an unwavering look. 'Don't say you still have feelings for him.'

She swallowed hard. 'I found it upsetting today, that's all. Sitting by his side, hearing him speak, seeing him smile even. It brought back the man I married, the man I loved once.'

And brought back all the anguish, too. This last year, she'd hidden it well, camouflaged beneath her nurse's uniform, beneath the harsh training and the relentless routine, but the truth was that she was still hurting.

'You do still want him out of your life, I take it?' The bed pans were neatly stacked to one side and Connie had thrown her a towel.

Daisy nodded.

'So when are you going to see Grayson Harte?'

'As soon as possible. I need to get it over with.'

She felt a whoosh of air as Sister Elton bustled into the room. 'No time for talking, nurses. You have patients to prepare for theatre.'

The ward sister allowed nothing to escape her. Daisy saw her glance towards Willa, still labouring through her pile of bedpans, but the older woman said nothing. From the days of initial training, Willa had constantly been at the rough end of Sister Elton's tongue, but since the news of her brother's death, Daisy had noticed a distinct softening towards her. There was a rumour that two of the brother's friends, also pilots, had been lost and everyone knew that Willa had a picture of one of them on her bedside table.

'From what you've said, Grayson seems a gentleman,' Connie continued to urge, as they made their way on to the ward. 'He's not likely to make you feel uncomfortable, is he?'

'No, I don't think he will, and that makes me feel worse. When we said goodbye . . . it was, well, difficult.'

'You didn't tell me it ended badly. I thought you'd both agreed it was best to part.'

'We did — sort of. It was more that he didn't understand why I couldn't make a new start. He tried to understand, but it just didn't work.'

'I can't see why not.'

'Neither could he. For him, the Indian episode was over. The bad people had been punished and my ne'er-do-well husband was dead, so what was stopping me?'

'He had a point,' her friend said judiciously. 'But, in any case he won't remember much of how you parted. It's not as if he's still pining for you, is it? You said he looked perfectly happy when you last saw him.'

Daisy had glimpsed Grayson one Saturday afternoon in Regent Street just before Christmas. Nurses had each been given a precious few hours to shop for presents, not that there was much to buy or money to pay for what there was. And there he'd been, strolling along the pavement outside Liberty's, with a laughing girl on his arm. She could still feel the fierce jealousy that had taken a sudden grip on her. She'd darted down a side street to get out of their way. And to recover. It was a shock that she could feel so passionately, when months ago she'd sent him away, knowing she could never give him the closeness he craved.

'I'm sure he is,' she managed to reply. 'Happy, that is. Things move at such a speed these days, they're probably already married.'

Joking was the best defence, and it was probably not even a joke. War was not the moment to hang about. People met, coupled, married and left each other, all within months, sometimes weeks, even days.

'So meet him as an old friend, an old acquaintance. You're asking him a favour, that's all.'

'It's quite a favour, don't you think? He's an intelligence officer and I'm asking him to aid a deserter. It's not something that makes me feel good.'

'You'll just have to get over it. After all, he's in an ideal position to help you. Who better? And if he finds it impossible or he's shocked to the core, he can say no. It's as simple as that. And then you can tell that dratted husband of yours that it's a no go and he'll leave you alone.'

Daisy sighed. If only it were that simple. But Connie didn't know Gerald, didn't know his persistence or his reaction when he didn't get what he wanted.

* * *

She had used the bombing as an excuse to stop seeing Grayson. It was true that meeting each other had become more difficult when, day after day, she was ferrying casualties out into the countryside and had virtually no time free. And with death all around, it was better perhaps to forget relationships, forget friendship for that matter, and concentrate on the work they both must do. But it was an excuse and a poor one at that. It wasn't the war that was stopping her. Not the fragility of existence, the gossamer line between life and death that she saw every day in the hospital, but the sheer awfulness of what had happened to her. She couldn't get over the betrayal. Her husband's betrayal, and even worse, Anish's, the man she had thought her dear friend. She could never again commit herself wholeheartedly to anyone.

From her earliest years, Daisy had lived a solitary life — at the orphanage, as a servant to Miss Maddox, as a working-class girl in Bridges' perfumery. She'd always been lonely and expected nothing else. And then Gerald had come along and, for a short while, a warmer life had beckoned. Her love for him, her friendship with Anish, had changed her, made her newly vulnerable, opened her to pain.

She could never be that girl again, but neither could she expect Grayson to understand. His life had been smooth. He'd lost his father at a very young age, she knew, but he had a mother who adored him, uncles who'd educated him, a job he loved and colleagues who were friends. If he survived this war, he would climb the intelligence ladder until he reached its very pinnacle, and he would have allies all the way. His was a golden life. He could never understand the raw wash of despair which at times could overwhelm her. The feelings of worthlessness, that in some twisted way she had deserved her fate. While she was working, she was happy. That first day of training on the ward, she'd felt a flow of confidence and that had stayed with her. She'd known she could do the job and do it well. But that was on the ward. Out of uniform, her self-belief could waver badly and, in an instant, render her defenceless. She had to protect herself from further hurt, and protect Grayson, or any man who came too close, from disappointment. That was the result of Jasirapur and the shattered dreams she had left there.

Daisy stayed on duty into the evening. Several of the nursing staff had gone down with bad colds and been sent to the sick bay. The hospital was very strict about nurses going off duty as soon as they fell ill, but it meant, of course, more work for those who remained standing. She stayed until past seven and, when she left Barts, daylight was already fading. The long evenings were still for the future. Until they came she sensed, rather than saw, her way home. In daytime, the city went busily about its affairs but at night the unaccustomed darkness altered its rhythm. You went slowly, feeling your way forward, hoping not to bump into walls, lamp posts, stray wardens or huddled strangers. Turning the corner into Charterhouse Square, she began to follow the path through the trees.

She was halfway across the square when the moon swam from beneath its dark cover. It was a full moon, too, and for a moment it bathed the area in white light, tipping the grass with silver and casting long shadows wherever she looked. A moment only and it had disappeared once more behind the banking clouds. But it had been enough to bring discomfort, enough to make her aware of those shadows and feel again eyes that followed her. It seemed a night for ghosts.

In fact, every night had been a night for ghosts, from the moment Gerald had risen from the dead to stand at her shoulder. Since then, she had seen unreal figures aplenty, imagined eyes watching from every corner. She knew it was a nonsense, but it didn't prevent her glancing over her shoulder as she turned the key in the lock. Nothing. You see, she told herself, there's nothing and, if you're not careful, you'll send yourself mad. In India, Gerald had tried to persuade her that her mind was losing its grip. All those accidents that somehow had a perfectly logical explanation, but only seemed to happen to her. They'd been a threat to her sanity as well as her body. Now he was playing with her mind again, and she must not let him.

Tomorrow, she must use her free afternoon to visit number 64 Baker Street. How was she to manage this unwanted encounter? Perhaps if she arrived near to the time that Grayson finished work, she might catch him at the entrance. That way she wouldn't have to brave the building or its gatekeepers. But if she had to, she would make herself walk through the door of the SOE headquarters and ask to speak to Grayson Harte. For good or for ill, it would be over — or so she hoped.

CHAPTER EIGHT

It had to rain, of course. The fine weather of the last week broke with a vengeance and Daisy was left struggling to raise a battered umbrella as she turned left out of the underground station. She had dressed as well as she could for the occasion in a woollen dress of olive green. It was the only dress she possessed that wasn't darned or mended in some way. Over it she wore her nurse's cape. It was forbidden to wear uniform off duty, but in the absence of a winter coat, she had little option but to break the rules. The rain was hammering down and she peered anxiously at her shoes, heeled and soled so many times that they were now perilously thin. They were bound to leak, she thought, and refused to imagine what she would look like by the time she made it to Grayson's office. And once this pair was completely ruined, there would be no more fancy footwear.

Since the start of the New Year, there had been shortages in just about everything. Food especially. Sometimes the nurses had gone hungry and several of them had complained, Lydia at the forefront, at the unfairness that gave labourers a larger food allowance. But Lydia had always been a troublemaker and, for the most part, people had shrugged and got on with it. But clothing was rationed now and their wardrobes were looking more tattered by the day. Shoes, especially, were expensive and scarce, and Connie had even taken to mending hers with Elastoplast. But should ever a new pair appear on the horizon, unlikely as that was, delicacy could be forgotten. It was stolid black lace-ups that ruled.

Splinters of water bounced off the pavement and soaked her feet and ankles. The wind had risen and the umbrella was beginning to look more dangerous than useful, but she battled on doggedly, taking what shelter it offered and counting down the street numbers. She had managed to keep her mind from dwelling on the meeting ahead, but now she could ignore it no longer. Stopping to face the glass doors of number 64, Daisy looked up at its facade.

White slabs of stone rose towards the sky, an aggressive contrast to the harmonious red brick of Mr Baker's first residential street. There was nothing to suggest the nature of the business conducted within its walls and, ordinarily, she would have passed the building without a second glance. But Grayson had mentioned all those months ago that the SIS had split into different sections, and from now on he'd be working with the Special Operations Executive. They had recently moved to a different headquarters and he'd be one of the *Baker Street Irregulars*, he'd said cheerfully. He'd seemed to relish the thought of meeting new colleagues, though Daisy had only the haziest idea of what their work might entail. It was sure to involve India since Grayson's experience there would be invaluable.

Fighting against an ever-rising wind, she yanked down the umbrella, and made a decision. There was no sign of Grayson and the storm had already taken its toll, her legs splashed with dirt and her face plastered in a frenzy of wet curls — there was little point in waiting for him to appear. She pushed through the revolving doors and into the dazzle of black and white tiles, outshone by the gleaming mahogany doors which stood to attention on either side of the ground floor corridor. On her left, a stone staircase wound its way upwards. Overhead she could hear the sound of feet tapping up and down its steps, a good five or six storeys above her, she estimated. Facing the stairs was a lift, its concertina door open, and inside its braided guardian perched on a stool. A reception desk barred her from going any further and a severe looking young woman, her hair scrunched back into a stubby knot, looked up from the file she was reading and arched her brows in enquiry.

'Can I help you?'

The woman's voice was as scrunched as her hair and Daisy struggled to find her tongue.

'I would like to see Grayson Harte, if it's possible.' She tried not to sound hesitant.

'Yes?' The eyebrows seemed to suggest that this was a privilege granted to only a few.

'I wonder is he in?'

'Do you have an appointment?'

'No, but—'

'You must have an appointment. I'm afraid you can't see him without one, Miss . . . You do realise this is a government building.'

'Yes, I do. But Mr Harte. It's important I see him.'

'I'm sure it is.' The woman smiled pityingly at her. 'Just make an appointment. I can give you his secretary's number if you wish.'

'I don't have the time for that.' Daisy decided that she didn't like the woman and would be happy to lie to her. 'If he's in, I need to see him now. It's urgent. A matter of national importance, you see.'

The woman's face changed, her expression chilled by Daisy's announcement, but she was still clearly unsure of this intruder. 'I'll see if he's available,' she conceded eventually, turning her back and muttering something into the telephone.

There was a pause of several minutes at the other end of the line, as though someone had gone away to check. What if they were checking up on her, Daisy thought? She'd just told a very big lie and, in the current desperate situation, they might not take kindly to such talk. What would Grayson think when he saw her standing there instead of the matter of national importance? Her stomach tensed. She couldn't do it.

She had to do it.

The woman replaced the receiver with a clang but said nothing further. Instead, she returned to her papers as though her unwelcome visitor had ceased to exist. Daisy caught the ring of shoes on the stone stairs. The footsteps were some way off, but coming nearer. They must belong to Grayson. He was walking towards her at this very moment. No, she couldn't do it after all. Snatching up the dripping umbrella, she plunged through the revolving door and out on to the rain-soaked street.

Her heart was jumping, but at least she was out of the building. She'd escaped. Soon she could lose herself among the crowds. She'd given no name; she was anonymous and untraceable. But she had gone barely three yards along the road when the sirens began their interminable wailing. High above she heard the roar of Spitfires as they began their chase of enemy planes.

Today, the Luftwaffe had not waited for night to fall and, when she looked back, a shroud of grey was already rising into the sky from the east of the city. An ambulance tore along Baker Street, its bell ringing furiously, closely followed by several fire engines. Black coils of stinking smoke chased through the sky and billowed overhead, while fragments of what seemed to be charred paper showered groundwards. Her ears were zinging from the noise of blasts that were coming ever closer. She stood for a moment and looked up, seeing in the distance English planes darting across the sky, like little silver fish in a great, grey pond. And amid the mayhem, a German fleet of bombers flying in majestic order, laying waste to the city below them.

The underground station had to be the nearest shelter. It was considered bad form to run, but she walked very quickly towards it. The authorities had been reluctant to allow stations to be used, but the public had taken the matter into its own hands and they were now London's largest air raid shelters, with miles of platforms and tunnels put to use. People felt safer under the ground, though in reality that wasn't always so. Marble Arch had suffered a direct hit earlier this year and, at Bank, the bomb had fallen right into the station and carried with it tarmac from the road, burning hundreds of people dreadfully. There was risk everywhere.

Even if the station were marginally safer, it was not a place Daisy wanted to be. The platforms would be overcrowded, fetid with the smell of unventilated bodies packed as close as sardines. But she had no choice, and could only hope her patients were right when they told her that stations had become more civilised over the last year, with sanitary closets and washing facilities installed. There was even talk that at some, mobile canteens had been set up to offer hot food and drink. At the entrance a queue had already formed and, as she waited, a small scuffle broke out at the front — a few men already merry from an hour spent in a nearby public house — but otherwise an orderly trail of people were making their way down into the depths of the oldest underground station in the world. It looked it too, Daisy thought. The Victorian tiling was dull and dirty, left uncleaned since the war began and the grind of ancient escalators no more comforting, jammed as they were from top to tail with people scurrying towards what they hoped was safety.

When she finally reached the platform, there were already hundreds crammed into the small space, and more streaming in with every minute. A mix of people, caught together in this flash of time, sharing the irritation, the defiance, the camaraderie, the fear. By the look of them, there were a large number of locals, people who spent every night here and who Daisy could see were already trying to organise the shelter into some kind of order. They had an almost impossible job. Some families had brought what appeared to be their entire household and were already setting up makeshift bunks, surrounded by their most valuable possessions. There were large numbers of women with small children;

a few suburban housewives caught out by the sirens before they could get home; and several men in dinner jackets, their ladies flashing expensive jewellery, detained on their way to an evening on the town. Old people, their faces lined and weary, young shopgirls and typists, a smattering of men in uniform. All wartime life, in fact.

The atmosphere was already thick and the noise intense. The trains would continue running until eleven o'clock that night and their constant rumble melded with the clatter of people shifting possessions, calming children, nursing babies, chattering over thermos flasks. One or two noisy disputes temporarily topped the ceaseless buzz, people quarrelling over what cramped space there was left.

Daisy tried to pick her way through to a small area she'd spied at the very end of the platform. It was a mere postage stamp of a space, but with luck, she might find fresh air funnelled from the surface. Inching forward, trying to keep her feet, she hardly noticed the people she moved through. They were simply bodies to negotiate, elbows to avoid, legs not to stumble against.

She was concentrating so hard that it came as pure shock when she felt herself pushed forcibly to one side. A man, her mind told her in the instant before she felt herself losing balance, it was a man who'd pushed her. A blank face, dark eyes. She teetered dangerously on the edge of the platform, hovering for a moment in the air above the live rail. Then out of nowhere, a pair of strong hands took hold of her arms and held her tightly. There was a voice from what seemed a long way away, but she could make no sense of it.

'Daisy?' it questioned. Then, 'It was you!'

CHAPTER NINE

She was finding it difficult to understand what had just happened. The push had almost certainly been deliberate, but why? And who had done it? There had barely been time to register a face — a blurred outline only. Now, she felt herself being steadied and looked up into a pair of deep blue eyes, eyes that she knew well.

'It was you at my office?' he asked, and this time his question needed an answer.

She drew a deep breath before she said, 'Yes.' The mysterious attacker was forgotten. It was almost a relief to own up to her visit.

'On a matter of national importance?'

The crinkle at the corner of his eyes and the familiar wide smile encouraged confession. She felt oddly light as the tension trickled away. 'I'm afraid I lied. How did you know it was me?'

'Miss Strachan gave me a detailed description. You made an impression on her.'

Miss Strachan had not been slow in making her own impression, Daisy thought, but perhaps now wasn't the time to mention it.

'She said you appeared agitated and hadn't wanted to wait. It takes some time to come from the fifth floor, you know. I was on my way.' His tone was only slightly reproving.

'It wasn't that. I would have waited but . . . I couldn't go through with it.' The words came out in a rush, ill-suited and too dramatic.

'Is calling on an old friend such an ordeal?'

Grayson made it sound so easy and she wished it were. Reaching up to push the damp curls from her face, her hand pulled at first one strand of hair and then another. 'It didn't feel right, that's all. I was there under false pretences.'

He didn't respond to this confession and his gaze remained steady. Then he took hold of her hand and, before she could protest, led her through the maze of family groups, towards the empty space she'd spied earlier.

'This is where you were making for, I think. We can talk here.'

Other people had been quick to spot the same refuge and it had shrunk to even smaller proportions. They settled themselves as best they could, squashed against the furthermost corner of the tiling before it lost itself along the tunnel. Daisy was uncomfortable, hemmed in on all sides, and swamped by Grayson's physical presence. She'd forgotten how cool and fresh his skin smelt. It was distracting at a time when she needed her wits about her.

'So why the pretence?'

'I had to see you and she — Miss Strachan — was insistent that I must have an appointment. But today is my only free day. I'm on duty for the rest of the week.'

'It sounds as though it might be something of national importance after all.'

'It's a personal matter,' she murmured.

So personal that now she'd arrived at the moment, the impossibility of conveying Gerald's demand hit her with an unforeseen force. She felt her breath stutter and words go missing.

'Tell me,' he urged. His hand rested lightly on her forearm, a gesture of friendship, of solidarity. 'You've braved meeting me again, so it must be serious.'

Daisy looked down at her hands and noticed they were clenching and unclenching. He must have noticed, too, and realised how hard this was for her.

'It was about your work,' she managed to say at last. At least, that was true, but far too vague. It was the best she could do, though.

'My work?'

'How is it going?' She'd ducked the question she should be asking.

'Fine.' His eyes narrowed. 'It's going fine.' An uneasy silence opened between them and, in her mind, it filled the entire station, blotting out the chatter, the laughter, the raised voices.

'Did I tell you that I'd jumped horses?' He was trying to fill the yawning gap and she was grateful. 'Not exactly jumped,' he continued, 'more of a sideways manoeuvre.'

'You said something about new colleagues, I think. I don't remember the details.'

'That's hardly surprising. Anyway, I'm working for Special Operations now. What's left of the SIS after last year's split is still with the Foreign Office, but I got lucky.'

'Why lucky?'

'The SOE is far less demure — it can even be a tad exciting. The Foreign Office seems positively staid by comparison.'

She'd always felt that Grayson was cut out for adventure, and it looked as though he'd found it. His masquerade as a District Officer in Jasirapur had never quite rung true.

'What do you do there?'

'Guerrilla stuff — getting operations going in occupied countries. Or at least, we try to.'

She forced herself to concentrate on what he was saying, but her mind refused to obey. Somehow she was having to hold one kind of conversation, while at the same time working to escape the one that really mattered. And, all the time, she was conscious of his warmth infiltrating the length of her body.

In a daze, she heard herself say, 'But I thought your work was with India.'

'It is. SOE is divided up, each section assigned to a single country and naturally I got to join the Indian sector. We set up the India Mission late last year. It's too distant for London to control directly, but I'm the liaison officer.'

'And that's exciting?'

'By proxy. We're building local resistance, helping groups in Japanese occupied territory. The station's due to move to Ceylon, to be closer to South East Asia Command, but I'll still be the liaison.' He paused for a moment and then with a slight awkwardness, 'Here, I'm rambling on far too long. You can't possibly be interested in all of this. Tell me, how's the nurse training going?'

Her ploy appeared to have worked. In his enthusiasm, he'd forgotten the urgent matter she wanted to discuss. She was being a coward, she knew, but with luck, the All Clear would sound before he remembered it. And if she could talk about her own work as engagingly, it might distract him a while longer.

'The training's going well. Studying isn't always easy, especially after a long day or night on the wards. But since I passed the Preliminary Exam, it's been better. I'm trusted now with quite difficult procedures, though I don't escape the drudgery — and bedpans are beginning to lose their allure.'

She gave a rare smile and he smiled back. 'Only beginning! But you must be gaining an immense amount of experience. And, once the war is over, you'll find that invaluable. I can see you making Matron in no time.'

Daisy didn't reply, but felt his eyes resting on her and, when he spoke again, his voice was gentle. 'Sorry, that sounded callous. I can imagine the experience has come at a price. Some of your days must be very distressing.'

She felt herself being tugged towards his sympathy. Don't look at him, she told herself, don't look into his face, into his eyes. She must not allow old feelings to surface. Not when they could be dashed at any moment, severed absolutely, if she was forced to admit the outrageous request she had come with.

'Some of the work is painful,' she agreed. 'Barts still operates as a casualty clearing station and the stream of bomb victims is pretty constant. But you're right. With local emergencies as well, the nursing is intensive, particularly as we've only a skeleton staff. Most of the nurses have been sent to Hill End, but I've been lucky. I was one of the few asked to stay in London.'

'And when the war ends, where to?'

He seemed as eager as she to keep the conversation going, so she obliged. 'I should be an SRN by then. I think I'd like to specialise in surgical nursing. I actually made it into the theatre the other day. One of the third year nurses had to go home — her mother is extremely ill — and I took her place. Operations are done in the basement now. They've moved all the linen, but it's still quite cramped. I found it so interesting, though, that I forgot how hot and crowded it was.'

He nodded almost absently and she felt his eyes fix anew on her face. He was thinking and that was dangerous. He was trying to read her, she could see. He hadn't forgotten the urgent mission she'd come on after all, and she couldn't imagine why she'd thought he would. He was an intelligence officer, wasn't he? It was his job to get to the bottom of things. She strained her ears; the All Clear was a long time coming, but it could still save her. If it sounded, she would say a swift goodbye and tell Gerald that she'd met Grayson as he'd asked, and had done her best to persuade but without success. It was a lie, but then how many times had her husband lied to her?

She crossed and uncrossed her legs, then glanced down at her watch. The second hand seemed hardly to have moved. Time was slowing down and she felt trapped. The people immediately around her had begun to settle themselves more securely. They must have decided the raid would be protracted or simply one among a series, and resigned themselves to spending most of the night from home. Limbs were spread more widely, shoes removed, coats bunched as pillows or tucked into the body as protection from the ferocious draughts that sailed in from either side of the tunnel.

Grayson watched these preparations with an indifferent eye but, when he turned back to her, his gaze was sharp and the quiet voice had become unyielding.

'It's been good to catch up with each other's lives, Daisy, but I don't think you came all the way from the City on your one free day to talk about my work or yours. What's going on?'

There was to be no escape then. When she dared look at him, she felt her eyes drawn to his and saw determination there, but kindness, too, and something a good deal deeper and warmer. What she had to say would anger him for sure. It might even hurt him and that was the last thing she wanted. But the confusion, the wretchedness, she'd felt these past few days, had reached a crescendo and in that moment it toppled and burst through the flimsy defences she'd built.

'Gerald is alive,' she blurted out.

CHAPTER TEN

She felt Grayson's body tense against her, saw his face stiffen to stone.

'Gerald is alive,' she repeated. She still hardly believed it herself.

'Gerald? Gerald Mortimer?' His bark of laughter was ugly, forced.

'Yes. Gerald — my husband.'

'But that's crazy. Why on earth would you think that?'

'I don't think it, I know. He's here in London. He came to see me.' It was getting easier now. Her breath was still catching, but she was managing to put one word after another.

Grayson wasn't so adept. 'But . . . but how can he be?' he stuttered.

'He didn't drown. He was rescued by villagers downstream.'

'That's impossible. The river that day . . . you saw the river, Daisy. You stood on its brink. No one could have survived that torrent.'

'He did,' she said flatly. 'Somehow he managed to hang on to wreckage from one of the festival floats. He was pushed into the bank some miles from Jasirapur, and the villagers found him and looked after him until his injuries were mended. Then he made his way back to England.'

'Just like that.' Grayson might still be stunned, but there was a sour edge to his voice.

'I don't think it was quite that easy. He hasn't told me much about the journey, except that it took months. He begged his way out of India, and then through Turkey and across Europe. He found a job in France, but then war was declared. And here he is.'

Grayson's legs twitched. He looked as though he would give anything to jump to his feet and disappear down one of the tunnels. Instead, his hands harrowed through the brown sweep of his hair until it almost stood to attention. His mouth was tight and his forehead creased; beneath its rigid lines Daisy could see a whole encyclopaedia of questions forming.

'But why? Why come to England, why not return to Jasirapur?'

'If he'd gone back, he would have been arrested. The military police would have arrested him.'

Grayson glared furiously at her, as though her remark was so self-evident it wasn't worth uttering.

'And he still *can* be arrested,' he was keen to remind her. 'The Indian Army will want a court martial for certain. He's brought dishonour on his regiment. But he's also guilty of a criminal act. He should stand trial for theft, even treason.'

Daisy nodded dumbly. He was not saying anything she'd not already told herself a thousand times.

'And now, of course, he can add desertion to the charge sheet.' Grayson was angry, very angry. 'Not to mention his treatment of you.'

'He did try to save my life,' she said in a small voice. 'You once reminded me of that.'

'That was when I thought he was dead.' His voice was savage. 'What possessed him to desert? Couldn't he for once have acted like a man, owned up to his crimes, taken his punishment?' Angrily, he jerked his body to one side. 'Evidently not.'

Daisy didn't know whether he was consumed by fury at Gerald's criminal follies, or whether it was simple jealousy of the man who'd returned to claim his wife. But, whatever the reason, he couldn't be much angrier. Why not then take her chance?

She made a soft clearing sound in her throat. 'It's why I've come to you.'

'You want my advice on how to live with a deserter?' His voice had lost none of its sting.

'No, yes. I want your help, Grayson. You're the only one who *can* help me. Gerald wants to go to a neutral country, to America where he'll be safe.'

'I bet he does. Tell him to apply through the usual channels.'

'You know he can't do that. He'd be arrested immediately.'

'And I should care?'

'I don't expect you to care. But I do. He's a soldier guilty of theft and desertion at a time when this country is struggling to survive. Think what my life will be like if my husband is tried for those crimes. And worse, if he's tried for treason.'

'It wouldn't be comfortable,' he conceded. 'But who knows, Gerald might get himself out of England and there'd be no problem. He's weasel enough. And no doubt you'll accompany him to whatever Shangri La he has in mind. England could fade to a distant nightmare for you.' Once more, he turned his body away from her, his jaw a hard outline against the fluorescent glow of the station lighting.

'I don't want him anywhere near me.'

The words formed themselves without effort. They were heartfelt and true. What she wanted most of all was a clean break, just as Connie had suggested. The realisation had been slow to come. Since Gerald reappeared, she'd been tormenting herself on what she should do, how she should feel, and it had been time wasted. Why had she clouded what was so beautifully clear? From the beginning she had been unhappy in her marriage and it had gone from bad to worse — and now, worse still. She had to cut herself free and, if Gerald made it to America, she would be. She would never need to see him again.

Grayson turned towards her as she spoke, his figure no longer frighteningly stiff. He reached across and took her hand in his and, for some time, they sat silent and unmoving. Then he gave her hand a squeeze.

'The sooner he goes, the better, Daisy. You've suffered enough from him and you mustn't be dragged into his murky little world again. How dare he even try!'

'I think he came to me out of desperation. He's no one else to turn to. When I first met him, he seemed the same arrogant Gerald, but underneath I believe he's scared. Really scared.'

'With good reason. The army usually get their man, even if SIS have too much going on to be interested in him.'

'He's convinced that someone is going to report him to the authorities.'

Grayson gave a low mutter. 'Who exactly? Who even knows he's in London? You won't bring it out in the open and neither will I, though by rights I should summon the Military Police immediately. I'm sure they'd be more than a little interested in Lieutenant Mortimer.'

'He's no longer Mortimer. He's reverted to being Jack Minns.'

'Ah, Jack Minns. That sounds about right — returning to the person he really is. He was such a little shit at Hanbury, I should have known what his future would be.'

She had never heard Grayson swear before and her face must have signalled her dismay.

'I'm sorry. I don't mean to distress you, but he's despicable. I wish you'd never met him. He's brought you nothing but ill fortune.'

She couldn't disagree. She wished with all her heart that when Gerald had walked into Bridges that day to buy perfume for another woman, one of her disdainful colleagues had stepped forward to serve him. Instead, the job had fallen to her and the moment she'd smiled across the counter at him, her fate had been decided. Was still being decided. And would continue to be decided until she found a way to get

Gerald across the Atlantic Ocean. A renewed sense of weariness rolled over her. Confessing her mission to Grayson had taken a toll and, in the end, it had been for nothing. He was sympathetic, but he wouldn't or couldn't help Gerald. He was too angry even to consider the possibility. Her husband would stay in London, a tormenting presence, a time bomb primed to explode at any moment and ruin the small success she'd made of her life.

But should she make a last effort to persuade? 'Gerald thinks he's being spied on by the men in the flat below. He's sure they mean him ill, and he seems more scared of them than of the Military Police.'

'Scared because he thinks they're spies?'

She saw Grayson's smile hover on the edge of sardonic. Then the faintest wail came to them, travelling through and around the hallways, the staircases, the tunnels. At last the All Clear. A number of people were staggering to their feet, methodically beginning to pack away blankets and pillows and crockery. The majority of those camped on the platform, though, made no move to leave. It might be better to stay the whole night, Daisy thought, particularly if there were further raids. Who would want to journey back and forth from house to shelter when they could be snatching a few hours' sleep? Perhaps, too, the solid tunnel walls, the cocoon of blankets, helped to blot out an unwelcome reality, the ever-present fear that there might be nowhere to go back to.

Grayson was already up and pulling her to her feet. 'Come on, I'll walk you back to Barts.'

She had no chance to refuse. He was heading for the exit and towing her behind him, and she could say nothing until the crowded escalator delivered them into the station foyer and, from there, out into the cold crisp air of an early April evening. They stood together in the darkened street and listened. The All Clear had faded to nothing and the traffic was stilled. There was no drone of planes to disturb the quiet, no roar of the guns that sought them. It was as though a mighty orchestra — planes, guns, sirens — had fallen silent. But not before they'd left behind an indelible imprint: whichever way Daisy looked, the sky was aglow with light, a sweep of glowering fire.

She wriggled her hand free; it was time to regain control. 'There's really no need to walk me back, Grayson. It will take you out of your way.'

'Only a very little. Or had you forgotten that my flat's in Finsbury?'

She was surprised. 'You're still in Spence's Road?'

'Why wouldn't I be? Did you think I'd moved back to Pimlico to be with Mummy?' The mocking note made her smile slightly. He adored his parent, but had always been careful to keep his independence.

'I just wondered. People's circumstances change so quickly these days.'

'Meaning?'

'I haven't seen you for nine months. You might have got married in the meantime.' She was grateful for the surrounding dark. He wouldn't have noticed the flush she'd been unable to prevent.

'Not guilty. You did a good job on me.'

'I'm not sure I understand.'

'Then don't try to work it out. I've said enough if I tell you the girls that I've knocked around with since you cut me adrift have been just that — girls to knock around with.'

She felt a perverse flood of pleasure. She'd told him to go his own way, hadn't she, and now she was feeling glad that he hadn't.

'So to Barts?' He offered her his arm.

'To Charterhouse Square. I don't have to work this evening.'

They moved off slowly, taking care to avoid the shrouded figures continuing to emerge from the station foyer.

'So tell me about the evil spies who live below Gerald's floorboards.'

She couldn't blame him for not taking it seriously. She found it difficult to accept herself. It was only the fact that

Gerald was the least likely person to be haunted by imaginary fears that made her give any credence to what sounded preposterous.

'You do know that everyone sees spies these days.' Grayson was enjoying himself. 'Since the Germans have been camped on the French coast with invasion likely, hysteria has reached danger level. Everyone suspects and everyone is under suspicion. Only last month some poor, benighted foreigner in Kensington was accused of making signals to enemy bombers by smoking a cigar in a strange manner. Apparently, he puffed rather too hard and pointed the cigar towards the sky.'

'I don't think Gerald's spies come into that category.' Why she was defending her husband's paranoia she had no idea, except that some deep instinct told her that he could be right.

'We get hundreds of reports of suspected fifth columnists, you know,' Grayson was saying. 'Strange marks daubed on telegraph poles, nuns with hairy arms and Hitler tattoos, municipal flowerbeds planted with white flowers to direct planes towards munitions factories. And so on. But in reality there are virtually no enemy agents here.'

'How can you be so sure?'

'Let's just say the Germans don't have an effective intelligence operation in Britain. Spies should be the least of Gerald's — sorry Jack's — worries.'

'They're not Germans. They're Indians. He heard them speak in Hindi.'

For a moment, Grayson paused in their slow walk. She couldn't see his face, but she was sure it wore an arrested expression. 'Does that mean something to you?' she prompted.

'Not necessarily. But it's unusual to find two Indians sheltering in the middle of London with a war raging. And particularly unusual at a time like this.'

'What's special about now?'

'You won't know, but India has recently surfaced again as a hot topic among the great and the good. Germany has been hinting it will guarantee Indian independence if the country doesn't join us in the fight, and Italy and Japan are likely to take the same view. It's only a matter of time, I think, before the Axis offer some kind of formal pact to our jewel in the crown.'

'But isn't the Indian Army fighting alongside us?'

'The Indian Army is magnificent, but we're desperate for men. The war has spread halfway round the world. We need more Indians to volunteer for the fight, just as they did in the Great War. Germany tried to stir up Indian nationalism then, as a way of causing trouble, but now we have Congress to contend with. So far, they've refused to cooperate unless we pay their political price — independence — and that's been rejected outright.'

'And if we can't persuade them to fight on our side, will it be such a disaster?'

'It won't be good. And if Congress should decide to join the Axis powers, then we *are* talking disaster.'

'I wonder if Gerald's Indians are involved in some way.'

'Unlikely. It's far more probable they're deserters, on the run like Gerald, or refugees drifting from place to place. There's been an influx of new people into the country and not just troops from the empire. The numbers making for London have swollen since the war began and the city has a very mobile population. After all, what better place to lose yourself and assume a new identity. Gerald should feel at home, shouldn't he?'

He hadn't been able to resist the taunt, she noticed, but she wasn't going to rise to the bait. 'Don't forget, the black market is thriving,' he went on, 'and plenty of refugees make a living from fencing stolen goods and selling them back to shopkeepers. New rackets and racketeers spring up every day. If your Indians are involved in that, they'll be keeping a careful eye on their neighbours. "Spying" on them, in fact.'

The moon had risen and though its light was dim, their path around corners and over uneven paving stones was becoming easier. He took her by the arm and steered her into Wigmore Street. 'I think Gerald has far more pressing problems than a couple of Indians. They won't want his attention any more than he wants theirs. I suppose he didn't hear what they were saying?'

Grayson might dismiss Gerald's spies as petty criminals, but she noticed that he was still curious. 'He didn't make much sense of their conversation,' she said. 'They seem to be agitated a lot of the time, arguing quite a bit. One of them always remained in the flat, and Gerald was sure that the other followed him whenever he went out.'

Grayson said nothing and she was moved to add, 'I know it sounds mad, but once or twice I've thought there was someone watching me, too.' And now someone trying to push me onto the line. But she wouldn't say that and sound even madder.

'How long have you thought you were being watched?'

She wasn't sure how to answer. 'Since Gerald popped out of his grave?'

'Yes, I think so. In fact, I thought there was someone that night, the night I first saw him when he came to the Nurses' Home, but I was probably imagining things. The shock of seeing him again has made me see danger everywhere.'

'Then we'd better get rid of him, hadn't we?'

CHAPTER ELEVEN

Was she hearing aright? Did that mean Grayson had made a decision to help? Daisy's throat went dry but, even if it meant he was willing, she couldn't allow herself to dance in the street. Not yet. Grayson had no idea of the shape or size of her appeal and when he did . . . but she had to go on with it, or how else was she to say a final farewell to Gerald?

Her stomach knotted in apprehension. The moment was crucial. 'Is it possible,' she asked in a low voice, 'would it be possible, to get papers for Gerald? To smooth his passage to America.'

Grayson stopped abruptly and she almost fell over her feet. 'You're not asking much, are you?'

'I know what I'm asking is huge, but I can't see any other solution.'

There was a long pause before he said, 'There isn't one.'

'Does that mean you'll try to get papers?' Could he really be about to agree? It seemed impossible and she had to tell herself to keep breathing.

'Yes, it means I'll try.'

Overpowering relief made her jettison caution. Without thinking, she threw her arms around him and held him tightly. They stood for a while, body to body, and then very gently he detached himself and held her at a distance. In the dim light, she could see his face, careful, serious. 'I don't know if I'll be successful. You'll have to give me a few days.'

'I will, but thank you, Grayson, thank you so very much.'

And, with a swift movement, she freed one of her hands and reached upwards, smoothing his cheek as she did so. The caress fleetingly touched his lips and she found them warm and firm. Old desires were woken and, in that instant, she wanted very much to kiss him, but he regained his clasp on her hand and brought it to rest in his. Before, she thought, she could do anything she would regret.

'Sorry guv'nor. Yer can't walk this way. There's still one of 'em down there.'

An ARP warden was blocking their path and pointing to a huge crater straddling the road outside what had once been a house. The sides of the building had been torn away, exposing crumbling inner walls and wallpaper that flapped in tattered strips. How long the warden had been there, she had no idea, caught up as she'd been in that moment of intimacy. Now she could see a large white barrier and could just make out its warning, Danger Unexploded Bomb. Beyond the barrier, a crew of weary firemen were hosing the still burning building, and the wounded were being helped to safety and 'a nice cup of tea' at the wardens' post.

It was mundane. Death itself had become mundane, mere figures on an ARP's casualty chart. Several of the wardens were still searching the rubble for survivors, while neighbours and bystanders worked frantically alongside. Everyone in London was a member of this civil army, she thought. The city depended on its inhabitants to keep it going. Even her erstwhile colleagues in the perfumery department, those girls who had been so scornful of her, were part of that army. Bombs rained down on Bridges as much as they did on the battery at Marble Arch, and the women, and thousands like them, who lived and worked in the streets of the city, were as much under fire as the soldiers behind the guns in Hyde Park.

'Where are yer goin' mate?'

'We're headed for the City, near St Paul's.'

The man shook his head. 'I dunno if that's been hit bad. But you can't walk this way. Best turn northwards and make a loop.'

Together, they turned in the direction of the Euston Road. The streets here were unfamiliar to them both and they were forced to travel more slowly, navigating the dense dark that once again cloaked the world. For the most part, they walked in silence, sunk deep in their own thoughts. Daisy was conscious that something unexpected had happened, that in some way she had taken the first tentative steps to bridging the gulf between them. The last time they'd met, she had been adamant she could never be more than his friend and, when he'd refused the offer of friendship, she'd retreated into a loveless world of her own. Yet, just now she had quite spontaneously broken through the isolation she'd imposed on herself; she had wrapped her arms around the man who walked beside her. It altered nothing, of course. Nightmares from the past would still haunt her and, whether Gerald left England or not, she would remain his wife. But something *had* happened, something she hardly dared put a name to. At least, not yet.

Grayson broke the silence. 'We should probably turn south here, drop down to Russell Square and then into High Holborn. Let's hope we don't meet more barricades or we could be a long while getting back.'

She hoped so, too. Her feet were already beginning to feel sore in the smart shoes she'd chosen for this encounter, and there was a definite blister forming on her small toe. She tried to think of something else. A loud hissing sound floating through the air towards them was nicely distracting.

'Steam engines,' he explained. 'They're waiting to leave.'

'Are we that close to the station?'

'It's just over the road. How's this for an idea? Why don't we stop for a short break. It's not late and there's bound to be somewhere open on the forecourt. We can grab a cup of tea — or something stronger, if you'd rather.'

'It sounds good,' she said, thinking how pleasant it would be to rest her feet, 'and tea will be fine.'

A few minutes brought them to the forecourt and the noise, caged within the station's four walls, was intense. Several long trains were waiting impatiently for their customers. Or was it for their victims, she thought fancifully. The trains were like prehistoric beasts, smoking and hissing under the huge, gloomy cavern of glass. Apart from rows of faint blue high up in the roof, there was no light in the entire station. The figures of porters moved like unworldly shades around the bales and packages which lay heaped in dark corners.

'Have you ever been to a London terminal at night since the blackout started?' Grayson asked. 'I always think it's a magnificent sight.'

'It's certainly a magnificent sound,' she joked.

Once they'd shut the doors of the station café behind them, the noise was reduced to a comforting shush. She settled herself on a bentwood chair while Grayson took his chance at the counter. He was soon back with two mugs of suspiciously grey tea.

'Hardly any milk,' he apologised.

'The romance of the railway isn't dead then?' She was feeling almost unbearably light-headed. It was relief, she knew, simple relief.

'It will return,' he promised. 'It's always been a great way to travel, at least in this island.'

She wondered if he was remembering India as he spoke and its interminably long train journeys. Anything up to three days of blistering heat and sweating discomfort. Days of noise, colour, chaos, before you arrived at your destination a wet and crumpled heap.

He stirred his cup. 'I never got to tell you, but I did some research. I think you might find it interesting.'

'Yes?' She couldn't imagine what the research could be, but if it took her mind away from India, she was happy to listen.

'I found some information on your mother. I know I promised you on board ship that I'd look, but then life got in the way. Recently, though, I managed to trace her to where she did her nursing. It could be the place you were born.'

Daisy felt an odd spurt of indignation. She should have been the one to find her mother. It wouldn't have been that difficult. She was a nurse herself now and there must be channels she could have followed. But she hadn't. She'd let it go. If she were honest, she hadn't wanted to find out, knowing instinctively that any search was likely to bring pain. The pain of not really knowing who she was.

'If I said Brighton, would it ring bells?'

'I don't think I hear any.'

'It's where your mother was nursing during the Great War. At the Brighton Pavilion. The palace was converted into a hospital for wounded soldiers. Interestingly, it was used for a couple of years for troops from the Indian Army, recuperating from trench warfare in France and Belgium. Your mother probably didn't nurse their wounded. There would have been male orderlies to do that, I think. And the doctors were a mix of Indian medical students and British doctors from the Indian Medical Service, who'd worked in India and spoke various languages.'

She barely heard his last few words. The mention of India had brought to mind the one photograph she had of her mother, wearing a brooch that replicated the image Daisy had seen amid the tumbling masonry of a temple. An image that decorated the neck of the goddess, Nandni Mata. Nandni Mata, she remembered — the words meant 'daughter'.

With difficulty, she wrenched her mind back to the present. 'If my mother wasn't nursing, what was she doing there?'

'There were several British nurses listed as working in the Pavilion hospital at that time, and my guess would be that they were used to train the Indian orderlies. The orderlies would be the same caste or religion as the patients they tended.'

An Indian orderly. Of course. A shaft of understanding flared, so bright that if it had been tangible, it would have shattered the café's gloom and sent the pieces flying. So that was the meaning of the jewellery!

'One of the orderlies could have given your mother the brooch, the one she's wearing in your photograph.' Grayson's words echoed her thoughts precisely. 'A gift, perhaps, for the help she gave him?'

Daisy nodded. 'That must be it.' She was turning the information over in her mind. 'I would never have guessed. Brighton. I always thought I had to have been born in the East End, but the details were missing from my birth certificate.' Like my father's name, she thought.

'We should take a trip down there one day and see if we can dig up anything more.'

She wasn't sure she wanted more. In her experience information usually meant an unpleasant shock and she'd sustained enough of those already. But, in any case, it was unlikely she would ever get to Brighton. After Dunkirk, the Kent and Sussex coastal towns had been closed to anyone but residents, and even they had to observe a night-time curfew. Casual visitors were strictly forbidden on pain of imprisonment.

That wasn't going to stop Grayson, though. 'We'd need a special permit to go,' he said, 'but it wouldn't be completely impossible.'

'A special permit or the end of the war?'

'Or the end of the war,' he agreed. 'Not much of a cup, was it?' and he gestured to her half-drunk tea. 'And perhaps we should go. We've still a few miles to cover.'

They dropped down from Euston into Bloomsbury and then on to High Holborn. Here and there were signs the bombers had come this way, dealing their random destruction. Glancing down side roads as they passed, Daisy could see little. The air was choking, a mixture of powdered mortar and fumes from the fires that still burnt brightly. A row of houses here, another there, had been obliterated, and rescue workers were combing the area in force, crunching through glass to toil away at the dust-covered rubble. Beside the main thoroughfare, bodies waited for collection, some covered in sacks, others by blankets and old curtains. An old woman dug desperately at masonry she had no hope of shifting. Daisy looked away. It was too painful to witness.

Grayson had not let her hand drop since they'd left the station. It was a necessary precaution, she told herself. She'd never walked these streets at night; they were as dark as pitch and every few yards the bombing had cast hazards in their path. But necessary or not, it was immensely comforting to have his strong figure by her side.

At last, they were nearing Charterhouse Square, and not a minute too soon for Daisy's aching body. The red brick of the Nurses' Home, just visible through the trees, was a welcome sight, but she would walk to its door alone. If Grayson were seen, and he was bound to be, it would cause gossip, and that was something she couldn't face. During the first six months of her training, she had met him only briefly and always well away from the hospital. He'd remained unknown to her nursing colleagues and that's how she wanted it to stay.

Daisy disentangled her hand as gently as she could. 'We can say goodbye here. I've only a few yards to go and you've still at least a mile before you get home.'

'What you mean, is that I'm getting too close to *your* home.'

'It's easier if you don't.'

He didn't ask her why, but accepted her decision. That was one of the things she liked about him. He didn't argue, didn't impose, didn't try to control. She supposed that was out of respect. Respect had been largely absent from her life and it was something Daisy cherished.

'I'll try and sort something out in the next few days.' He looked down at her as he made the promise.

She couldn't see the expression in his eyes, just the dim outline of his head. An almost desperate longing to take his face in her hands and kiss his warm, firm mouth, caught hold of her, astonishing her with its force.

'Be prepared for disappointment,' he was warning, 'though I'll do my best.'

She stepped back to a safer distance, shaking herself free of the unwanted emotion. 'It's more than I deserve. Thank you again.'

'It's far less than you deserve, Daisy, but we won't quarrel over that. If I'm not to come here or to Barts, where do you want to meet?'

She couldn't quite forget the sense of being watched, and searched her mind for somewhere innocuous. She had told herself that the shadow she'd seen was probably an innocent passer-by, or a trick of the light, but she would be careful — just in case.

'Would a Lyons tea shop suit?' she hazarded.

'Sounds good to me. Can you make the one in the Strand? That would be halfway house for both of us.'

'On Thursday I can. I've an extended shift the day before and should be able to take a couple of hours off duty that afternoon. That is, if Thursday isn't too soon for you.'

'I'm pretty sure to know one way or another by then. Three o'clock? If you're not there, I'll know you're still being a ministering angel. Then I *will* have to come looking for you!'

CHAPTER TWELVE

Daisy stepped through the oak door into a scene of confusion. Her mind was already unsettled from the encounter with Grayson, and the last thing she needed was to walk into turmoil. The narrow hall seemed over full with people. One or two girls were hanging from the banisters while several others were bunched at the foot of the stairs, but all of them seemed unable or unwilling to intervene in the furious argument that had erupted between Willa and Lydia Penrose.

'You snitched, you cow. Don't deny it.' Lydia, her face tight and red, was advancing against the other girl who had backed further and further towards the wall, until she was now cowering flat against the post boxes.

'It wasn't me.' Willa's voice was barely audible. She had put up her arms as if to defend herself from the blows she was expecting, and Daisy felt slightly sick at the sight.

'It was you, all right. It always is. You're lousy at your job and you can't bear it that I'm good at mine.' Lydia's voice was shaking with anger. 'You have to tell tales about me to make yourself feel better.'

The trembling girl could only shake her head, her silence seeming to infuriate Lydia even more.

'Not talking now, are you? Worn yourself out gossiping behind my back.'

'I haven't. I didn't. I've never said anything bad about you.' Willa had found her tongue, but her protest was feeble.

'You did. You must have. No one else would. You're pathetic — look at you. You call yourself a nurse. You can't even wear the uniform right. The only way you'll ever get on is to suck up to Sister and tell tales. I wonder what else you've been saying — about all of us.' And she pointed to the girls looking on, their eyes wide, their mouths slack with surprise. 'I bet they'd like to know. Tell us, why don't you?'

Willa was shaking and her face was the colour of laundered sheets. Daisy walked towards the pair of them, intent on stopping Lydia's flow of invective.

'What exactly is she supposed to have done?'

Lydia whirled to face her, momentarily forgetting her prey, and the pause allowed the crouching girl to pull herself upright. 'I'll tell you what she's done, Nurse Driscoll.' Her tone was sneering. 'I went out for a fag. After an eight-hour shift, I bloody deserved it. But no, apparently not. Little Miss Suck Up here seized her moment. She told Sister that Lydia had been a naughty girl.'

'I didn't,' Willa repeated and her voice was a little stronger. Daisy's presence seemed to be steadying her. 'I didn't, Daisy, honestly.'

Lydia turned to face her victim again and her expression had lost none of its venom. 'Someone did. If it wasn't you, who was it?' she spat out. 'Was it one of you, girls?' She surveyed the half dozen faces looking at them from the other side of the hall. 'No, I thought not.'

'Why don't you just admit it, Willa, and say sorry,' one of the nurses suggested.

'Yes, say sorry. Then we can all get some rest,' said another. The girls had so far remained neutral, but now they'd made their decision. They were tired and desperate for sleep, and none of them fancied being on the sharp end of Lydia's tongue.

Willa looked from one to the other, a flicker of desperation passing across her face. She licked her lips with her tongue. 'Sorry.' The word crept out, barely reaching the ears of her listeners.

But they'd heard enough and nodded, satisfied. The group dispersed, most turning to go back up the stairs, but one or two of the girls coming towards Lydia and patting her on the back. Willa was deliberately ignored.

'You know what,' Lydia complained bitterly to them, 'because of that bitch I've got to work for two weeks without a break. That's my punishment — but what's hers?'

'We'll think of something, Lydia, don't worry.' They smirked at each other and the three of them made for their rooms, leaving Daisy with a still trembling Willa. She looked at the girl's face, puffed from weeping, and took her hand.

'Are you all right?' It seemed inadequate after the scene she'd just witnessed.

Willa didn't answer, but instead said again and again, 'I didn't tell. I didn't tell. Honestly, I didn't.'

Daisy hugged her, smoothing her tangle of hair in an attempt to quieten her agitation, but now she had begun to talk, Willa couldn't stop.

'Someone must have reported her, but it wasn't me. I've often seen Lydia go out for a smoke, so why would I say anything today. Why? Why?'

'I think you should try to forget the matter,' Daisy soothed. 'Lydia will, I'm sure. In time, she'll come to realise it wasn't you. You've just been the scapegoat. She had to have someone to blame.' And wasn't that always the way of the world, she thought wearily, the weakest, the most vulnerable, were called to shoulder the blame. 'Come on, I'll walk you to your room. You need to sleep. Work will be as hard as ever tomorrow.'

They were platitudes, but all she could offer.

'What do you think they'll do to me?' Willa asked in a wavering voice as they reached the door of her room.

'Nothing, it's all talk. What could they do? They'll be far too busy even to think about what happened tonight. You mustn't let it play on your mind. Promise me, you'll try to sleep. Remember we're on duty again at seven. Think of all those breakfasts to serve, beds to make, floors to clean before Sister walks in to read prayers. Who's going to have time to think of petty tit for tats?'

'I suppose so,' the girl agreed miserably. 'I suppose you're right. Thank you, Daisy.'

'I've done nothing.'

'You have. You were here,' she said simply. 'And it's helped.'

* * *

Daisy shut her door, collapsing wearily against it, grateful to be back once more in the small, bare room. After the strain of meeting Grayson and this latest unpleasant incident with Willa, she needed to be alone. Needed time to think. First, though, she must jettison the shoes that were pinching remorselessly and stretch her poor, bruised toes. Willa's problem was soon dispensed with. It was a simple spat, she decided, one of many that erupted at regular intervals in the Home, a result of being cooped together, working and living under the most intense conditions. Lydia Penrose was always going to be an awkward addition to the nursing team. She came from a wealthy family and liked people to know it. She was proud of 'doing her bit for the war' as a humble nurse and liked to remind them of that, too. Often she was the driving force behind any trouble on the wards or at the Home. And whenever there was trouble, it seemed that Willa was always the target.

Daisy wished the girl would stand up for herself, but she understood why she didn't. She had met Willa's stepfather briefly and sensed in an instant the emotional bullying he employed against his stepchildren. From an early age, Willa had been brainwashed to believe she was stupid. It was a brutal tactic stopping short of physical cruelty, though having seen the girl's raised arms tonight, Daisy wondered.

Whatever methods the man employed, his stepdaughter had learned her lesson of humility too well. It was better to be an orphan, she thought. She had always longed for a family of her own, but in its absence she had grown strong and independent in a way that Willa couldn't match.

The girl's troubles drifted from her mind as soon as she began to undress, quickly since the bedrooms were unheated and the chill was penetrating. She threw on her nightdress and climbed swiftly into bed, tucking the covers tightly in place and rubbing her feet up and down the cold sheets to create at least a jot of warmth. She couldn't sleep just yet. There was too much thinking to do. Thinking about Grayson, whether she wanted to or not — their walk tonight had raised uncomfortable questions.

She still had to pinch herself to believe that he'd agreed to help. His decision to procure papers for Gerald must flout every one of his principles, and yet he'd most definitely agreed to try. To try for a man he'd loathed since boyhood, and a man he should be denouncing to the authorities. For the first time, she wondered what would happen to Grayson if it ever became known he'd aided a felon. Daisy didn't want to think too much about that; nor did she want to think too much of why he'd agreed to her request with hardly a moment's hesitation. It made her feel shabby, almost unclean.

She'd played on his feelings, aware all the time that she was unable to repay any debt that might come owing. If he was hoping that by seeking him out she was signalling a new beginning, those hopes would soon crumble. She was unable to feel the way he wanted. There was no denying the physical pull between them. She'd felt his attraction ever since their first meeting, even at a time when she'd been a new bride, and tonight he'd stirred emotions in her that she would rather forget. She could recognise desire when it came calling, but it was not enough and it never would be.

And Grayson wanted more. He wanted her heart and her soul, and she no longer had those to give. She'd given them once and they'd been returned to her in small pieces, and that's how they'd stay. It wasn't a lack of trust. Once, that might have been the case, but no longer. She trusted Grayson completely, and she couldn't understand why she was unable to let go and allow her heart to feel again. But she couldn't. It was a barrier she was unable to leap and she knew she would always disappoint him. When she'd realised that — what was it, nine months ago? — she'd said her goodbyes, feeling immensely sad but resigned to the inevitable solitude. She was used to it.

On a very few occasions she'd grown close to people, but never for long. Even Connie would eventually drift out of her life, she knew. Jocelyn Forester already had. The young girl with her boundless pleasure in life had brightened Daisy's world for a brief period, but that light was now all but extinguished. Her single ally in Jasirapur had married and was once more living back in India. She hadn't wed her Indian Army soldier after all, but a planter from Assam, who she'd met at a tea dance in Hove while she was staying with her Sussex relations. The news had caused Daisy a wry smile. Their correspondence had always been desultory, and now war made communication even more difficult. She doubted she would see her friend again. And that was for the best. After the wretched end to Daisy's life in India, she couldn't see herself exchanging girlish chatter with the colonel's daughter.

She wouldn't want to tell Jocelyn a lot of things — Gerald's desertion, for instance. It would be unfair to place such a burden on her. And she could never speak of Grayson's illicit help. Unfair again. But she was allowing her mind to run ahead and she shouldn't. It was by no means certain that he'd be able to help. Despite his explanation, Daisy had only the haziest idea what the SOE did. She presumed they must manufacture papers for the spies they sent abroad and wondered if someone would do that for Gerald. But he wouldn't go as a spy, surely. The United States was a neutral country and presumably you didn't send spies there. Or did you? There was little point in speculating. She must just wait and hope.

CHAPTER THIRTEEN

'How did it go?' Connie's smiling face appeared in the doorway, just as Daisy was about to dim the light. 'You did meet him, didn't you?'

She bounced into the room and shut the door with a decided thud. Daisy hastily scrabbled something together that would satisfy her friend. It would have to be a severely trimmed version of events, but sufficient to stop Connie prying further.

'You didn't go, did you?' Connie marched forward and, even in the fluctuating light of the small bedside lamp, Daisy could see accusation writ large on her face. 'You funked it!'

She looked steadily at her friend and said in a quiet voice, 'I went.'

In an instant, Connie had rushed over to the bed and was enveloping her in the warmest of embraces. 'Well done! And so very sorry I was a doubting Thomas. I should have known you'd find the courage to beard the beast.'

'Grayson isn't a beast.'

'No, but what you had to ask him was.'

'Don't heap me with praise.' It was time to come clean. 'I was only a little brave.'

Her friend looked sceptical and she tried to explain. 'I went to Baker Street, I even went into the building where

Grayson works and asked for him. But then I got cold feet and when the receptionist rang for him to come down and meet me, I ran away.'

'So, you didn't see him after all?' Connie's face had gone pink. 'You screwed up your courage so far and then you chickened out.'

'I know, but don't be cross. Eventually, I did get to meet him.'

'But how?'

'There was an air raid just as I left the building. I rushed to the underground station with everybody else — it was the nearest shelter. Grayson must have been coming after me. I imagine he wondered who his mysterious visitor was, and decided to find out. Anyway, when the siren went, he had to take refuge in the station, too. And that's where I saw him.'

'How serendipitous. Is that a word? But there must have been a huge crowd down there. How did you find him?'

There *had* been a huge crowd and one of its number had almost killed her. From time to time, Daisy had thought about that moment. At first, she'd been sure the push was deliberate, but now she wasn't so certain. It seemed such a foolish notion, lacking any kind of sense or reason, and she wasn't about to worry Connie with the tale of a mystery attacker. She would be better to forget him.

'I didn't go looking. I'd no idea he'd be there. We just bumped into each other.'

'There you are, serendipitous.'

'I suppose so, but it took me an age to get round to asking him for help. In fact, I didn't until we were on our way here. I don't think he believed me at first when I told him Gerald was alive, but then walking back home somehow . . . things loosened up.' That was the least embarrassing way she could put it. She wasn't about to confess she'd flung herself into his arms. 'And then I asked him.'

Connie's eyes widened and she seemed to be holding her breath. 'How did he take it?'

'Amazingly well.' Her conscience pricked again at how little Grayson would get in return.

'So he wasn't *too* angry then — or he'd have refused you.'

'I hope not. In any case, he said he'd do what he could.'

Her friend squealed and Daisy hastily shushed her to silence. The bedroom walls were thin and the last thing she wanted were eavesdroppers.

'That's wonderful. Farewell Gerald. Yippee to that!'

'I'm not out of the woods, yet,' Daisy warned. 'I can't be sure Grayson will be able to help, even if he's willing.'

'If he can't, nobody can.' Connie repeated her earlier conviction. 'But why are you looking so glum? At least there's a chance now of losing the loser.'

'I hated asking Grayson. I felt I was exploiting his good nature.'

'What you mean is you hated exploiting his feelings for you.'

Connie had hit the nail on the head.

'It made me feel bad. Then, when I got back, there was Willa, too,' she said distractedly.

'What about her? What she's done now — or not done more likely.'

'I walked into the most tremendous row — between her and Lydia, as always. Lydia was convinced it was Willa who got her into trouble, sneaking to Sister about her smoking. She's been punished by having all her frees taken away for the next two weeks.'

'Serve her right. Lydia Penrose thinks she's Queen of the May, that she can do anything she likes and get away with it.'

'I don't believe it was Willa who told tales.'

'Who then?'

'I don't know, but Willa would never have had the nerve. And she's much too sweet natured to harm anyone deliberately.'

'And if the Penrose wasn't so wrapped up in herself, she'd know that. So how did it end?'

'Lydia slunk off with her cronies and Willa went to bed. To cry herself to sleep, if I'm any judge.' Daisy stared moodily into the distance. 'I didn't know what to do, Connie. She's such a frail soul. She lost her brother only a few weeks ago and, I suspect, someone else she was close to as well. And nursing doesn't help her. I don't think she's cut out for the profession, and certainly not for the rough and tumble of this place.'

'Perhaps the row will make her realise it at last,' Connie said comfortably, 'and then she can forget nursing and go home.'

'I don't think her home is very welcoming either.'

'You can't take the troubles of the world on your shoulders. Forget Willa for the moment and look forward to freedom. It's around the corner and I've got just the thing to celebrate.'

With a magician's sleight of hand, she plunged into her cape and from its folds pulled out a single bottle of beer.

Daisy laughed. 'Where on earth did you find that?' Alcohol was scarce at the best of times and at the Nurses' Home non-existent. 'Don't you think a celebration might be a mite premature?'

'You think so? For you maybe, but not for me.'

Daisy looked at her friend more closely. 'Is it *you* that's doing the celebrating? Now I come to think of it, you looked unusually sunny when you came in. So what's happened?'

'Dr Lawson.'

'What about him?'

'I've got myself a date.'

'With Dr Lawson?'

'Who else? With the scrumptious doctor.' She pulled the regulation chair up to the bed. It was made of basket weave and groaned loudly as Connie's plump form settled into its meagre space. 'Don't breathe a word though, will you?' Her voice was barely above a whisper. 'I don't want the other girls to know. I don't want them on my back, especially not Lydia and her crew.'

'But how? I thought he was married.'

'He's as single as you or me. Well, me at least. And he's delicious and no one else is going to touch him. It was the whizziest bit of luck, Daisy.'

'Go on, tell me.'

Connie's face was alight and she leaned forward until she was almost lying against Daisy's shoulder. 'There was a mix up tonight on the medicine trolley, and I had to stay behind and help Sister sort it out. Just as I was finishing, Dr Lawson — I suppose I can call him Colin now, at least to you — anyway Colin walked on to the ward to talk to Sister. But then the phone went and she had to walk to the other end of the ward to answer it. So, that left him and me with nothing to do but talk.'

Daisy was amused. 'About what?'

'He asked me if I was just coming on duty or off and I said I'd had to stay, but I was looking forward to getting my supper and he said, what's the food like at the Home, and I said pretty bloody awful — well, without the bloody — and he laughed and said the doctors didn't eat much better, but at least he wasn't getting fat and being hungry a lot of the time meant he danced well! Which was an odd thing to say, and now I think about it, I reckon it was a definite ploy. And I said do you like dancing and he said he loved it and I said I did too and he asked me what I was doing Saturday evening and I said absolutely nothing (my fingers were crossed behind my back in case Sister decided to bung me another shift) and he said the West End is still jolly, plenty of dances and hundreds of people on the street even if you can't see anyone and would I like to go with him to the Astoria? And I said, yes not half. Well actually I said, *That sounds delightful, Dr Lawson*. And he said *Call me Colin, at least off duty*. And I said *Call me Connie, at least off duty*. And he said he loved my name. Which is more than I do, but how about that?'

Her friend came to a breathless stop. Daisy had been listening attentively and, by the time Connie's monologue was finished, she was wearing a broad smile. 'And I thought Dr Lawson was my beau,' she teased.

'It's too late now. You had your chance and you didn't want him. In any case, you've got a husband,' Connie teased back.

'But not for long, I hope.'

'Amen to that.' She produced a bottle opener from a concealed pocket in her nurse's apron and poured half of the beer into Daisy's night glass.

'What if he's a brilliant dancer,' she mused. 'I'll need to practise my steps. There's bound to be a great band at the Astoria. I know Snakehips Johnson was due to play there, but they were at the Café de Paris when it was bombed. Perhaps Art Gregory will come back. Where did that old turntable go?'

'It's still in the sitting room as far as I know. Beneath a dozen nursing manuals and a ton of dust.'

'I must get it out. There were some Glenn Miller records somewhere, too.' She bounced up from the bed, bottle in hand, and began to dance around the small room with an imaginary partner, humming *Tuxedo Junction* out of tune.

'And what should I wear?' She stopped dead. 'I've nothing to wear.' She saw the olive green dress that Daisy had taken off and scooped it up, dancing it against her ample form. 'If I can get into this, can I borrow it?'

'Of course you can, though I'm not sure it will be quite right for the dance floor.'

'Needs must. It's better than anything I've got in my wardrobe and it's modest enough for Colin. I think he'd like modest, don't you?' And her friend prattled on, imagining how she would dance with her doctor, what she would say to him, what it might lead to, and then horrors, what if she had to work?

'I'll do the shift for you if that happens,' Daisy reassured her.

'You're a brick. I hope you won't have to, but I've absolutely got to go to that dance.'

'You've got to go now. It's already past eleven and we're up again in six hours.'

'Oh God! You're right.' She swallowed the rest of the beer in one gulp and made for the door.

'And take the bottle with you,' Daisy called after her.

The door shut and Daisy wriggled back under the covers. She couldn't help smiling. Connie was so pleased. Dr Lawson, or Colin as he must henceforth be known, had been in her friend's eye for some time she knew, although Connie would never admit to it. But this evening she'd come clean and with good reason. Her campaign to bag him had advanced hugely, and Daisy guessed that she was already making plans to introduce the hapless doctor to her family. She was happy for her friend but envious, too. Connie's life was so beautifully simple.

CHAPTER FOURTEEN

After watching Daisy out of sight, Grayson turned north towards his flat in Spence's Road. Despite the thick darkness, he walked briskly, hardly hesitating as he swerved lamp posts, pillar boxes, pavements that veered suddenly to the right or left. His mind would not be still, one thought chasing another, while all the time his limbs moved mechanically as though they belonged to a second man who walked alongside. When Miss Strachan had announced his unnamed visitor, he'd had an instant reaction. Instinctively, he'd known, even as he'd walked down the stone staircase, that it was Daisy waiting for him at the bottom.

There was a cord that joined them, had always joined them, since the moment he'd picked her up from the ship's deck after that catastrophic fall. From the outset he'd recognised her fragility, but in time he'd come to know the strength that lay within, her refusal to be broken. Something bad had happened on board ship, he'd guessed that, though at the time he'd asked no questions. It was much later he discovered she had lost her baby, another loss to add to those she'd suffered. And there were more to come — her husband, for instance — though he could hardly be called a loss when she had never possessed him. Gerald Mortimer, Jack Minns, whatever he wanted to call himself, would never be possessed. He belonged to no one but himself, interested only in his own well-being and prepared to do anything to guarantee it. He was a worthless creature.

And he hadn't changed. Daisy had looked well, had looked beautiful. Even in the dim light of the station, he could see the bloom on her cheeks and the glint of health in her dark curls. But beneath the surface, he'd known that something was wrong. There was a tension running through her like a thread of steel, pulling and pinching, shattering any peace she may have found.

It had taken him some time to get to the nub of it. He'd allowed her to dally, talking about his work, her work, but all the time he'd been aware she was prevaricating. Eventually, she would get to what it was that had brought her in search of him. It had to be important. Their parting had been final and she wouldn't otherwise have braved meeting him anew, nor flung herself into his arms when salvation seemed near. When he'd learned what ailed her, he'd said yes. Said yes immediately, even though he hadn't a clue how he was to proceed. It was enough that she was in trouble and needed his help.

* * *

By the time he walked into his Baker Street office the next morning, he'd decided what he had to do. Mike Corrigan was already at his desk and looked up in welcome. The Irishman waited until his friend had slung his jacket over the battered coat stand and tipped the pile of papers he carried on to the desk, before he spoke.

'Everything okay?'

His face must give him away, Grayson thought. His colleague had immediately sensed it wasn't.

'Things are difficult,' he replied evasively.

He wasn't sure just how much to confide. Corrigan was a close companion and he trusted him implicitly. The man could more than keep a secret. He'd worked for SOE for years, many of them in the field where he'd braved real danger. A badly scarred right hand was testimony to that. But this was an extraordinary situation and he didn't want to involve Mike in something that could land his friend in trouble.

'How difficult?'

'I met Daisy last night,' he said baldly.

Corrigan knew all about Daisy. He'd followed the ups and downs of their romance and been unhappy for Grayson when Daisy had walked away. Unhappier still when his friend had begun meeting the flame-haired Diana, a secretary working in the Foreign Office. *She's a nice enough girl*, Mike had said, *but she's not the one*.

Now he was looking quizzical. 'And was meeting her a good thing?'

'I'm not sure. In the long term, maybe. But for the moment, it's not so great.'

'You're sounding like the Delphic oracle, my friend. What's this about?'

He supposed it wouldn't hurt to tell him Daisy's startling news. Perhaps retelling would help him believe it himself. He was still finding it hard to accept that Gerald Mortimer was alive. And he wasn't alone. Daisy was having the same difficulty, he knew. Last night he'd seen it in her clenched hands, her ramrod back, the constant twisting of her hair.

'Her husband is back.'

Mike gawped, 'But—'

'I know. He's risen from the dead, apparently. He never drowned.'

Corrigan scratched his jaw in disbelief. 'That must have been a shock for her, to put it mildly.'

It *was* putting it mildly, Grayson thought. Gerald had 'died' nearly two years ago and, by now, Daisy must be attuned to her widowhood. So, how must it feel having the new life she'd so carefully constructed blown apart, having her feelings plundered once more and brought, raw and squealing, to the surface?

'I can't even guess how she must feel. Last night, she appeared pretty definite that she never wanted to see the man again. Maybe a little too definite.'

When she'd spoken those words, Grayson had heard them with an upsurge of relief, delight even. Yet, realistically, she was bound to react with anger to the miracle of her husband's reappearance.

'I'm not surprised she doesn't want to see him.' Mike got up from his desk and collected the empty mugs from the top of a filing cabinet. 'What wife would? From what you've told me, the man was behind every plot against her — even tried to convince her she was going mad.'

'Worse! He led her to the lions' den, led her towards her own death. And then at the very end, tried to rescue her.'

'She won't forget what he did. She might forgive, but she won't forget,' Corrigan said sagely.

Grayson rapped a sharp tattoo on the desk, his fingernails catching at the wood. 'I'm sure you're right. But where there's forgiveness, there's also love.'

He remembered vividly how Daisy had sung the praises of her lieutenant on board the *Viceroy*, until he'd thought that no man could ever live up to such adoration. And he'd been right. Not that Gerald Mortimer was any kind of man. He was a worm who'd come crawling home to avoid just punishment, and then callously involved his wife in his web of deceit.

'So, what are you saying? That you've no hope of a future with her?'

He didn't answer directly. 'Gerald has asked her for help and she's agreed.'

'And how does that involve you?' Mike had arrowed to the heart of the matter, as Grayson had known he would.

'The man is a deserter — he never returned to his regiment after the "incident". He could be charged with theft, too, and maybe even treason. He wants to save himself by going abroad and he's desperate to get to America.'

'I don't blame him,' Mike said humorously. 'But he's got a gnat's chance of that.'

'Ordinarily, yes. But that's why she came to me. Daisy wants my help.'

Mike stopped in the doorway, mugs in hand. 'How the hell are you to help? You can't mean . . . you can't mean to help him get there? That's outrageous. It would involve you in all kinds of shenanigans.'

'I'm well aware of what it involves. A new identity, new papers, a valid reason for him to travel to the States.'

'You can't do it.'

'If I pull some strings . . . but I don't want you knowing a thing about it.'

He had to make sure he protected his friend. Corrigan might be furious with Ireland's neutrality and determined to see Britain win the war, but there were those at Baker Street who didn't trust the Irishman in their midst.

'You might be able to get papers for him,' Mike admitted. 'You could pull in some favours. But what reason could there be for him to sashay off to America in the middle of a war? And what the hell is Carmichael going to say when he discovers the intrigue you've landed in?'

John Carmichael was their boss, a highly intelligent man, incisive and skilled at his job, but a man who didn't suffer fools gladly. And a man who demanded absolute loyalty.

'I can't think about Carmichael right now. But I've an idea of how to get this despicable man across the ocean.'

The murky world of forged papers and forged identities was one with which Grayson was familiar, but he'd never thought he would be using his knowledge for the benefit of Gerald Mortimer.

'And that would be?'

'I'm saying nothing more. It's too dangerous. Forget what I've said.'

'Think about this, Gray.'

'I have,' he said flatly. 'I've thought about it all night. And I know what I'm going to do. Case closed.'

Corrigan was about to raise another round of protests when Bertie Sandford's cheerful voice echoed boisterously along the corridor beyond. Sandford shared their office and was a jovial companion, but a man whose discretion could not be relied on.

Grayson bent his head over the files on his desk, thankful that Bertie had arrived — it would save an argument with Mike. When the telephone rang, Sandford went to answer it while Corrigan disappeared to make tea. A secretary knocked and delivered a sheaf of new typing to his desk. He tried to concentrate on the information she'd brought, but made a poor job of it. All he could think of was Daisy and how to rescue her. Grayson knew he was a fool. He didn't need to be told. He'd never succeeded in capturing her heart, though goodness knows he'd tried. Why couldn't he just accept defeat? It was because he'd hoped for so much more, he thought, had truly believed it was possible.

When they'd arrived back from India, he'd had hardly any time with her before he was recalled to Jasirapur to give evidence against the gang who had attempted to kill her. The trial itself dragged on far longer than he'd expected. Prosecution papers were a mess and the defence constantly delayed proceedings on the grounds that they'd not been given access to evidence. It was a good three months before he'd returned to England and, when he did, he found Daisy changed.

She was living in a gloomy bedsit and seemed to have retreated into her shell once more, eking out her small widow's pension with odd jobs that were as tedious as they were aimless. He met her as often as he could, hoping to bring back the girl who'd begun to blossom on their sea voyage home. But he failed. She'd been friendly enough, interested in him and his work, but always a little distant. Then, out of nowhere, he'd been recalled to India again. The Station Manager at Jasirapur was dangerously ill in the British hospital in Delhi and a temporary administrator was needed. At a very sensitive time, with Britain on the threshold of declaring war, Grayson was the right man to send to India. That had been another six months wasted.

He'd written to Daisy, of course, and occasionally received a letter in return, though they'd told him little. Once more back in London, he'd been determined to pick up the threads of their friendship and delighted to find her happier and more purposeful. It seemed she'd woken from the long daze she'd fallen into and taken charge of her life, having been accepted for nurse training at St Barts. He'd thought it a new beginning for them both, but the hope was soon extinguished. The rigours of hospital training made meeting difficult and that seemed to suit her. As the months passed, Grayson had felt her drifting further and further away.

And things hadn't changed. Last night she'd talked to him of his work, but shown little interest in his personal life. When he'd mentioned girlfriends, she hadn't reacted. Instead, she'd talked matter-of-factly about his possible marriage. It all pointed one way. She was still in thrall to the man she'd married, and Gerald's resurrection from the grave could only strengthen her feelings. Grayson might fume, expend useless energy in raging at the unfairness of it all, but he could do nothing to change the situation. Anger was pointless, jealousy was pointless and, though he knew he could destroy the man with one telephone call, he wouldn't do it. He couldn't hurt her in that way. Instead, he would try to rescue Gerald Mortimer. He must be mad, he decided, mad or still in love with her. He knew the answer. Whatever he did, he would be doing it for Daisy.

CHAPTER FIFTEEN

'I tell you, she's a threat.' Rohan Sweetman thumped the table, the Hindi words stiff with suppressed anger.

'But to try and kill her . . .'

'I didn't try. It was to put her out of action — just for a while. An accident.'

Hari looked at his companion. Sweetman had become increasingly zealous in the weeks they had been in London and it made Hari uncomfortable. 'But it could have killed her. If she'd hit the live rail, if a train had come out of the tunnel.'

'I took that chance. It was necessary.'

'But she's a nurse.'

'For God's sake, Mishra, what's that got to do with it? She's a threat. Can't you get that into your skull? That man upstairs, what's his name—'

'Minns. It's Minns on the door.'

His colleague hardly paused for breath — 'that man Minns has been watching us for days. He's been listening, too, and he understands Hindi. Why else would a man who speaks our language rent the room above? He belongs to the British Secret Service, for sure. He even looks like one of their agents.'

'He looks down and out,' Hari Mishra said mildly.

'But that's a disguise, can't you see? He's got to look rough, he's got to fit in. The area's wretched and this place is a hovel.' He kicked the nearest chair in disgust.

Hari couldn't disagree. Looking too closely at the dirty, brown space depressed him, so he tried not to look. Instead he spent as much time as he could reading. Anything that came to hand, used newspapers Rohan picked up from park benches, odd books he stole from second hand bookshops, flyers that came through the door. It made the wait more bearable and his English had improved by leaps and bounds. When this was all over, he thought . . .

He'd accepted he had to remain within doors — his dark face made him conspicuous — and it would only be until they could put their plan into action, but his incarceration was beginning to grate. And Rohan Sweetman didn't make things any easier. He was a wearing companion, always serious, always wound tight, lecturing him endlessly on Indian independence and the perfidy of the British. That was the strangest aspect of the whole business, if you thought about it. Shouldn't he, Hari, be the one doing the lecturing? He was Indian after all while Rohan's parentage was a mystery. The man passed for English, but his true background remained unknown and that was probably as well. Hari had no wish to delve too deeply. They had a job to do in London and the sooner they did it and left the country, the better.

'He wouldn't be living here unless he had a purpose, and we're the purpose.' Rohan was still harping on the man upstairs.

'Maybe,' Hari conceded, 'but the woman might have nothing to do with it.'

'She has. That's evident. She's his contact. You've got to be stupid not to see that. He's a British agent and she's his contact. A nurse is the perfect cover. Nobody suspects a nurse and in that uniform she can move around without drawing attention. It's clear what's been happening.' Sweetman walked to the window, then back to his chair, and back again to the window. 'This Minns, though I doubt that's his real name, tells her what he's overheard listening at our door or through the floorboards. Then she contacts someone in Baker Street to relay the information.'

Hari shook his head. 'It seems a bit far-fetched. Why doesn't he report straight to Baker Street?'

'Far-fetched!' his colleague almost screeched, then remembered his earlier words and lowered his voice. 'It's the way they work. She went to the Baker Street building, didn't she, asked for a man who's in the Indian section there? I heard her with my own ears — I know that for a fact.'

Hari Mishra looked downcast. 'I suppose you're right,' he conceded gloomily.

'Of course, I'm right. Why else would she go there? It's nowhere near where she works or lives. She can't know the man personally, so what other reason could she have for going to meet him?'

'Except she didn't. You said she left the building without seeing him.'

Rohan looked temporarily discomfited. 'I can't work that out. Maybe she left a message for him to meet her outside, and then the air raid siren went and she had to shelter in the station. But he followed her, he definitely followed her. And they did meet. I saw them.'

'And she talked to him?'

'Yes,' his companion growled. 'I couldn't prevent it.' He began to pace up and down again, pulling all the while at the thin moustache that lay beached on his upper lip.

'So, all you did by pushing her, was to warn her that we know she's an agent.' Hari felt a glow of satisfaction at having for once wrong-footed his colleague.

'She didn't know it was me,' Rohan retorted. 'She's never seen me. I've been careful to keep out of sight all the time I've been watching her. Anyway, there were so many people bunched into that station, she wouldn't have known who'd pushed her. In all probability, she believed it was an accident.'

'I doubt it,' his friend muttered. 'If she works for the Secret Service, she'd be suspicious. I reckon our cover is broken.'

Sweetman gave a loud *tsk* of exasperation. 'One minute you're criticising me for trying to protect us, and now you're wailing our cover's destroyed. You need to get a grip and *we* need to get on with the job we were sent to do. She'll have passed on her information by now, and it could be damning. We need to act before the Service can respond.'

'When do we go?'

Rohan pointed to the ceiling, lowering his voice even further so that it was barely a whisper. 'The plan goes live the day after tomorrow. That's when Patel has a first meeting at the Foreign Office, but only with a junior minister. It's the right time to strike. If my sources are right, he'll be travelling to Whitehall in a cab. No official car.'

'How will we manage it?'

'Leave that to me. I've been working on it. Chandan Patel won't be well guarded. It's only an initial meeting and, though the Service may fancy there's something afoot, they won't think the information serious enough to warrant much attention. They've other priorities at the moment.'

'And what do we do with him?' Hari whispered back.

'We hold him — until it's too late for him to make the meeting or any other meeting. When he doesn't turn up, the British will say Congress aren't serious about negotiations, and Congress will say the British are up to their old tricks and ask what the government has done with their representative. A perfect storm, you'll see!'

* * *

Their words were spoken softly enough that the man living above them heard nothing. Gerald hadn't been beyond his front door for two whole days. He'd locked himself in, the minute he'd got back from seeing Daisy, and intended to remain in his rooms for at least another twenty-four hours.

By then, there should be some news, and he would make his way as unobtrusively as possible to the corner shop in the hope of finding a letter. He was being very cautious. He hadn't forgotten his return from the meeting in Hyde Park.

For a moment, he'd hovered outside the downstairs flat and listened intently. He hadn't caught much of what the men had been saying, but he'd sensed that the disagreements between them were coming to a head. When that happened, he must be miles away. He was still convinced they were the spies he'd told Daisy, though it was just possible they weren't spying on *him*. He couldn't be certain.

The white feather they'd pushed beneath his door was clearly an omen of something bad to come, but of what Gerald had no idea. It might be they couldn't agree among themselves. Their situation was dubious. Would those in authority believe them if they came with some tale of a deserter living close by? Indians in the East End of London were unusual and, at a time of national emergency, might be viewed with suspicion. It was more than likely they had something to hide, and that was what was staying their hands. He needed those hands to be well and truly stayed, at least for a few more days. Just long enough for Daisy to get those papers. Whatever the men were up to, they were welcome to continue. He wanted no part of it. What he did want was to sail as far away from his past as possible and reach safe harbour.

Everything depended on Daisy's powers of persuasion and surely she could do it. Grayson Harte had always been a pushover where she was concerned. He'd known that from the moment she started talking about the District Officer she'd met on board ship coming out to India. But he'd managed to turn the tables, even when the sainted Grayson had saved her from that cobra. Somehow he'd managed to twist the unpromising encounter to suit himself, suggesting Harte knew a little too much, had arrived on the scene a little too pat. Sowing the first seeds of doubt in her mind.

He'd always been good at manipulating. He'd had to be, growing up in such wretched surroundings. It was a survival skill he'd had to learn. From an early age, he'd manipulated his parents and they had been good people. That was it really. You could only manipulate good people, people like Daisy. Like Grayson Harte. In the past, he'd forced a young Harte to do his bidding and he would again. But the last time would be the best. Harte's feelings for Daisy would blackmail him into organising those treasured papers.

It shouldn't come as a surprise, Gerald thought sourly, the man should be familiar with blackmail from his school days at Hanbury. Senior boys had most often used physical pain to bully the younger into jumping to their tune, but he never had. He'd never needed to. He'd used guile instead. He'd discovered early that Harte was at Hanbury by virtue of his uncles. His father was dead and his mother had been left without a penny — it was the uncles who paid for his education. And that meant that Harte couldn't afford to step out of line or he would be letting them down. Of course, he did step out of line. All boys did from time to time. But Jack Minns was there watching him, minute by minute, watching out for every slight infringement of the rules. And the rest was simple — *do this for me, do that for me — or I tell.* And the boy, conscious of the debt he owed his relatives, always did. He might be a man now, might be some crack officer in the intelligence service, but Gerald could still make him do what he wanted. And he wanted those papers.

CHAPTER SIXTEEN

Daisy felt tension returning as the time grew near to meet Grayson. It wasn't too dramatic to say that her whole future depended on their meeting. If Gerald were able to leave the country, her nursing career could flourish, her life, too. But if he were trapped, daily expecting a knock on the door, followed by arrest, trial and imprisonment, she could forget any chance of making good. She would be out of a job almost certainly, unless she took up service again. In wartime, there was such a shortage of servants that employers were unlikely to be particular about references, but even then she would have to forge her own. It would be a nightmare life, worse than anything she had known so far.

And that wasn't her only worry. Meeting Grayson again made her ill-at-ease. She remembered rather too clearly their walk together, and knew she had to keep him at arms' length. It was unfair on both of them to do anything else. A Lyons tea shop was the most unromantic setting for a tryst but, even so, she knew the encounter would be uncomfortable. If he'd been successful in his mission, she would want to kiss him in gratitude and, if he hadn't, he would want to kiss her in comfort. Either way, it was going to be a difficult half hour. That was the time she'd allotted in her mind. A quick cup of tea, a brief conversation, and then back to the hospital to finish the rest of her shift.

This morning she'd been on the ward long before seven, eager to get the day started. The sun had risen just as early and, for once, was flooding the long ward, filling its high windows with a pink and golden glow. There were thirty beds in the room, fifteen on each side, and nurses were strictly allocated to one side or the other and not permitted to wander. Daisy gathered together several screens and walked to the furthest of her beds. She enjoyed this time of day. After the long night, patients were glad to see a fresh batch of nurses come on duty, glad to gossip as they were made ready for breakfast.

'How are you, my dear?' The elderly woman's face puckered into a wide smile and, despite her worries, Daisy smiled back.

'Not too bad, Mrs. Oliver. How was your night?'

'Oh, you know. A few hours' sleep and an awful lot of staring into the dark.'

A week ago, Mrs Oliver had been bombed out of her house and lost everything: her home, her possessions — and her husband. She was recovering from broken bones, but her broken heart was something else.

Daisy balanced an enamel bowl on the small bedside table. 'Let's see if a warm wash will perk you up.'

'It always does,' the old lady said cheerfully, 'leastways when you do it, love. Not too keen on some of the others.' And she nodded meaningfully down the ward where Lydia was impatiently clanging screens together.

Daisy ignored the hint and began to wipe the lined face with a warm flannel. 'I'm afraid this towel has seen better days,' she apologised, gently patting the woman dry. The hospital's linen had not been replaced and much of it was now thin and rough.

'Like me then.' Mrs Oliver gave a hoarse chuckle. 'So, will I be seeing you all day? You'll be here?'

'Apart from a few hours this afternoon.'

'Ah, off to see your sweetheart, I'll be bound.' The old lady smiled and when Daisy's cheeks flushed pink, she said, 'See, I'm right. And why not? You're a real looker — that's what they say these days, isn't it? But even better, you're a sweet, kind girl. The very best.'

'I'll be certain to come to you for a reference,' Daisy responded gaily, moving the screens on to the next patient.

From the corner of her eye, she caught sight of Willa half in and half out of the sluice room. This morning, the girl had been given the task of boiling up the huge, oval fish kettles in order to sterilise the instruments and kidney dishes that had been used overnight. In mechanical fashion she was lowering the items into the furiously boiling water. She was very pale, Daisy noticed, but seemed composed, and she hoped the girl had taken her advice and was attempting to forget last night's ugly incident. She would try to keep an eye on her in the next few days, but it was difficult with so much to do on the ward and the need today to rush to the Strand the minute she was given her free time. She took no lunch, working without a break until two o'clock, in the hope that Sister Elton would feel duty bound to let her go, without discovering a new set of chores.

Daisy thought it unlikely, since she was rarely in trouble with the hospital hierarchy. She was the ideal nursing recruit, she'd been told: mature and reliable. And even though she couldn't match her fellow trainees in either education or background, she had the right manners. The manners of a superior domestic servant, she thought wryly. In general, Sister was strict but fair and only very occasionally difficult. Like many women of her generation, she had lost her fiancé in the Great War and, at forty, had little chance of marrying. Her job was everything to her, and it was easy to see how petty annoyances on the ward could escalate into resentment of the young women under her charge.

The ward sisters at Barts were 'ladies' and, from her days in service, Daisy was sensitive to their position and understood how best to deal with them. The knowledge had afforded her a relatively easy passage through the daily tribulations of hospital life. At times, she'd had to bite her tongue — when she was asked to work again and again, long after she should have been back at the Home. But in wartime there were no rules. You did what needed to be done, and only then venture to put up your feet.

Except there would be no putting feet up today. She had a long walk from the City to the Strand, although the going should be easy. It was daylight and the roads were clear; there had been no further bombing since the time she'd taken shelter in the Baker Street station.

Once out of the hospital, she walked briskly, making good time along Holborn, past Chancery Lane and into the Strand, arriving at the tea shop, slightly out of breath but on time. Grayson was already sitting at a table in the window and waved at her as she came through the door. His crisp white shirt and immaculate grey flannels made Daisy feel shabby. Before leaving, she'd changed her pinafore and pinned on a newly starched cap, but the rest of her was looking decidedly frayed. And would continue to look frayed, she thought, since the uniform must serve her for months, if not years, to come. The tea room was looking just as threadbare, its wallpaper faded to an indeterminate sludge and, beneath the brave polish, the dark wood of its tables and chairs wounded by myriad scratches.

Grayson rose and pulled out a seat. 'I've ordered tea, but I wasn't sure what you'd like to eat.'

It hadn't been her intention to eat anything. The shorter the interview the better, but she found she was ravenous. Her last meal had been nine hours ago and hardly generous. The poster advertising breakfast wasn't helping either: porridge, bacon and fried bread, dry toast and marmalade and a pot of tea for one shilling and sixpence.

She scaled back her dreams. 'A scone and butter would be fine.'

He raised his hand to beckon the waitress over, while Daisy watched him covertly. He seemed cheerful. Did that mean he'd been successful? Or was he preparing her for failure, pretending the matter for which they were meeting was of little importance? Her stomach pitched unpleasantly. A young woman, neat and well-laundered, arrived at their side in the familiar black and white uniform. A wide smile revealed the whitest of teeth. Daisy, her mind spinning this way and that, found herself wondering if Nippies had to pass a tooth test before they were employed.

As soon as the girl left, Grayson said, 'I should put you out of your misery. The papers for Gerald will be ready in two days.'

A strange choking filled her throat. There was astonishment that he'd pulled it off, and even greater surprise that events were moving so quickly.

'How?' she stammered. 'Where?'

She knew she must sound slightly unhinged, but his announcement had sucked the breath from her body. Before he could reply, the Nippy returned with porcelain cups and saucers and a large pot of tea. A plate of appetising scones and two white napkins were placed side by side in the centre of the table. A small oasis of civilisation in an uncivilised world, she reflected, as Grayson skilfully poured the tea. She eyed the scones with interest, but he was speaking and she needed to pay attention.

'In two days' time, the Foreign Office will be sending a new ambassador to New York. He'll take with him a large team of advisers and supporting personnel, including a tranche of secretaries and Gerald has been recruited as an additional member of the secretarial team. According to the official record, his duties will be to keep the ambassador's diary and arrange some of his appointments. The least sensitive, naturally.'

Daisy's spirits drooped with disappointment. She looked down at the floor, tracing what pattern remained on the scuffed linoleum. The plan was unlikely to work, she thought, it was almost impossible to imagine Gerald as a secretary.

'Of course, he won't do any such thing,' Grayson was continuing smoothly. 'Once he gets to New York, he'll disappear. At least that's the idea, and we can only hope he sticks to it.'

That was better certainly, but she could still see flaws. 'The ambassador, though. Won't he find it strange when he suddenly loses a member of his staff?'

'He's been briefed. I imagine His Excellency will be only too pleased to be rid of the man.'

Grayson was smiling and she felt bad that she couldn't stop finding fault. It meant too much to her, that was why. 'But how will Gerald be able to disappear? When he gets to New York, he'll be penniless.'

'He'll be provided with a new set of clothes, a new passport, and sufficient money to keep himself for a month. After that, it will be up to him.'

'That's very generous.'

'Yes, it is.'

'How did you manage it?'

'With difficulty. I had to sweet talk the section that deals with America and they in turn had to sweet talk the Foreign Office. I painted it as an operational emergency, saying that Gerald had been one of our men in India, but had got into hot water during his work there and we needed to spring him or else he might reveal some embarrassing secrets.'

'You lied.'

'I lied,' he confirmed. 'It helped that this week the Indian sector has been in turmoil and the whole of SOE has known about it. My story about Gerald didn't sound too improbable.'

'What kind of turmoil?' She willed herself to believe it wouldn't stop Gerald from fleeing the country.

'Congress have sent a representative from Delhi for negotiations over independence. Do you remember, I told you Germany is determined to woo India, and we've been battling their propaganda? Anyway, Congress finally agreed to our request that they send someone to talk, and this is the chap. His name is Chandan Patel. We were given numerous demands before he arrived and we've been running around trying to fulfil them: the best hotel, a secretarial staff, high level security which is still up for debate and, naturally, access to top ministers. Congress appear windy. They want to talk but not too eagerly, and they don't want anything to befall their man. They should be windy,' he said meditatively. 'They're trying to ride two horses. Always a dangerous thing.'

'But lucky for me. I mean lucky that this Congress person has arrived at just the right time.'

'Congress wallah is the term being bandied around my section.'

'Congress person,' she said firmly. 'His coming to London is the greatest good fortune. As you say, it will deflect people's attention. Nobody will bother to find out whether Gerald really was an SOE man in India.'

There was a small pause and Daisy thought this might be the right moment to thank Grayson profusely and leave. But then he turned to her and his gaze caught hers. She tried to look away, but found she couldn't.

'Tell me, how you've been since we braved the raid together.'

The words were oblique, but she knew they hid a question he wanted answering. He wanted to be clear about her feelings, and she shouldn't be surprised. When they'd last met she'd been a storm of contradiction, throwing her arms around him, lifting her lips to his, and then as quickly withdrawing into the shell she'd built, determined to keep him at a distance. He must feel bemused. But then so did she.

'I've been fine — enjoying the unaccustomed peace.' She'd deliberately misunderstood his question. 'Not a sound since that raid. I wonder if the Luftwaffe have decided to stay home.'

'They'll be back soon enough. But it's certainly been a treat to be free of wailing sirens.' He'd decided to play along with her.

'The last time I sat here, there were incendiaries falling out of the sky, dropping the entire length of the road. I remember that they hit with a curious plopping sound — I'd never heard it so distinctly before — and then sizzled into a bluish white flame. A man, from the Home Guard I think, covered one with a steel helmet which went a bright red, then hot white and finally fell to pieces. The news vendor, the one you can see outside now, was watching the helmet disintegrate. He had a broad smile on his face, but never once stopped bellowing *Star*! *News Standard*! *Get your evening paper here*! . . . and all the time incendiaries carried on raining down.'

The anecdote moved Daisy as much as it amused. It summed up the spirit of London during these long, weary months. There were bad people, of course, racketeers who used the war for their own purposes. Such people had always existed. There were even those who scavenged bombed out buildings for anything of value, despite the fact that looting carried the death penalty. She remembered how stunned she'd been when she'd read of the Café de Paris bombing, a shocking transition from glittering luxury to wholesale destruction. While the women were having their wounds bathed in champagne, looters had moved in, breaking glass cases to steal jewellery and taking valuables from the bodies of those who had died. But these were the few, the very few. The great majority soldiered on through hardship, through fear, bound together by defiance as much as sorrow.

Grayson sat in silence and she wondered what was coming. At last, he leaned across the small table and took her hand in his before she realised what he was doing. 'I need to ask you something and you may not agree.'

CHAPTER SEVENTEEN

'What?' He was worrying her.

'Once the papers are ready, I must hand them to you personally. It would be too slow and too dangerous to post them. I think we should make the handover as innocent as possible.'

She nodded agreement. This was not so worrying after all. 'Where would be best to meet?'

'I think we should go dancing.'

She retrieved her hand and her lips opened to sound a silent 'Oh'. If ever there was a mad suggestion, this was it. Go dancing. With Grayson. She hadn't danced with him since coming home aboard the *Strathnaver*. In truth, she hadn't danced at all since then. It was Connie who danced. She had a momentary vision of them dancing elbow to elbow with her friend and Dr Lawson.

'I know it sounds ridiculous, but dancing is what everybody does. It's an activity least likely to attract attention.'

'Do we need to be that cautious?' she managed to say. It was a weak response, but he'd startled her and she was grappling for a way to say no.

'I'm not sure, but better safe. Don't forget that Mortimer told you he was being spied on by his fellow tenants, and you believed him.'

'But you didn't.'

'Shall we say I remain to be convinced? At one time, though, you thought you were being followed, too. And I confess that at the moment I'm feeling a tad jumpy. Mortimer's false papers have nothing to do with India, but the men he's worried about might have other ideas. With Patel in town, I don't want to take any chances.'

It still seemed mad. Daisy had more or less dismissed from her mind Gerald's Indians, as she thought of them. She'd begun to believe that Grayson was right when he said they probably had things to conceal and were in hiding themselves. But then there was the strong sense she'd had of being watched, and that push on the underground platform. She'd almost convinced herself it had been due to a surge in the crowd, but a niggling doubt still remained.

'If you're right that Gerald is being spied on — and by association, you as well — my plan is perfect,' Grayson was saying enthusiastically.

'How is that?'

'The men we're talking about are Indian and they're most unlikely to go dancing.'

'We could go for a drink. They wouldn't drink either. We don't need to dance.' The thought of being held in Grayson's arms was far too alluring. If they sat at a bar, she would feel a great deal safer.

'We could, but bars are public and hotbeds of gossip. A dance and dinner will be far more exclusive.'

'I'm not sure they do dinner at the Astoria.' She was still thinking of Connie's forthcoming evening with Dr Lawson.

'Not a good idea. The Astoria is far too public and way too cheap. Anyone can gain admittance and sneak in and out without being seen. We'll go to the Ritz.'

She laughed, but then she saw he meant it. 'Does SOE pay you that well?'

'The short answer to that is no. But this is by way of being an emergency. No one who shouldn't be in the hotel will get past the doorman of the Ritz.'

Daisy was unconvinced. Part of her wanted very much to say yes, but caution was uppermost. She'd already vowed that once this business with Gerald was over, she would see Grayson no more. Dancing with him was hardly an appropriate prelude.

He watched her changing expressions closely. 'I'll reserve a table, we'll eat dinner and whether we dance or not will be up to you,' he said calmly. 'It will look perfectly natural for us to be there together. I'll pass you the papers just before we leave, put you in a cab to the Home and then, I'm afraid, you're on your own.'

That didn't have a good sound. If someone was showing too much interest in Gerald, it wasn't comforting to think she might meet that person when she went to the corner shop to leave the papers. But she could see that she was the one who must do it. She would hardly be noticed in the district, her uniform making her indistinguishable from any other nurse on the street. And there were plenty of those, more and more as the war progressed. Dozens of nursing staff were out and about during the day, walking in the fresh air, smoking a cigarette, joining a queue. If a man really had been following her these last few days, tracking her to the Nurses Home and maybe across London to Grayson's office, he could do it again. But what would he discover, if he followed her to Gower's Walk? Nothing, as long he had no knowledge of the papers. All he would see was a nurse entering a small shop and making a small purchase. Better, then, to do as Grayson suggested.

He was looking expectantly at her.

'I'll come to the Ritz,' she said.

'Good girl. I'll make sure you get a decent meal out of it.'

There was nothing remotely lover-like in his response and that was a comfort. He had a job to do and she had one, too. The plan he'd devised was one he thought most likely to work. He'd gone to huge trouble in getting those precious papers, and she must do whatever she could to ensure his efforts hadn't been in vain.

'I must be off now.' He pushed back his chair. 'But on Saturday take a cab from Charterhouse Square to the Ritz and I'll be waiting. Say seven o'clock? We'll give the bar a quick look-in beforehand, just to make sure it's free of undesirables.'

When he'd left, she called the waitress over and asked if by chance the tearoom had paper and envelopes. They were scarce commodities, she knew, but occasionally a restaurant or hotel would build a small stock and make them available to customers. In a few minutes, the Nippy was back, smiling and bearing one sheet of paper and one small envelope. Daisy wrote swiftly:

Dear Gerald,

I should have the papers you want by Saturday evening and will deliver them to the corner shop as soon after as I can. It will depend on the free time I'm given.

Daisy

Her most pressing problem now was how to deliver the letter. It was important Gerald knew as soon as possible that salvation was near, but she couldn't take the message herself. As it was, she was in danger of being late for the rest of her shift. Fearing Sister's ire, she hurried from the tea shop and straight away broke into a run, attracting little attention from passers-by on the Strand, who assumed she must be responding to an emergency call.

She'd reached the Aldwych and was about to cross Kingsway, her eyes fixed blindly ahead in the effort to reach Barts on time, when a car came from her left. It appeared out of nowhere and was being driven at high speed. She had taken several steps into the road and the car swerved to avoid her, then slalomed its way round one vehicle after another, tyres squealing and the smell of burnt rubber filling the air. Daisy came to an abrupt halt, her heart pounding at the near miss.

In the distance, she saw the saloon pull out once more, this time to swerve around a black taxi, but then it came to a complete stop sideways on, blocking the entire left side of the road. The taxi was forced to slam on its brakes and she saw the cabbie lean out of his vehicle and gesticulate at the other driver with an angry, raised fist. Something odd was happening and, despite being late, she remained watching from the pavement. The stand-off between taxi and saloon car seemed to go on for a considerable time, though in reality it must have lasted only seconds, before a fire engine appeared from the opposite direction, slamming to a sudden halt as it met the car blocking its passage. And almost immediately, the harsh clang of its warning bell was joined by the wail of an advancing police car. Another player was about to join the drama.

The driver of the saloon, who had scrambled out of his car, spun around and, seemingly taking fright at the sound, ducked back in and slammed the door shut with extraordinary violence. With more squealing of tyres, he reversed the vehicle in a wide arc, mounting the kerb behind and ignoring any pedestrians unlucky enough to be passing. Wrenching at the wheel to turn full circle, he put his foot down hard and roared along the opposite side of the road, back towards Daisy. In seconds, the car had vanished, but not before she caught sight of a pair of eyes as the car raced past. Those eyes seemed vaguely familiar. Which was absurd, wasn't it?

Her mind continued to brood over the face she'd seen, until she became aware that she was still standing on the pavement. Shaking herself awake, she broke into a run once more — she was now hopelessly late. By great good fortune, an ambulance, making its way up Kingsway, stopped to offer her a lift. With luck, she thought, she might just make it back to Barts in time. And even better, the driver happened to live a few streets north of Gerald's corner shop. He knew Rigby's well, he said, and once he'd returned the ambulance to its home station, he'd be going off duty. He'd take her envelope with pleasure — he could see if the shop had any cigarettes while he was at it. He was getting a bit short.

* * *

Grayson returned to Baker Street feeling happier than he had for months. It was possible that Daisy was on her way back to him, though he wouldn't allow himself to hope too strongly. At the moment, he was needed — he was crucial to rescuing her wretched husband — but once it was done and dusted, she might disappear as quickly as she'd done before.

One thing, though, had given him pause. He'd seen the way she'd looked at him — the night they'd walked back together through the dark streets and today, sitting side by side, in the tea shop. The lingering glance, the softness in her eyes, suggested she wasn't as indifferent as she liked to make out. And that was unexpected. Grayson had tried to forget her, tried very hard. He'd gone out with several of the girls he'd met through work. The fling with Diana, for instance. But that could never be described as anything more than a fling and he'd been relieved when it was over. He'd decided then, that for the duration of the war, he'd concentrate on the job and let women go hang. That was until he met Daisy again.

Looking up from his desk, he was conscious of Bertie Sandford watching for him.

'How did the party go?' his colleague enquired lazily. His tone suggested something akin to a bacchanalia, rather than the chaste setting of a Lyons tea shop.

'Fine.'

'Only fine?'

'What do you want me to say? I had two cups of tea and a scone. And I passed on the message.'

At times, he had to try very hard not to get irritated with Bertie. Everything was a joke to the man and that could be intensely annoying. But Sandford was never cast into gloom by setbacks and there were certainly plenty of those. The unit needed people like him, particularly at a time when the country had lost so many good men at Dunkirk and Britain stood isolated, fighting for its very life.

Bertie leaned back in his chair, his hands behind his head. 'I think it should be a little more dramatic than that, old chap. After all, you face dismissal if the truth ever comes out.'

'I don't think I need a reminder.'

In the end, it hadn't been possible to keep negotiations secret from his immediate colleagues, but so far Bertie had remained uncharacteristically quiet. Michael Corrigan looked up from the document he was annotating and drummed his pencil on the desk, wondering, it seemed, whether or not to intervene.

'But is she worth it, old sport?' Bertie was not giving up. 'Don't like to rain on your parade and all that, but somehow I doubt it. No woman's worth your job, even the divine Daisy. And she must be divine or else why lay your future on the line?'

The man's words were genial, but Grayson knew there was more to them than their surface shine. Snobbery was rife in the unit and, for that matter just about everywhere in the Service, and Daisy's background had long been a topic of wonder for his colleague, ever since Grayson had mentioned she'd been brought up in an orphanage and worked behind a shop counter. God knows what Sandford would say if he knew she'd once worked as a housemaid. He had made it clear enough that he thought Grayson's attachment to a working-class girl of uncertain origins an aberration. But Bertie was Bertie and couldn't help himself and, though he might hate the man's attitude, he knew his best course was to ignore him. He was grateful, though, when John Carmichael strode into the office and put an end to the conversation.

'While you've been out, Harte, there's been a bit of a problem,' Carmichael began. 'Have your colleagues filled you in yet?'

'No, sir. I've only just returned. There hasn't been time.'

Carmichael nodded. 'There's been an attempted kidnap. In broad daylight and in the Strand.'

Grayson was taken aback. He'd been in the area only minutes ago.

'Have you any news on the victim, sir?' Mike asked. 'We've been given no positive ID yet. Is it anyone we should know?'

'You could say that,' his boss said drily. 'The victim was Chandan Patel, on his way to the Foreign Office. A meeting with a junior minister.'

Bertie whistled through his teeth while the others looked at each other in astonishment.

'He was travelling alone?' Grayson found it almost incredible that such a high profile visitor would be unchaperoned.

'Completely alone and travelling in a London taxi,' Carmichael said sharply, and Grayson heard a distinct click of his teeth. It had evidently been against Carmichael's advice.

'There must have been witnesses, sir.' Corrigan began to tap his pencil once more.

Their boss raised a hand and ran it wearily through already thinning hair. 'The police have interviewed Patel, but he was too shaken to have seen anything useful. They've got the cabbie at Bow Street right now, but I imagine he was busy controlling his vehicle and won't be much help. Most people in the vicinity melted away and we can't put out a call for witnesses without alerting the world — and by that I mean unfriendly powers — to the fact that Patel was worth kidnapping.'

'So there's nothing to suggest who was behind the attack?' Grayson had the most uneasy feeling, though he hardly knew why. It was an uneasiness that went beyond the concerns of his unit.

'There was a bobby on duty. A pretty sharp young man, by all accounts. Immediately after the incident and off his own bat, he called on nearby businesses and managed to find one person who'd seen the whole thing. The man has been carted off to Charing Cross police station, but I doubt he'll be able to add anything more to what he's already said — that there were two men in the car and at least one of them looked oriental. He couldn't say what kind of oriental. Could be Chinese, Japanese. Or even Indian. And, if that's so, I'm sure I don't need to underline what that might mean for us.'

There was silence in the room. 'Did this chap get a car number?' Bertie asked, suddenly galvanised.

'No, he didn't. But in any case, they'll have changed it by now. Or dumped the car. I'll keep you posted when anything else turns up.' Carmichael turned on his heels and walked out of the office.

'Well . . .' Mike let out a long breath. 'Fancy a beer anyone? I think we need it after that. You must, Gray. All that tea! Too much of it addles the stomach.'

Grayson smiled. 'The Barley Mow?'

'You're on. How about you, Bertie?'

'Got some stuff to finish up, old boy. Might join you later.'

CHAPTER EIGHTEEN

Once they were settled in a corner of the pub, glasses of beer on the table, Corrigan asked, 'What do you make of it? The Patel thing.'

'I'm not sure.' Grayson took his first sip. 'It's going to give us problems obviously but . . .'

'But what?'

'I think they may turn out to be a great deal worse than we think.'

'What makes you say that?'

'Again, I don't know. Maybe a conversation I had with Daisy a few days ago. There are a couple of Indians living below the sainted Gerald who might just be renegades.'

'You didn't mention it back there.'

'It's a wild card. And I can imagine what Sandford would make of Daisy's story.'

'You shouldn't let him wind you up.'

'I don't. Well, only a little. But he's getting a bore.'

'Getting? Hasn't he always been?'

'I know he's harmless,' Grayson conceded. 'I know it's just Bertie talking, but I'm getting tired of his views on Daisy.'

'You're not the only one.' Corrigan raised his glass. 'Let's drink. To Daisy!'

'To Daisy,' he echoed.

'So how did it go — your meeting this afternoon?'

'It went fine.' Grayson saw his friend's amused expression. 'More than fine actually. I'm not stupid, Mike. I know she's come back into my life because she needs something from me, but when I'm with her it doesn't feel that way.'

'What does it feel like?'

'I don't know. Good, I suppose. Being with her feels good. It always has done. She's like no other girl I've ever met. She has such spirit, she's such a grand fighter, but caring, too. And very lovely.'

'That helps.' Mike smiled over his glass. 'But also very married, my friend, or had you forgotten?'

'How can I? It's her miserable husband I'm laying my neck on the line for.'

'So . . .'

'So, with any luck, in a few weeks he'll be in America.'

'But she'll still be married.'

'Not forever. There's such a thing called divorce. If he takes flight and leaves her behind, she can sue for desertion in a few years.'

'And do you think she will?'

'To be honest, I've no idea,' he confessed. 'Sometimes I feel she truly cares for me but, at others, I'm just as sure that having once given her heart, she'll never give it again.'

The pub had grown steadily noisier as people left their work and decided on a few convivial pints before making the difficult journey home. You needed quite a few these days to set you up, Grayson reflected. With every month that passed, the alcohol level of the beer decreased.

'You know, Bertie's right about one thing,' Mike said thoughtfully, as they were pushed further into the corner by the press of people.

'Only one thing — surely not. Isn't he right about everything?'

'He's right when he says you've put yourself in danger by hustling for those papers. If Carmichael finds out, you're done for.'

'I'm going to tell him.'

'What!'

'I've thought about it — a lot. I've decided it's my only option. He's a decent man, a generous man. He'll hear me out.'

'That's as maybe, but he'll still skin you alive, and that's if he doesn't get you dismissed from the Service.'

'It's a chance I have to take. There have been too many secrets and I can't live with one as big as this. Secrets are the reason for the mess I'm in, the mess Daisy is in. If one day we *are* to marry, I want a clean sheet. And that includes the work I love.'

Mike drained his glass and stood up. 'If you're absolutely determined, all I can say is the very best of luck.' He didn't sound too hopeful.

* * *

Rohan Sweetman was angry. The kidnapping had gone wrong and his partner had done nothing but whimper ever since. Why had he been landed with Hari Mishra? He was another pair of hands, and that was about all you could say for him. Physically he wasn't that strong. The foot damaged by an explosion in the Pioneer Corps had seen to that. And psychologically he was weak — very weak. He was forever putting obstacles in their way and, after this latest setback, had been wringing his hands, often literally, at every opportunity. It was a mystery to Sweetman how the man had ever summoned sufficient nerve to work with high explosives.

'It was a stupid idea,' Hari was saying for the umpteenth time. 'Stupid to think we could kidnap a high-ranking envoy in the middle of London and get away with it.' He wiped his forehead with a none too clean handkerchief.

Sweetman would like to have hit him and hit him hard but, with considerable effort, he managed to curb his rising temper. 'There's a war on, Mishra, and the city barely functions much of the time. All kinds of strange things happen every day and people have got used to it. Ordinarily, they wouldn't have bothered even to look.'

'It was still stupid.' Mishra sat down hard on his bed and bent almost double.

'People hadn't noticed anything untoward, had they?' Sweetman asked belligerently. 'And it would have gone well, except for that damned fire engine.'

'And the police car,' his annoying henchman reminded him.

'Okay. But they weren't after us, were they? They were racing to an emergency call and it was our bad luck to meet them. We'd have had him otherwise. Patel was completely unprotected. And what the hell's the matter with you now?'

His companion was rocking himself back and forth on the bed. 'My stomach hurts. And it wasn't bad luck,' Mishra muttered rebelliously in between rocking. 'It was an omen.'

'An omen of what?'

'An omen of trouble. Big trouble. It's telling us we won't succeed and we should stop now and go home. The plan is in ruins. Patel was due to meet the Foreign Secretary in three days, we know that, but now they could shift the meeting. They could make it immediate — tomorrow, the next day — if they think someone is after him. How are we going to stop Patel with no time to organise and half of London's police force after us?'

Sweetman's jaw clenched and he spoke with a forced restraint. 'Now who's being stupid. No one saw us, Hari. No one is looking for us. All we need is another idea and I'm working on it. There'll be time.'

'A kidnap again? Let's hope this one goes better than the last.' The man grimaced with pain.

'Not a kidnap. But don't doubt I'll come up with something. Something spectacular.'

'And what about the girl?'

'What about her?'

'You say no one saw us, but she did. I saw her clearly and if I saw *her*, she saw *us*.'

Sweetman walked over to the bed and bent over the perspiring man. 'What she saw was a car,' he enunciated carefully. 'A car that is now in a ditch in Stratford. When the time comes, I'll steal another.'

'But she looked straight at us.'

The man was in a funk, Sweetman thought. His pains were almost certainly imagined. 'Even if she did, she couldn't have seen us properly. We were travelling too fast for anyone to recognise our faces.'

'I don't know,' Mishra mumbled unwillingly and fell back on the bed, his legs drawn up to his chin.

'But I do and I'm telling you, she was too concerned with her own safety to worry about who was in the car. Now, for God's sake, leave it and let me think. There's a lot of planning to do and it will be me that does it.'

Mishra pulled the covers up to his chin and closed his eyes. Sweetman would not admit it aloud, but he was concerned by what his companion had said. There was the very slightest chance the girl had taken note of their faces, his face in particular. And just possibly matched what she'd seen to the one she might have glimpsed in the shadows these past few weeks. It was unlikely though. Whenever he'd been following her, he'd made sure he was out of sight. He was fairly certain she hadn't realised she was being watched but, even if she'd been aware, she'd find it difficult to match face to figure.

Sitting down at the table, he drew an empty writing pad towards him. Slowly, he sharpened a pencil, allowing the wooden curls to float to the floor. He could hear Mishra beginning to snore but he needed to think. He lifted the pencil, poised to write, but nothing came and the page continued ominously blank.

The underground station, he thought, Baker Street. The girl had enjoyed a much better view of him there. What if she put all those sightings together and made four? And what, if then, she decided to pass on her suspicions? If she was the spy Sweetman thought her, she would call on her contact and tell him. She'd tell the man upstairs, Minns or whatever his name was. She'd describe to him the man she'd seen, describe the men she'd seen today. It wouldn't take much for Minns to recognise his fellow tenants. In the East End, the pair of them stood out like a red flag in snow. He could usually pass for white but not always, and Mishra certainly couldn't — it would be an Indian that she described. Minns might not be sure how it all added up, but he'd pass on the information to his masters. Or get the girl to. She would go to the intelligence officer Sweetman had seen her with at Baker Street. A knock on the door was already sounding in his head.

Panic gripped. They should get out of here, leave while the going was good, except he had no idea where to go. At short notice, it was impossible to find another room they could afford. They might have to sleep rough for a few nights. He could steal a car perhaps, and they could sleep in that. No, that wasn't the answer. Stealing a car too early might lead to detection. The park, that was a better solution. They would have to sleep in the park. It would only be for a very short time, three days if Patel's meeting with the Foreign Secretary wasn't brought forward. The shock had galvanised his mind and a scheme had begun to form — an audacious scheme. But first, they must escape the trap.

'Hari?' He went over to the bed and shook his companion awake. 'You have to get up.'

'What, why?' The man's half-closed eyes were hazed and Sweetman could feel the heat coming off him.

'We have to go. Don't worry. I've a new plan, a superb one, but right now we need to get out of here.'

Mishra groaned and doubled up. 'I can't. My stomach hurts too bad. And I'm cold.'

He could see the sweat beading the man's forehead and dribbling in broken lines down his face. He probably *was* ill, but they couldn't stay here.

'Look, you'll be better soon. We need to go,' he insisted.

'Go where?' Mishra groaned again.

'Anywhere, the park. We can sleep there. It's April and warm enough. And it's only for a few days.'

Mishra closed his eyes. 'You go. I'm staying.'

'What the hell use is that? Come on, get up!'

But Hari Mishra had had enough and proved unexpectedly determined. 'I'm not moving,' he muttered thickly.

In frustration, Sweetman flung himself away from the bed and set to pacing up and down the bare boards. Very gradually, his panic began to subside. Perhaps Mishra was right, perhaps it was madness to sleep rough when they had a roof of sorts over their heads. After all, it was a long shot that the woman had recognised him. She might have an inkling, but she couldn't be sure and, if she did decide to tell what she'd seen to the man upstairs, Sweetman could watch for their meeting. He'd know what to do. In the meantime, he must hope she hadn't acted independently and that no one had thought to join the dots. He sat down at the table again and began to write. With every minute, his strategy was becoming clearer. But he'd say nothing to Mishra. Not yet. He might delay telling him what he intended until the day of the meeting. That way, the man wouldn't have time to get cold feet.

CHAPTER NINETEEN

Connie caught up with her at the end of their shift. She was stacking the last pile of rolled bandages on to an empty shelf when her friend bustled into the small storeroom.

'Come on, Daisy, time to go. We'll grab something to eat and then you can tell me everything! But nod if things turned out well.'

She nodded obediently.

'Attagirl!' Connie squeezed her arm and tossed her one of the capes she carried.

'This calls for a celebration,' she said, as they tripped down the stairs. 'And what better than Woolton Pie for supper? Again. It was only last month Cook added it to the menu and we've had it half a dozen times already.' She gave a groan. 'I suppose it's possible that one day I might grow to love turnips.'

They were at the front entrance of the hospital when Daisy hesitated. 'I think we should wait for Willa.'

'She left for the Home ten minutes ago.'

'If you're sure . . .'

'Stop worrying. She seemed perfectly fine when I saw her. Just hungry, I guess.'

But when they walked into the dining room, there was no sign of the girl. 'She was certainly on the ward earlier and I'm sure I saw her beetle off,' Connie said. 'Perhaps she couldn't face the Woolton. If I weren't so darned famished, I'd be dipping out too.'

She took Daisy's arm and steered her towards the long counter. 'Let's get this dreadful stuff down us and then we can talk. Imagine it's steak and kidney pie without the steak or the kidney.'

Daisy wasn't exactly looking forward to the talk. Once Connie was sure that the precious papers were on their way and her friend could look freedom in the face, she wouldn't be too interested in the details. She wouldn't want to know about the letter Daisy had sent or the ambulance driver who was delivering it or the tea she'd drunk or the scones she'd eaten — well, perhaps the scones. What she'd really want to hear was what Daisy had said to Grayson and what Grayson had said to Daisy. She'd want to have every second of their meeting recounted. It would be a shame to disappoint her with an outcome that was so unromantic.

But, an hour later, when her friend heard the word 'Ritz', her green eyes danced and her smile shone. 'The Ritz! Wonderful! And a dinner dance! How the upper classes live.'

'Hardly,' Daisy protested.

'He wants to spoil you,' her friend went on. 'Wants to impress, too, so make sure you are impressed. But don't forget to eat.'

'It's got nothing to do with spoiling. Meeting at the Ritz is the best way, he said.'

'I bet he did. The best way to woo you.'

They threw themselves onto the most disreputable of the sofas lining the nurses' sitting room. It was the furthest from the door and the least likely place to be overheard.

'You're impossible.' Daisy tucked her legs beneath her and unpinned the starched cap, shaking her hair free.

'And Grayson is a wily fox. I can see that. I can't wait to meet him.'

'You aren't going to. I agreed to go to the dance because I think he's probably right. It will be safer to hand the papers over during dinner at the Ritz than anywhere else.'

'Safer? What are you talking about? How could it be dangerous?'

'I don't know. It may not be. It's just a suspicion. But there's definitely something going on, something to do with Gerald, though I've no idea what. On my way back here, the oddest thing happened. I was at the Aldwych, crossing the road and a car nearly knocked me down, then it swerved out to overtake half a dozen vehicles on Kingsway and ended up blocking a taxi so the driver couldn't move. It was only when a fire engine came along in the opposite direction that the cab could get going again.'

Her friend was looking nonplussed. 'And that has to do with Gerald?'

'No,' Daisy said slowly. 'It can't have. It sounds stupid now I've said it aloud, but at the time I connected the two things. The mind can play strange tricks, can't it?'

Connie bounced up and down impatiently. 'You've been working too hard, that's the problem. It was just one of those stupid events that happen every day in London. The chap in the car obviously didn't like taxis.'

She wished she could believe it was that simple but, before she lost herself in worry, her friend had moved closer. 'So tell me about the Ritz.' Connie beamed expectantly.

'There's nothing to tell. We'll have a meal there — and yes, I will remember to eat — then afterwards, Grayson will hand me the papers and I'll come back here. Nobody will notice a thing. In fact, nobody will be at the dance who shouldn't be. And I'm to take taxis both ways so I can't get into too much trouble.' She let out a small sigh. 'I must admit, though, I'll be glad when this whole affair is over.'

'And it will be, poppet — very soon. But you must have at least one dance while you're at the hotel. Colin, Dr Lawson, says they've got the most stupendous band there.'

Daisy looked at her friend, the edges of her mouth curving into a smile. 'So, you've been hobnobbing with Colin again while I've been pounding the city streets?'

'He looked for me on my break. We had a cup of tea together.'

'And . . .'

'And I do like him, Daisy.' For once Connie's cheerful face was serious and a slow flush began its climb to her cheeks. Then she was back to the Ritz. 'Promise me, you'll have that dance.'

'Maybe.' It wasn't exactly the endorsement her friend had been looking for, but Connie took not the slightest notice. 'You'll have to have a new dress. You can't dance without a new dress.'

Daisy gave up. 'And how am I supposed to do that?'

'There's a lovely black lace number in Harper's window. Low neckline, tiny sleeves and a swishy skirt. I saw it today and wanted it desperately. But it wouldn't fit me. But you . . .'

'I've seen it and it's gorgeous, but it will stay in the window. I've no coupons left, not to mention money.'

'You may not need coupons.' Connie lowered her voice. 'I know for a fact that the woman who runs the shop will sneak you a dress without them, as long as you pay the right money.'

'Well, that's just dandy. I've all of three pounds in my purse. That might just buy the sleeves.'

'I've got the money my uncle sent me for my birthday. He's very generous and, with your three pounds, it could be just enough. If it isn't, we could promise to pay the rest over the next few months.'

'I'm not letting you do any such thing. Spend your money on a frock for me! It's for one night, Connie.'

'But what a night! Think how gorgeous you'll look.' Her friend was already far into the dream, but then her practical nature took over. 'In any case, I need your olive green, so you can't wear that. I've already tried it on — sorry, but I didn't think you'd mind — and I can just get into it.'

'And the black lace?'

'Not a chance. But it will be stunning on you.'

Daisy shook her head. 'I can't let you squander your birthday money,' she said again.

'Yes, you can. Cinderella, you *will* go to the ball!'

* * *

Gerald was feeling happy. He'd managed to coast down the stairs and out of the front door without making a sound, and was now on his way to Victoria Park. He hadn't wanted to go to Rigby's to check for Daisy's letter, but it had been worth it. The owner was a surly piece of work. When Gerald had first moved to Ellen Street, he'd asked the shopkeeper for a job. He'd needed an employer who'd ask no questions, and a corner shop that was keeping his post for the few pence he could ill afford, was a good bet. But the shopkeeper had looked him up and down and told him, *no work for you*. Not for your kind, that's what he'd meant, not for a coward.

Gerald had felt fury at the insinuation. He was no coward, not in the ordinary sense. But what good would be served by giving himself up? He wouldn't be fighting for his country, he'd be locked away in some filthy jail, punished for a crime committed thousands of miles away. The irony was bitter. Lack of money had destroyed the life he'd known in India and now, with barely enough left to pay the next week's rent, it had threatened to destroy him all over again.

But not anymore, or not for much longer. Today, the owner of Rigby's had been his usual uncivil self but Gerald didn't care. He had Daisy's letter tucked into his pocket and was making for the park, where he could sit and read without the need to look constantly over his shoulder. As if to celebrate, the sun had decided to shine and the trees to remember it was April. Time to shake off winter's sleep and embrace life again. And that was just what he intended to do himself. He had no doubt the letter contained good news. Daisy wouldn't have written so soon unless she had something positive to say. He found a bench a little way into the park and sat down, careful to ensure that his back was to the railings and he had a good view in all directions. You couldn't be too safe. He needn't have worried, though. This morning only a handful of people had been enticed to one of the few green spots in the East End: several dog walkers, the park warden making his rounds picking up rubbish as he went, and a couple working on the allotments that most of the park had been given over to.

Gerald spread the note across his knee. It was brief but he didn't mind. It said all he wanted it to say. Daisy was promising to get the papers to him as soon as she could; he was sure that he'd have them within days. She would be glad to see the back of him, he imagined. Well, he'd be glad to go. He'd thought of taking her with him, if she were willing, and he might have enjoyed a reunion of sorts, but really a chap did better on his own. He stretched out against the back of the bench, an expansive smile on his face. He'd almost found safety, and an unexpectedly strong feeling of relief spread through him.

He'd been very scared, he realised. He hadn't wanted to admit it, had tried to suppress the thought, but there had been a quiet voice in his ear that said he'd never escape. That he'd be forced to face the past and its sins, and pay for them all. But that was over now. He could look forward, not back, and didn't he deserve to? All credit to Daisy, though. She'd done a splendid job in persuading Grayson Harte to perjure himself, but he deserved some credit, too. And that's what he'd never been given. Quite the contrary. He'd tried to save her life, hadn't he, but there'd been no praise for that. Instead, he'd been hounded from place to place and was still being hounded in his own country.

Okay, he'd done wrong, he'd admit it, but it hadn't been his fault. He'd got in with the wrong people, that was all. Anish, for instance. Why on earth had he made him his friend? He was a brother officer, a graduate of the Indian Army Academy, and he'd appeared to be a true gentleman. How could he have known the man was some kind of mad patriot who would involve him in criminality of the worst kind? Involve him to the point that he lost everything he'd ever cared for. Made him behave in a way that was wholly out of character. All those accidents that had haunted Daisy. Accidents that weren't accidents. He hadn't liked knowing. Not at all. But he'd been forced to go along with them, and he knew she would never forgive him for it.

But she'd been as much to blame. If she hadn't been so stubborn, so wilfully determined not to take his advice, she wouldn't have suffered. If she'd gone to the hills for the summer with the other wives, as he'd told her, none of it would have happened. The stolen arms would have left the bungalow without a problem and, when she returned home in the cool season, she would have found nothing untoward. He'd have paid off his debts at last, and life would have gone on as usual.

But she had to pry, didn't she, poke her nose into what didn't concern her and end up in danger? And he'd had to go to the rescue. It was bad enough standing by while she coped with dangerous snakes and flying rocks and saddles that mysteriously failed, but he couldn't ignore cold-blooded murder. He'd had to try and rescue her. Nearly died doing it, and branded himself a murderer in the process. So yes, he deserved her help. He deserved those papers.

Tucking the envelope into his shirt pocket, he sauntered out of the park, weaving a slow path through traffic-filled roads towards Ellen Street. The calm he'd enjoyed this morning lasted until he turned the corner and saw the gothic face of number seventeen lurch into view. From this position, its three storeys loomed over the squalid cottages at its feet, the dense black roof a dark pall threatening the entire neighbourhood. If the house were no longer there, he thought, the road might look homely, inviting even. Well, perhaps not inviting, but certainly not as menacing. He almost wished the Luftwaffe would pay the building some attention on their next visit.

Pushing at the blistered paint of the front door, Gerald edged it open. It swung back easily. He tried never to use the large brass knob in the centre of the door. It was rusty and, when turned, filled the air with a loud, grinding noise. He was keen to avoid noise at all costs. His nerves were back on duty and he felt his stomach jumping in tune with his breath. Inching his way up the stairway, he made sure to give the door of the first floor flat a wide berth.

Last night, there'd been another row. Something bad had happened, that was certain, and the two men had raised their voices at each other for minutes on end, forgetting they could be overheard, forgetting that he might pick up a Hindi word here and there. He hadn't. He'd cranked up his radio and deliberately played it at full volume just to tell them that he wasn't listening. Now, though, their flat was utterly quiet and, if anything, it felt more ominous than the shouting. Gerald eased his way upwards and into his own front door without incident. Once inside, he pulled Daisy's envelope from his pocket and settled it carefully on the stained wooden mantelpiece, sliding it behind the clock stuck permanently at three minutes past ten.

The letter was his talisman and, while he had it, nothing could harm him.

CHAPTER TWENTY

'I should have gone into supper and sat with Willa.'

This Saturday evening, both girls had crammed into Daisy's room and their outfits for the evening were strewn across the narrow bed. The small desk was covered with pots of every shape and size. Connie had emptied her drawer of anything she thought might vaguely help their preparations for the grand night out.

'Stop fussing,' she chided. 'You couldn't have gone to supper. You couldn't have eaten a thing.'

'But Willa wanted to talk to me,' Daisy insisted. 'She caught me at the front door, just as I was coming in, and I said I'd try to meet her.'

'She knew you were going out, didn't she?' Daisy nodded. 'Then she'll understand. You can speak to her in the morning. Tonight the Ritz awaits. And to make things even more peachy, I've just seen tomorrow's shifts — neither of us are on until nine. How lucky is that?'

She only half heard Connie's words. She was remembering the almost desperate note in the girl's voice. 'Willa braved the dining room tonight,' she went on, 'that was my chance to speak to her.' She jumped up from the chair and stood, irresolute. 'I could go to her room now.'

'You can't. There's no time. If you start listening to her troubles, you'll make yourself late for your taxi.'

'Then I'll call another one.'

Daisy couldn't get the unfortunate Willa out of her mind. They'd been on the same ward today and, when she'd asked, the girl had said she was fine, but her white face and tight mouth told a different story. And her eyes . . . her eyes had made Daisy shiver — they'd been blank, hardly alive. Then, returning to the Home this evening, the girl had twitched at her sleeve, her head bowed, seeming unable to look into Daisy's face.

'There won't be another taxi.' Connie planted herself in front of the door, barring the way. 'Willa has problems with a capital P and she'll still have them tomorrow. You can talk to her then. Tonight's too special. Now, are you going to let me make you up?'

Daisy felt unhappy. Surely, she could spare the poor girl a few minutes. But the clock was ticking, the evening about to begin, and her stomach was already fluttering with excitement.

Tugging at her arm, her friend was trying to steer her towards the inadequate mirror and she gently shook herself free. 'Thanks, Connie, but I'd rather do my own make-up.'

'Suit yourself. I intend to be bold and go to town with the red lipstick. The lighting at the Astoria will be blindingly bright and I don't want to be bleached out.'

She settled down at the desk, humming quietly to herself, while Daisy watched, her mind elsewhere, thinking of all the ways in which she could have been a better colleague. In ten minutes, Connie had finished and swivelled round to face her. 'Well, what do you think?'

'You'll certainly make your mark.' Her friend had found a vivid green eyeshadow and used it to complement the blood red lipstick. Her hair, hennaed the previous night, shone brightly copper.

'Is it too much?'

'You said yourself that artificial light leaves you looking a ghost,' she replied diplomatically. Connie could take strong colour, she thought, and this evening looked positively vibrant.

Her friend scooped up the olive green dress and funnelled it over her shoulders, tugging it hard to fit over ample hips. 'It doesn't look that great,' she mused, moving this way and that in front of the small mirror. 'Still beggars and all that . . .'

'You look fine.' Daisy hugged her. 'Colin will know you've made a tremendous effort and be flattered. And so he should be.'

The girl smiled cheerfully back. A small thing like a tight dress wasn't going to spoil her evening, though Daisy hoped she would get her one decent frock back with the seams intact. Except, it was no longer her one decent frock.

'Let's see the black lace then.'

She slid the wispy confection over her head and shoulders and pushed her feet into her best shoes. They had nearly crippled her the last time she'd worn them, but then she'd walked miles. This evening she would have the luxury of taxis both ways.

She became aware of Connie staring at her. 'What?'

'You look sensational.' Her friend drew a reverent sigh.

'I do?'

'Take a look,' and she stepped to one side so that Daisy could view herself in the mirror. At any one time, she could only see a small part of her image, but it was sufficient. Her eyes travelled slowly downwards, taking in her barely made-up face, her dainty waist and finally, as she backed across the room, the remainder of the dress in all its splendour. Even with a shrunken mirror, she could see how it flowed effortlessly, swirling and swishing in a way that no wartime dress should. The amount of material it used was profligate, an utter and complete extravagance. And she loved it. She would keep it forever, she decided.

* * *

The taxi dropped her at the front entrance of the Ritz at a minute to seven. Piccadilly seemed alive with people, but every street they'd driven down had seen crowds out to enjoy themselves. Clubs featuring live bands, theatres staging the latest shows, all full to capacity. Max Miller was at the Holborn Empire, she noticed, and a fabulous new singer, Vera Lynn, was performing songs from her radio programme, *Sincerely Yours*. She must remember to tell Connie. Nurses were frequently offered free tickets at short notice and she knew her friend watched the board outside Matron's office assiduously. A Vera Lynn show would be special.

As soon as the cab drew into the kerb, she saw Grayson's tall figure through one of the stone archways. He was standing in the lobby of the hotel, but moved quickly through its swing doors towards her. Daisy was used to him always looking smart. Even in the searing Indian heat, his shirts had been immaculate and his shorts knife-pleated. But tonight in evening dress, he appeared more elegant than any man she'd ever seen. And she matched him! she thought giddily, sending a silent thank you to her friend. Connie had been right about the dress.

Grayson took her arm and ushered her into the sumptuous interior. The lights might have been switched off outside but behind the blackout curtains, chandeliers blazed amid a cocoon of red and gold silk. He eased her nurse's cape from her shoulders and immediately a uniformed receptionist glided forward to take it. To hide it more like, Daisy thought wryly, imagining the worn garment slowly suffocating beneath a tide of cashmere and furs.

Grayson had turned and was looking at her properly for the first time. For a moment he seemed stunned, unable to speak. Then the familiar smile flitted across his face and he said simply, 'You look sensational.' Connie's exact words, but now doubly precious.

His hand found her elbow and guided her towards an archway on their left. 'Our table will be ready in half an hour, but first let me show you off in the bar.' A rich, dark space opened up before them, lit by even more chandeliers, though this time dimmed to a subtle warmth.

When the waiter had taken their order, she looked around at the scattering of dark wood tables and silk cushioned chairs. The room was divided into separate spaces by arches of ornamented mahogany, which made it impossible to see most of the people who shared the bar with them. Grayson sat upright in his chair, his eyes fixed on her, unable it seemed to look away. She roused herself to speak, to break the spell that seemed to have him in its hold.

'Did you check the room for spies beforehand?' She was only half joking.

'No time, I'm afraid.' Her taunt had woken him. 'I should have, though. All kinds of dubious characters infest cocktail bars. Usually fashionable wasters, though, who make their living from scams or, even worse, blackmail.'

The waiter placed two fluted glasses on the table in front of them. 'A martini cocktail,' Grayson explained, once the waiter had left. 'I hope you like it. And perhaps we should carry out an inspection now. That man over there, for instance, what do you reckon?'

Daisy looked across at the corner seat he was indicating. The man in question wore the extravagant military dress of a country she couldn't name.

'He's in uniform,' she said doubtfully.

'Exactly. What better disguise for a spy?'

'Apart from a dinner jacket and bow tie you mean?'

'Or a frock of the most enchanting black lace?' She blushed. She was enjoying the power of the dress, but she hadn't quite bargained for its full effect.

'Perhaps we shouldn't be too facetious,' he cautioned. 'There was a serious incident yesterday, possibly the work of spies, although as yet we don't know.'

She took a cautious sip of the martini and felt it kick against her throat. 'Where? What happened?'

'A kidnapping. Or rather an attempted kidnapping.'

The alcohol was loosening her mind, freeing her thoughts to wander and make unexpected connections. The incident in the Strand came back to her with force. Surely not.

'It happened on Kingsway.' Grayson continued. 'Chandan Patel, you remember the Congress chap I mentioned. He was on his way to Whitehall. He was due to have a preliminary meeting there with a junior minister when he was pounced on. Apparently, a saloon car overtook his cab and forced it to a halt.'

Daisy took an even longer sip of her drink. 'And was he successful, the kidnapper?' she asked, already knowing the answer.

'As it happens, no. Patel was lucky. Or rather we were. A fire engine just happened to be racing from the opposite direction to answer a call, and found its way blocked. And behind the fire brigade was a police car — it must have been a serious blaze. Our would-be kidnapper took fright when he realised what he had to deal with. He spun his car and sped off before anyone thought to stop him.'

Grayson gestured to the waiter and two more martinis glided gracefully on to the table.

'I know,' she said quietly.

When they were alone again, he leaned towards her. 'What do you mean, you know?'

'I was there.'

'Good grief!'

'I was on my way back to Barts from meeting you, and just crossing over from the Strand when a car nearly knocked me down. It must have been the kidnapper's car.'

'Did you see anything?' Grayson was eager. 'Anything at all that might suggest a clue to the man's identity. We've given Patel extra security, but we still need to find the blighter.'

'He wasn't alone. There were two of them — there was a passenger in the front seat,' she said. 'I'm sure of it.'

'And?'

'I thought the driver looked familiar.'

'Go on.'

'That's all, really. I thought I might have met him somewhere, but I've no idea where. Nothing else.' Grayson looked deflated. 'I'm sorry to disappoint you, but I only saw him for an instant — when the car flew by on the opposite side of the road. I thought he snatched a glance at me as he sped past, but that was probably imagination.'

He took her hands and held onto them tightly. 'Think for a minute, Daisy. We need this man at Latchmere House, behind bars. We need to question him. And soon. Intelligence that's stale is like food, it does more harm than good, so we must strike now. Where could you have seen him?'

'I really don't know.' She shook her head sadly. 'I'm sorry, I can't help, Grayson.' Then, 'I wish this was all over.' The words came out sounding more anguished than she'd wanted.

He stroked the hand he was holding. 'It will be very soon and I'm sorry to have pressed you.' He relaxed back into his chair. 'I presume Gerald knows by now that you've secured his future.'

She heard the note of bitterness that he couldn't quite conceal. 'I wrote to him straight after you left the café and gave the note to an ambulance driver who lives in Gerald's district. He promised to deliver it, and I'm sure he'll have done so.'

The head waiter materialised beneath the mahogany arch, his podgy hand waving graciously in their direction and beckoning them to follow.

'Good. Food at last.' Grayson got to his feet and again offered her his arm. 'Let's go and eat. I'm ravenous.'

Following the black-suited maitre through several adjoining rooms, each eerily quiet, they arrived at the top of several flights of steps, naked brickwork on either side. The staircase they were descending was badly lit, increasingly so, and soft carpet soon gave way to a rough drugget and then to unadorned stone. At the bottom of the staircase, a passage stretched before them, bare and deserted, punctuated by a series of grubby doors. Here and there sandbags had been packed against scaffolding poles painted in the colours of the Union Jack. It seemed an extraordinary way to begin dinner, and Daisy began to wonder if this was some kind of joke. If it was, Grayson must be in it. At the end of the passage, they came to a halt outside a closed door. Inclining his head towards them, their guide flung the door open with a flourish and instantly they were engulfed in noise: a deluge of chatter and clatter and music, vibrating around and through the cavernous space.

'La Popote,' the maitre announced.

'What?' She looked startled, unsure of where she was.

'It's the grill room,' Grayson explained. 'All the posh hotels have these underground restaurants. I imagine the space used to function as a store for provisions, but this last year or so it's adopted a new role — as a safe place to eat.'

The walls of the room were thickly padded, Daisy noticed, and packed with more sandbags kept in place by wooden props and naked metal struts. Candles burned in the necks of empty wine bottles sitting atop the utility tablecloths, while a candelabra of more bottles had been constructed to light the modest space allocated for dancing.

They were shown to a table a little distance from the band, but on the far edge of the dance floor. Behind the stage where the musicians were playing, a mural of the Western Front in 1914 had been painted and, on another wall, caricatures of Hitler and Goring.

'We won't make this a late night, I promise. I imagine you have to be up at first light.' Grayson said with a smile.

'I've some of the morning free, in fact.' A blissful nine o'clock start, Daisy remembered. 'But several hours of fire duty after my shift. That means a long day.'

Everyone had been forced to fire watch since the government made it compulsory. But the rota was not popular, particularly when nurses had to take their turn after a gruelling day on the ward.

Grayson frowned. 'I'm surprised you have to do it. It must be better for porters and orderlies to be on the roof.'

'It probably is, but there aren't enough of them. There aren't enough men in the hospital. The doctors are spread thinly and, of course, there aren't any male nurses so we women have to do our share. And it's not too bad — now the hospital is better equipped. We've a roof full of sandbags and stirrup pumps, and last month they gave us helmets to wear, just like real wardens.'

A waiter glided sideways up to their table and with a flourish produced two glass bowls, piled high with something that Daisy thought looked exciting. He served the iced dishes alongside neat quarters of bread and butter.

'It looks pink,' she said, peering intently into her bowl. 'What is it, do you think?'

'Lobster cocktail would be my guess.'

'Goodness!' and without another word she gave herself up to the pleasure of eating.

For once, it was food she could savour, despite the miasma of expensive cigarettes that swirled in the air. Restaurants allowed diners to eat off ration, she knew, and the food was always going to be far superior to anything served in canteens or indeed in a nurses' dining room.

They ate in companionable silence, until Grayson put his cutlery down and gave a small sigh of pleasure. 'That was good. And there's partridge with bread sauce to follow, and all kinds of vegetables — though hopefully not a turnip in sight. We don't get anything like this at Baker Street.'

'Nor at Barts,' she added with a smile.

He was leaning forward to speak again, when the band struck up a foxtrot. She could feel her toes begin to tap beneath the table, but tried hard to appear indifferent. The music was too reminiscent of their nights on board the *Strathnaver*. Such memories, though, held no fear for Grayson. He laid his napkin to one side and got to his feet. 'The main course will be a while yet. Let's snatch a dance before you have to flee the ball.'

She started to find an excuse, but had mumbled only a few words when he strode around the table and lifted her out of the chair. 'Come on, Daisy, it's one dance, that's all.'

CHAPTER TWENTY-ONE

Several other couples were already swaying their way around the small space, clearly enjoying the sounds and rhythm of a top class dance band. Everybody it seemed was out to have fun, bent on thrusting a monochrome world aside and, for a short while, losing themselves in colour.

And Daisy was no exception. She wanted so much to sink deep into this haven of pleasure, to be enchanted by the candles' soft light, the bubble of conversation, the sparkle of the women's jewels. It wouldn't be for long, she decided. It would be fun to dance steps she hadn't practised for a very long time, to lean into the music and allow its seductive melody to wash over her. But then she would lead the way back to their table, eat another delicious plate of food, and leave with Gerald's papers tucked in her handbag.

Grayson was a good dancer. She'd forgotten just how good, and they'd made several turns of the floor before she was even aware of him holding her, or aware of the harmony of their steps. But then, as he moved closer, she smelt the tangy freshness of his skin, the smell she remembered so well from all those months ago in India, and felt herself begin to lose her determined control. The foxtrot, though, came to an end before her body could wander into dangerous territory, but almost immediately the band began to play again and this time the music was sweet and smoky and languidly soft.

'One more dance?' he said quietly in her ear.

Before she could refuse, he'd pulled her close. She liked the feel of him so very much and wished she didn't. His face settled against her dark curls, his mouth brushing her cheek. Neither of them spoke, and she allowed her body to float, her feet to flow by instinct. Round and round the small floor they drifted, their bodies growing closer, their limbs shadowing each other. They seemed to be dancing in a dream. With every minute Daisy felt herself melt a little further, felt herself absorbed inch by inch, two figures slowly transforming into one. She had lost any strength to fight back. Every dormant nerve, every fibre that had slept for months, was kicked into life and craved satisfaction.

He had both his arms around her and she laid her head on his chest. If she looked up, she knew she would meet his smile. He would be looking down and his lips moving towards her. He would kiss her. She wanted that kiss. She looked up and there was his smile, his lips. His head bent towards her, but the kiss never came.

The air was rent. A siren, two sirens — one must be the Ritz's own, she thought, dazed by the sudden shattering of the moment. Their piercing wail brought the scene to a close. The band stopped playing. Dancers stopped dancing. Waiters abandoned food on the nearest tables and began ushering their customers across the room to a second doorway. Along with everyone else, she and Grayson were hustled into a passage, almost identical to the first, and with a similarly large number of doors leading from it.

'Dormitories,' Grayson said briefly, as they passed empty rooms to right and left. 'The hotel needs to ensure its customers stay safe.'

The head waiter emerged from out of the crowd and tapped Grayson on the shoulder. 'Mr Harte, this way please.'

They followed him into a much smaller room. It was sparsely furnished: a table, several chairs and two camp beds which, to Daisy's astonishment, were dressed in matching sheets and pillows of blue and green linen.

'Why have we been put in here?' She felt uncomfortable.

'I imagine for reasons of security,' Grayson answered easily. 'The management know why I'm here. They've a good idea of their clientele, but there's always a very small chance that a rogue might slink through their defences. And, in this situation, he could cause trouble.'

Her eyebrows formed a question mark. There had been no mention before of security being a problem at the Ritz.

'It's nothing that should worry us too much,' he reassured her, 'but since the attempted kidnapping, I've gone up the scale as a potential target. My interest in Patel will be pretty widely known in some quarters.'

Daisy wasn't sure if she *was* reassured by this. 'The Ritz know who you are? I mean, that you work for SOE?'

'They do. They had to. The game has recently become a little more urgent, and I needed to take a few precautions. This playpen we've been allocated is about as secure as you can get.'

'And where is everyone else?'

'You must have noticed how many rooms there are. People will have been given beds here and there, and I guess most of them will make a night of it. No doubt the women have brought a nightdress and toothbrush with them. Nowadays, it seems quite the thing for girls to go out to dinner equipped for an air raid.'

'I didn't,' Daisy said faintly.

The sight of the beds, narrow as they were, was reinforcing how foolish she'd been. Tonight was supposed to have been a pleasant dinner and a swift return home. Instead, she'd allowed herself to be persuaded onto the dance floor, and then behaved like a moonstruck girl in the throes of her first passion. She had clung, it was the only word she could use, clung to the man who stood just yards from her. Lifted her lips to him, craved his touch.

'The raid will be over soon, I'm sure, but for now we'd better stay put.' Grayson's voice was soothing and cut across the unwelcome thoughts. She was certain that he'd read her fears. 'As soon as the All Clear sounds, you must be on your way.' He shrugged himself out of his jacket and draped it around a nearby Windsor chair. 'It's sad we missed the partridge, though.'

* * *

But the raid wasn't over soon. It was the worst they'd endured for months, in fact the worst Daisy could remember, so overwhelming that even in this bunkered room, she could feel the thud and groan of the bombs as they fell. They were miles below ground and she ought to feel safe, but she didn't. In this windowless room, she felt trapped, the sound of danger muffled, but its assault on her mind intense. If only they'd remained in the bar, she would have had a grandstand view. She would have seen what was happening, seen the devastation taking place and somehow it would have felt better. Her eyes would have told her to accept the very worst, rather than suffering the frightening images her imagination was building. Minute after minute, from every direction, the dull crack of massive explosions breached the room's false calm. Several times she felt her pulse grow erratic and had deliberately to slow her breathing.

'Try and rest. It's got to end soon,' Grayson repeated.

Daisy had her doubts. It was as though the entire might of Germany was being thrown at them in one single night. But she knew he was right. There was little benefit in continuing to perch on the hardest of chairs. She walked across the room to one of the narrow beds and laid down. Grayson followed suit, lying full length and motionless, his eyes fixed on the whitewashed ceiling.

'This evening hasn't exactly ended as we thought,' she ventured. If she talked, it might soothe a panic she was still finding difficult to control.

He turned his head to look across at her. 'It hasn't,' he agreed. 'I'm still thinking of the partridge.'

She found herself giving a nervous giggle. 'Do you think they're still in the oven?'

'I sincerely hope not. The smell of incinerated bird is the last thing we need right now.'

Not when incineration was spread for miles around, she thought. What would they face when they finally found their way from this cellar? It sounded as though the entire city was being obliterated.

She checked her watch. It was a few minutes past midnight. 'Do you think a taxi will manage the journey once the bombing stops?' She was thinking of the mission she'd had to abandon.

'To be honest, I'm not sure if any vehicle will get through. We'll have to decide what best to do when we see the level of damage outside.'

He, too, was imagining a hardly recognisable city and she shivered at the thought. He saw the shiver and rolled off his bed, dropping down to his knees beside her.

'Try not to worry too much.' His voice was gentle but resolute. 'We're safe, and we'll stay safe, and so will those wretched papers.'

She smiled a little wanly and he took her hand and held it in his. 'Come what may, you'll find a way to deliver them. I promise.'

Her smile grew a little stronger. The warmth of his touch was bracing. 'I'm being defeatist,' she admitted. 'I'm sorry. My life has seemed such a mess since Gerald returned that I'm starting to let things get on top of me.'

'I know how hard—' he began to say, when an almighty crash sounded from close by, its echoes resonating along the passage beyond. It was wholly unexpected and, for a moment, she went rigid with shock.

'What on earth was that?' she whispered.

'I've no idea but whatever it was, we must stay put.' He wrapped his arms fully around her, as if to protect her from the unknown danger.

'Then we'll be trapped here.' Her fears, never far away, began to surface again.

'If we leave the room, we'll face even greater danger,' he reasoned. 'We have to keep our nerve. I know you can. I've seen you under pressure and you were magnificent.'

'I was? Right now, I'm not feeling too magnificent.'

There was another loud crash from somewhere above, then a loud tinkling sound. 'I think that's probably the chandeliers,' he said.

A violent trembling she couldn't prevent took over her limbs. It must be the result of these last few weeks, she thought. She wasn't a coward, she wasn't easily daunted, but this massive raid coming on top of everything else was proving too much.

Without saying a word, Grayson got to his feet and climbed onto the bed beside her. His arms once more wrapped her round. 'Tell me to go if you don't want me here.'

She didn't tell him to go. His body lying close, his arms encircling her, gave the comfort she needed. They lay side by side listening as the thuds and crashes crept slowly nearer, eventually surrounding them on every side. They lay in a circle of noise, in the very centre it seemed, of destruction.

'What about fire?' she whispered. The threat of being trapped so far below ground still terrified her.

'We'll have to hope there hasn't been a direct hit, and that the wardens and fire crews are working overhead.'

It was a desperate hope, but he was right. There was nothing they could do. Closing her eyes, she found a comfortable niche on his shoulder. and was so weary that despite the enveloping noise and fury, she drifted into an uneasy doze.

Until a knock sounded and a waiter put his head around the door. 'Sorry to disturb you, Miss. Just checking that you're okay.'

She noticed that his black-suited uniform was smeared with crumbling, white plaster. 'Is the raid over?' How long she'd slept, she had no idea.

'Just about.' The waiter gave her a friendly nod and disappeared.

Grayson had been asleep too, it seemed, and was now stretching himself lazily awake.

'So, it's finished,' he said. An uneasy quiet reigned in the building. 'Are you feeling brave enough to venture out?'

'Of course, I am. And I'm sorry I was so feeble last night.' She gave him a small hug. 'Thank you for being a rock.'

He planted a light kiss on the top of her head. 'If it's a rock that I am, then so be it. Come on, we should make a move. These beds are damned uncomfortable.'

'I don't think they're meant to sleep two.'

'I'm sure they're not but so much nicer, don't you think?'

'Yes, I do.' Her face flushed and he looked at her, surprised.

For a moment their glances locked, then he leaned across and kissed her on the lips.

'That's my prize for being a rock,' he said softly.

'Mine too,' she said even more softly, and kissed him back. She hadn't meant to, but something was driving her, a desperation to know his touch before they parted again, and this for the last time.

He seemed to feel the same desperation for, in an instant, his arms were round her, enfolding her in the tightest of embraces, his mouth finding hers. A long and tender kiss. Then another and another. What was she doing, she thought dreamily, kissing Grayson? A slow heat was suffusing her body, the black lace slipping from her shoulders. And a harsh world was forgotten.

CHAPTER TWENTY-TWO

They seemed not to need words, but lay for long minutes safe in each other's arms, tired and elated, barely able to believe what had happened between them.

Eventually, he said, 'How are you?'

'I'm well.' An understatement, but true. Daisy was well, better than well.

'No regrets?' He sounded anxious.

No regrets. How could she have? She was a married woman with a renegade husband to spirit from England. Making love to a secret service agent was possibly not the cleverest thing she had ever done, but it was certainly the best. Ever since she'd met Grayson, she'd felt a connection with him, one that went beyond friendship. It had gone unacknowledged by them both, but she'd sensed that beneath his engaging smile and upright bearing, a passionate man had his being. And her intuition had been right. He was a passionate man. For the very first time, she understood emotions of which she'd only previously read. She was a wife with virtually no knowledge of physical love. One drunken, fumbling night with Gerald, had been her sole experience and she could never have imagined how utterly consuming such feelings could be. But tonight — this morning rather — she knew.

'We should get going, although I think I might have said that before.'

'You're right, we should,' she murmured, but snuggled back into his arms.

It was the knock at the door that eventually forced them from the bed. The head waiter stood on the threshold and coughed apologetically.

'Will you be requiring a cab, Mr Harte? They're rather short on the ground this morning.'

Grayson untangled himself and threw on the shirt that lay crumpled on the floor. Daisy could not remember it coming off but there it lay, along with the black lace and the best underwear she possessed.

'Thank you, Porson. Just one — a taxi for the lady. We'll be out in a jiffy.'

'Certainly, sir. I'll make sure the cab is waiting.'

Daisy scrambled into her abandoned dress, then looked around for her shoes. Grayson retrieved the errant pair from under the bed. 'You must have kicked them off before you did your dormouse act and buried yourself under the blankets.'

She felt her skin tighten at the memory of the raid. 'That was the most terrible night.'

'Was it?'

'I meant the raid.' She couldn't prevent herself blushing and, seeing it, he scooped her up in his arms and kissed her on the lips. 'I love it when you blush. And you always do. Your feelings are writ large, Daisy.'

'If they are, I should be looking anxious. I'm not feeling happy about the day ahead.'

'You mustn't worry. I've the papers here.' He fished an innocent brown envelope from the inside pocket of his jacket and passed it to her. 'And other than you and I, only a very few people know about them.'

She was looking down at the envelope, her forehead wrinkled slightly. 'These are the papers?'

'What did you expect? A parchment scroll with a wax seal?'

'No, not exactly. I'm being silly, I suppose, but after the trouble they've caused, I expected something more . . . significant.'

'It's better they're insignificant. Bury them in your handbag. The cab can drive you straight to the shop — what was it called, Ripley's?'

'Rigby's.'

'The cabbie can wait and then take you back to St Barts. I'll make sure he has his fare.'

'Thank you.' She'd been uncomfortably conscious that her handbag contained nothing but small change.

'There's no need for thanks between us. Not now.'

'I suppose not,' she said shyly, but felt a twinge of misgiving, even as she agreed.

Grayson held her hand as they made their way along the deserted passage and across a frowsy looking restaurant, still uncleared from the previous night's revelry. She snatched a glance at him and felt her body soften in response. But she should stop feeling for a moment, she told herself, and think carefully. She had been determined she would never again make herself vulnerable. Yet last night she'd done just that. It was unwise.

The fence she'd been busy erecting, ever since she and Grayson had stepped off the *Strathnaver* at Southampton eighteen months ago, had been under strain several times before, but last night it had splintered irrevocably. And she'd delighted in every moment. No doubt it was the extraordinary setting, the extraordinary events they'd been caught up in, that had spurred the collapse. The fear of death was a powerfully disruptive force, Daisy knew. That was how she must think of their time together. It was what had propelled her into Grayson's arms and nothing more serious. A release from the tensions of the past few weeks: the war, the bombs, Gerald. But even as the words came to mind, she felt a small shift in her heart.

They'd reached the hotel foyer and a scene of grand destruction greeted them. There had been no direct hit on the hotel, but the reverberations from the intense bombing had loosened the fastenings to the chandeliers and at least three were lying smashed on the silk carpet.

'How sad,' Daisy said, as they skirted the debris.

'Chandeliers can be mended. People can't — at least, not always. We were lucky to escape the worst. I think you might see some very difficult sights on your journey this morning.'

As Porson had promised, the cab was waiting for them and Grayson handed her in, bringing her hand to his lips as he did so. It was an old- fashioned act of gallantry to warm her on this bleakest of mornings.

'When can we meet?' He was leaning into the taxi, his eyes bright, despite lack of sleep. 'I know you'll only be able to make an hour or so.'

'Tuesday probably. In the afternoon, though I can't be entirely sure.' She could not reasonably refuse to meet him, and she was honest enough to know she didn't want to. But she would need to tread very carefully.

'Tuesday then. I'll come to the Square after lunch and lurk.'

She smiled up at him as he slammed the cab door shut. And then the taxi was on its way.

* * *

Grayson had been right about distressing sights. From east to west of the city, a shroud of smoke still hung in the sky and, wherever she looked, there was huge devastation. The cabbie had switched on his radio as soon as they'd pulled away, and through the glass partition she could faintly hear the voice of the newsreader: last night's raid had been the worst of the war so far. For most people, radio news was their sole communication with the world, the only way they knew what was happening to friends and relatives fighting abroad or battling on the Home Front. No casualty figures were given this morning, no precise details of the damage inflicted on London, but that was far from unusual. The BBC were always careful never to broadcast anything that might sap morale. The fact that they'd mentioned the ferocity of the bombing told people all they needed to know.

The cab slowly wound its way through the narrow back streets of Mayfair. Daisy tried to keep her eyes fixed ahead, but her gaze was continually drawn to the disfigured landscape they were passing. Every road was littered with a mountain of rubble and, on all sides, there was scarcely a building left with its windows intact. At times, the vehicle was forced to a halt by the piles of earth and plaster, bricks and tiles, that spilled across the road, but then the driver would wrench his wheel left and right and somehow weave a pathway through. Several times he had to change direction completely, to avoid huge waterlogged craters which had sprung from nowhere. A bomb had breached the Tyburn stream, for centuries trapped underground.

After the firestorm, the streets were unnaturally quiet, empty of human life except for the occasional 'lady of the night' who continued to stroll the shattered pavements, finely dressed and wholly indifferent to the wreckage she walked through. It was hardly surprising she continued to ply her trade, Daisy reflected. Not when the demand for prostitutes was so high, and a woman on the street could earn fifty times as much as the girl in a shop.

They had been travelling towards the river and now turned onto the Embankment. Idly, she glanced to her right, then jerked herself upright, staring blindly through the cab's window. She couldn't quite believe what she was seeing, for the Thames was changed out of all recognition. It was scarlet — scarlet water. In fact, not water at all it seemed, but a thin wash of red dye. Fires raged fiercely on each of its banks, their demon glow mirrored in the depths of the ancient river. It was too horrible to look on and Daisy slumped back into her seat. But fire was inescapable; it was everywhere.

As they approached the City, she could see the red blaze highlighting the dome of St Paul's against an overcast sky, a doomsday silhouette. Around the cathedral, great gaps had been torn between rows of houses; those left standing stared blindly and darkly at nothing. The few small gardens had been desecrated, with earth and rubble and fragments of furniture piled high where once sooty flowers had bloomed. The taxi crunched its way over street after street of splintered glass. Twice, maybe three times as many houses, had been destroyed or damaged than she had ever seen before.

Wardens were out in force, still scouring the worst hit areas. Hours ago they'd rescued the living, and now came the grim task of collecting body parts and taking them to the mortuary in the hope of identifying those who'd perished. Daisy looked away, averting her eyes from the sacks that stood ready at the side of the road. On into the East End and the streets were a little busier, though for the moment the business of everyday life was suspended. Groups of exhausted bystanders had emerged from their overnight shelter and were standing motionless on street corners, gazing dumbly ahead. It was as though by continuing to stand and gaze, they could convince themselves that they'd come through, that they were still alive.

Daisy needed no convincing. She had never felt more alive, wonderfully alive. But it seemed wrong that she should feel this exhilarated when others were bowed in grief. For the first time that morning, she thought of Connie and prayed that the Astoria had been spared. A spasm of guilt took hold that she hadn't thought of her friend before. Back at the hospital, her first task must be to go in search of her. The taxi was barely moving now. It had entered a down-at-heel road where, by a strange quirk of fortune, most of the properties had survived undamaged. She glanced up at the street sign. Gower's Walk, her destination. Halfway down the street and hemmed in by houses on either side, was the shop Gerald had described. It was a drab building of dirty yellow brick, with a striped awning which had been shredded by the elements and flapped dolefully in the breeze. The woodwork seemed never to have seen a brush stroke of paint and, when she peered into the shop's one window, its grime was so thick that she was unable to make out any goods for sale. Not that there were many, she could see, once she'd pushed the door open. It appeared that Mr Rigby was as penniless as his neighbours.

The bell clanged and the man behind the counter looked up unsmilingly. When she handed him the envelope, he grunted. When he looked at the name, he spat on the sawdust floor.

'You will give it to Mr Minns when he calls,' she said anxiously.

'He'll get it, don't worry.' His voice was incongruously high. He spat again. 'No justice in the world,' she heard him mutter in the same high voice, as he trailed off to the rear of the shop with the envelope in his hand.

She had no idea what he meant, but it was clear that Gerald was not a favoured customer. She wondered if the man might know her husband's address. If so, she could deliver the papers personally but he didn't come back and, when she heard him shuffling and mumbling in the distance, she thought better of it. It was more than likely the shopkeeper didn't know — Gerald had been careful never to say where he was living. And if, by chance, she found the address, he might be angry if she turned up unannounced. She might even put him in danger by doing so. The Indians that he feared were sure to be in the house still, and she couldn't dismiss his worries as readily as Grayson had.

Since the kidnapping attempt, though, it appeared that Grayson himself was having second thoughts. It seemed incredible that Gerald's supposed enemies were the very same men who had tried to abduct the envoy the SOE were protecting. But there couldn't be that many Indians in London. And if that were so, were they the very same people who'd been following her? If indeed she *had* been followed. Daisy was still not entirely certain there'd been anybody, and not sure either why her mind connected a possible stalker with what had happened in Kingsway. She'd had a vague feeling that she'd seen the driver of the saloon before. But where?

Of course, she couldn't have. She walked quickly back to the waiting cab and scolded herself for silliness. She couldn't have recognised the driver of the speeding car. She'd been only vaguely conscious of a figure watching her, a shadow really, and always on the periphery of her vision. But if there had been someone watching her and he was still watching . . . no, she was sure that no one had seen her go into the shop with the envelope, or leave without it. All would be well. Grayson had told her that Patel was meeting with a senior government minister mid-week for final negotiations. Congress would decide then whether or not to involve India in Britain's fight and, once the talking was finished and the deed done — one way or another — any threat was bound to vanish, whether to her or to Gerald or to Grayson.

Her heart gave another of those peculiar little bounces as her mind sounded his name. The knowledge that she would see him very soon trumped the weariness snapping at her heels. Tuesday was only two days away and already her mind was busy working on how best to get the necessary time off duty. She'd begun to count the hours before they were together again, she realised, and that was ridiculous. They were closer now than she could ever have imagined, but her deepest feelings remained unchanged. She would never again commit herself, not in the way she had as the young woman who'd flung herself body and soul into what she'd believed the love of her life.

They would be loving friends, nothing more, and she hoped he would accept it. For months she'd kept her distance for fear of the hurt she might cause, but last night had changed everything. Distance was no longer possible. Last night they'd embarked on unexplored waters and Daisy could only hope they would each find their own safe harbour.

CHAPTER TWENTY-THREE

Her spirits were still bubbling when she walked on to the ward an hour later. The sight of Connie talking to a patient at the far end of the room filled her with relief. But it was clear that every nurse was working at full stretch, both on the ward and in the adjoining corridor, where a line of stretchers had been temporarily parked. Many of those injured from the night's wreckage had already been patched up or sent to theatre, but more victims were arriving all the time. Nurses rushed back and forth, fetching water and towels, fielding kidney dishes, pressuring wounds that were pumping blood at an alarming rate. Or simply sat and held patients' hands in an attempt to console and comfort. Daisy made ready to plunge into the fray.

'A word, Driscoll.' Sister Elton had appeared at her shoulder and was beckoning her towards the small glass office to one side of the ward.

Daisy went with a heavy heart. She had no difficulty in foreseeing the interview to come.

'Sister Phillips tells me that you did not return to the Home last night. And you are an hour late coming on to the ward.'

'I'm sorry, Sister. I was invited to supper and was caught out by the bombing raid.'

'Do you think you are the only nurse who went out on Saturday evening?'

'No, Sister,' she murmured, her eyes downcast.

'Others have managed to return and report for duty on time. Why not you?'

'I was at the Ritz.' Sister Elton's eyebrows twitched. 'They wouldn't let us leave the hotel . . .' The sister's eyebrows twitched even more rapidly. Daisy staggered on, '. . . they insisted we took shelter below ground and I wasn't able to get away until this morning.'

The senior nurse said nothing more but walked over to her desk and began, sheet by sheet, to flick through a sheaf of papers piled high on its surface. Then, methodically, she rearranged the sheets and placed them into a manila folder. All the while, Daisy waited for her sentence to fall.

'My nurses are not in the habit of visiting the Ritz, Driscoll, and I have no idea of the arrangements that pertain there. But since you will not have worked your full shift, you will have no time off for the next three days.'

'But Sister—' Tuesday's delights were dwindling into the mist.

'You have something to say, Nurse Driscoll?'

'No, Sister.'

'Then go back to the ward and work. You are needed.'

And needed she was. For the next six hours Daisy worked without pause, her mind bristling with resentment that she would be unable to meet Grayson as they'd planned, while all the while her hands mechanically bandaged limbs, stuck plasters and swabbed wounds.

She was passing down the ward towards the sluice room, carrying yet another bowl of water turned crimson with blood, when Mrs Oliver called her over.

'You're not happy today, nurse.' The old lady's eyes were sharp.

'I'm fine, Mrs Oliver. It's been a little frantic.'

'That it has. And no wonder. The noise last night! Truth to tell, I thought it was all up with us, thought I'd be seeing my Edward sooner than I expected. But somehow the bombs missed.'

'The hospital was lucky.' Daisy rested her bowl on the bedside table. She dare not stay talking too long or Sister Elton would be at her shoulder with another reprimand.

'And the bombs missed you, too, my dear. Wherever you were.'

She had no wish to get into another conversation about her whereabouts. She gave the old lady a gentle smile and made ready to move off. But Mrs Oliver hadn't lived for eighty years without learning to read below the surface.

'Don't let that Sister upset you. You'll get to see him — I'll make sure of it.'

Daisy looked astonished.

'That's what it's about, isn't it?' Mrs Oliver heaved herself upright against her pile of pillows. 'I saw Missus Frosty Face take you into the office. You were positively glowing when you came on to the ward, but after she'd finished with you, you looked as though you'd had a good whipping. I know you were seeing your young man last night. It had to be about that. Am I right?'

Daisy couldn't deny it, but marvelled at how transparent she must be. And all the time she'd thought herself so discreet.

'When were you supposed to meet?' Mrs Oliver asked.

'The day after tomorrow. After lunch. It's when I usually get my free time except—'

'Except there's no free time now,' the old lady finished for her. 'I've got a little plan. I've been working it out and it's simple. On Tuesday, I'll play up a bit. The nurses know me for a placid old soul, so they won't know what to do with me if I misbehave. They'll call the dragon over to help, and I'll keep her busy. You can steal out and have a few words with your beau, and she won't even know.'

'Mrs Oliver — you are a wicked woman!'

'If that's my only sin, I'll be up in heaven alongside Edward in no time at all.'

Daisy squeezed the old lady's hand and continued to the sluice, smiling inwardly. She didn't know if the ruse would work but she was grateful, and it was certainly worth a try.

By teatime, the trickle of new patients was ended and she was able at last to retreat to the nurses' station. She had begun to feel dangerously light-headed and there would just be time to snatch a slice of toast and a cup of tea. As she was finishing stacking her china, Connie appeared in the doorway with a knowing smile on her face.

'Who's a naughty girl, then?' she whispered provocatively.

Daisy felt the annoyingly familiar blush gather strength, but she decided to put on a bold front. 'I've no idea what you're talking about.'

'Not much, you don't. I came to check you were okay last night. And guess what, no Daisy. And no Daisy this morning either.'

'The raid was really bad, you know that. It prevented us leaving the hotel.'

'I bet it did.'

Her friend's eyes looked suddenly alert. She had spied Sister Elton, who had slipped into the nurses' station and was now advancing on them. At least, that spared her further interrogation, and Daisy was grateful. 'You're to tell me every single detail — this evening.' Connie hissed, as she made a rapid retreat. 'No excuses. Fire duty is off.'

Her friend was right — fire duty was off. A cluster of incendiary bombs had been dropped on the hospital roof the previous night, and those nurses acting as wardens had donned their tin hats and rushed to do battle. Between them, they'd put out every single fire, but a great deal of debris had been left behind and the fire watching rota had been suspended until such time as the male orderlies could gain access to the roof and clear it of any danger. Daisy received her reprieve thankfully. She was utterly fatigued, and the thought of spending five or six cold hours on an exposed roof was uninviting.

* * *

'You're not going to slink off to bed. Don't even think of it,' her friend said, as they filed into the dining hall. 'We'll have this ghastly meal and then we'll talk.' It was evident Connie was bursting to spill her news — the evening with Colin Lawson — as well as discover Daisy's secret.

As usual, supper was nondescript and left Daisy thinking longingly of the partridge, but mercifully as short as it was bland, and they were soon making their way towards the nurses' sitting room. They were about to walk through the door, when a girl came flying out, almost cannoning into Connie who was a step ahead.

'Steady on.' Connie disentangled herself and stepped back to see her assailant. 'Lydia Penrose, I might have known. What's sent you into such a steam?'

'Ask her!'

Daisy had followed her friend into the room and, at the anger in Lydia's voice, she turned to look over her shoulder. Willa Jenkins was crouched into the corner of one of the upright chairs and was blinking rapidly.

'What's she done now?' Connie asked wearily.

Daisy went over to the girl and bent down by the side of her chair. She'd promised to talk to Willa and she hadn't. There'd been no time, but she felt guilty that in some way this was the result.

'What's the matter, Willa?' she asked in a quiet voice.

'What's the matter, Willa?' Lydia taunted. 'She's a cheat, that's what. She's copied my last homework project word for word. Look at it.'

There were two sets of papers on the table and Lydia jabbed her finger at one, then the other. 'See. She's copied my work. And now I'm in trouble with the physiology lecturer. Have I cheated, he asked me. How dare he! How dare she! Have I cheated? I don't need to cheat, not like that brainless moron.'

Daisy looked at Willa. As the words rained down, she had balled herself even smaller. There seemed little left of the person she had first known. A husk, she thought, that's what Willa had become.

'Did you copy Lydia's work?'

The girl stared at her as though she hadn't heard.

'Did you copy it, Willa?' she repeated. 'If you did, it's better to own up now.'

The girl remained silent, staring glassily ahead.

'Of course she did. Look at her. Can you imagine *that* actually writing an essay?' Lydia advanced on the chair and prodded her victim with a sharp finger. Her voice was shaking. 'I've had just about enough. If you cross me once more, Jenkins, I'll make you more sorry than you've ever known. Whatever you've had dished out so far, won't touch it.'

'What do you mean, what she's had dished out? What have you been doing?'

'Never mind goody two shoes, Driscoll. It's not your business. But I forgot, not so goody two shoes after all, I hear. A married woman who sleeps around. There's a four letter name for that beginning with s and ending with t.'

'How did you . . . ?' She'd thought only Connie knew of her marriage and Connie would never have told. The girl must have eavesdropped on their conversations. Lydia Penrose was despicable.

'Leave her, Daisy,' Connie said, as Lydia pushed past them.

'Yes, leave me. Do as Ginger says and keep away.' The angry girl turned at the door. 'I'm not surprised you always defend Jenkins. You belong with her. You're both aliens.'

Daisy's bemusement caused Lydia to walk a few paces back into the room. She pointed her finger first at Willa and then at Daisy. '*Her* brain is a mishmash, and so are *your* genes.' When Daisy continued to look mystified, Lydia said, 'Don't you realise? Take a look in the mirror some time, Driscoll. You're hardly pure bred.'

A flash of enlightenment and Daisy was suddenly back in Jasirapur, back at the Officers' Club and hearing a woman, Margot Dukes that was her name, announce to the entire room that in her opinion the newcomer had *a touch of the tar brush* about her. It had been a devastating moment that she'd worked hard to expunge from her mind, but now here was Lydia, not just reviving the dreadful memory, but giving it new life.

Connie grabbed her by the arm and hurried her away. 'You're to take no notice. Penrose is a cow, the most unpleasant woman I've ever met. Come on, I've got things to tell you.'

On the other side of the room, Willa rose to her feet and walked mechanically out of the door. Daisy knew she should go after her. She still hadn't had the talk with her that she'd promised and now would be an ideal moment. But she was too upset by Lydia's words, too incensed, to give Willa the attention she needed. Instead, she allowed Connie to lead her to the battered sofa they'd made their own.

Slumping down on its cushions, she brooded in silence, while her friend sat beside her and waited. Eventually, though, she could wait no longer and burst into speech.

'It was amazing. Last night, I mean. Colin was amazing.'

Daisy roused herself to take an interest. 'He's a great dancer,' her friend breathed. 'A regular shincracker. I had difficulty keeping up with him and I must have stood on his toes plenty, but he never mentioned it, not once. He's a darling. We danced for hours, or at least it seemed like that, and then the siren sounded and we had to beetle out and find the nearest shelter. We were stuck there for an age, but it didn't matter. It was scary, though. The noise was horrendous — a sort of screaming through the air alongside the sound of the bombs. Colin said it was JU88 dive bombers. He knows such a lot. And we talked and talked, and there was this funny, little old man who'd brought his accordion along to the shelter and was playing tunes and we sang along to them.'

'Is Colin an amazing singer, too?'

'Don't make fun. No, he isn't, but he's a great sport and you needed to sing, to keep up your spirits. It was the most tremendous raid.'

'I know it was. Have you seen all the destruction?'

'Not really. I've been on the ward all day and last night we walked back in the dark. Some of us had a bed to go to. Our own bed.' And she looked pointedly at Daisy.

'The Ritz has rooms underground.' She tried very hard not to redden. 'Rooms to shelter in,' she added.

'And what else?'

There was to be no escape. Connie could read her too easily. 'What was it like?'

She knew her friend wasn't referring to the underground room. 'Wonderful,' she said simply, 'wonderful.'

Connie gave her an enormous hug. 'So you're together now.'

'Don't go too fast.'

'Not go too fast. What do you think you were doing last night?'

'I don't know. And I don't know how it will end. All I know is that I feel free and happy and . . .'

'Wonderful!'

They fell about laughing and were shushed by a nurse at one of the tables, a stack of textbooks at her elbow.

'I knew he was for you,' Connie whispered excitedly.

She didn't answer, but instead looked across at their studious colleague. 'Perhaps we should play a game of cards,' she suggested. 'As long as it doesn't get too noisy.'

'You really are goody two shoes,' her friend scoffed.

Daisy walked across to one of the groaning cupboards that lined the sitting room wall and rummaged, disgorging half its contents across the threadbare carpet before she held aloft a pack of cards.

'There! I hope it's worth the effort.' She threw the pack down on to one of the side tables.

'Tut, tut, Nurse Driscoll. Everything should be shipshape.' Connie clucked an imitation of Sister Elton.

'Gin rummy?'

'I think so. This time I'll slaughter you.'

They played for an hour or so in a spirit of friendly rivalry, Connie interrupting play every so often to recount snippets of her magnificent evening with Colin, or to persuade Daisy to divulge the intimate details of her night. Several nurses drifted in and out, the student packed her books and departed, and a doctor looking for Sister Phillips poked his head around the door. When he'd gone, Daisy stopped playing.

'I need to go to bed,' she yawned.

'No, you need to go to sleep,' Connie mocked.

They had cleared the table of cards and were piling the moth-eaten cushions back on to the sofa, when the door banged open. The only other girls left in the room, who'd been chatting quietly together in the opposite corner, looked up.

It was Lydia again. She stood immobile in the doorway.

What now, was Daisy's first impatient thought. But then she noticed that Lydia's complexion was deathly white and her face frozen. Her jaw seemed trapped, trying ineffectively to work itself free.

She rose quickly, tipping the pack of cards across the floor. 'Lydia?' she queried uncertainly. 'What is it?'

By now, Connie, too, had become aware of the little drama being played out in the doorway. 'Come on, Lydia. Stop being Lady Macbeth,' she joked. 'What's up?'

'It's Willa,' the girl managed to say at last and her voice came gratingly, barely a whisper. 'Willa.'

'What about her?'

The other nurses had stopped chatting and were looking anxious.

'She's, she's . . .' but Lydia could not go on.

Connie pushed past the traumatised girl and took the stairs to the bedrooms two at a time. Lydia remained a statue in the doorway and Daisy was forced to take her by the hand and lead her to a seat.

'Look after her,' she said to the nurses who were hovering, uncertain what to do, then turned and followed Connie out of the room.

At the top of the stairs, she met her friend coming out of Willa's room. 'Don't go in there.' Connie was looking sickly and her voice did not sound her own.

'Why not?'

'Stay there. I've to get Sister Phillips.'

'But—' Daisy moved towards the door.

'Don't!' Connie screeched. 'Don't look.'

'But Willa—'

'She's . . . she's dead.'

And it was then, through the open doorway, that Daisy became aware of the soft sway of a body and a pair of feet where they shouldn't be.

CHAPTER TWENTY-FOUR

The morning following Willa's death, Daisy was on the ward at seven o'clock. Sister Phillips had made it clear that despite the dreadful thing that had happened under their very noses, every nurse would be expected to fulfil her duty roster. Daisy was fulfilling it, though she was hardly conscious of doing so. She washed faces, tidied bedclothes, dusted lockers, and smiled. She smiled constantly, though inside she was crying and could not stop. It wasn't just for Willa that she cried — poor, sweet, incompetent Willa — to die in that dreadful way and so very young. It was for herself, for the terrible guilt permeating every pore, until she felt she was rotting from within.

Guilty, guilty, guilty. She could have saved the girl if only she hadn't been so wrapped in her own petty affairs. Willa had cried out for help and none had been forthcoming. And she'd heard the cry, yet offered nothing, distracting herself instead by playing out romantic fantasies in an unreal setting.

That was a bubble well and truly burst. She would never think of the Ritz again without thinking, too, of Willa, and those feet swinging a few feet above her head. With a shock, she realised she would never think of Grayson either, without recalling the terrible price her colleague had paid. Willa had needed support and, out of all the nurses in the Home, the girl had come to her. Knowing nothing of Daisy's history, she'd nevertheless sensed a kinship, believing her promise that they would talk, that Daisy would listen to whatever Willa feared and try to advise. Yet, in the next breath, she'd broken that promise, too dazzled to make time for her. She could have gone to the girl's room on Saturday evening, but instead had put on make-up, donned a fancy dress and gone to the Ritz, telling herself that she would see Willa tomorrow. But she hadn't seen her — she'd been too busy on the ward. And last evening, she had failed again. She hadn't followed Willa, so obviously distressed by Lydia's accusations, but had sat with Connie and talked to her — of Grayson.

Grayson was the problem. He'd distracted her from what was most important and she'd allowed it to happen. He was not good for her; they were not good for each other. Trouble seemed to follow them and always would, and that was something she'd known instinctively. She'd tried to keep her distance, tried to protect herself, and him, by pulling free. But then what had she done but propel herself back into his orbit and allow the old attraction to flare? Meeting again had proved disastrous, in just about every way. That night — she could hardly bear to think of it, the night she had spent with him — the joy, the delight, were no more. Ashes, was what she knew. The taste of ashes.

She hardly saw Connie all day, though her friend was somewhere in the background. She didn't, in fact, see anyone. Willa's face superimposed itself on every moment and it startled her when, after dinner, Connie took her hand and led her to the nurses' sitting room and their favourite sofa. Twenty-four hours ago they'd laughed here over a game of cards, full of life, full of love.

'You look dreadful, Daisy.' She didn't know how to respond. Looking dreadful was the least she could do, she thought dully. 'You mustn't take this so hard,' her friend coaxed.

Daisy swivelled to look at her. 'How am I supposed to take it?' she asked fiercely.

'It's sad, terribly sad, but life has to go on. Our lives have to go on.'

'But not Willa's.' Daisy pinned her arms against her stomach and stared down at her feet.

'No, not Willa's. But I doubt if she'd want to see us sitting around in this moping way for too long.'

'How do you know what she'd want? How do any of us know?'

'Daisy—'

'It's true isn't it? None of us were too concerned with what she wanted when she was alive. And now she's dead and past wanting.'

'You're taking this too personally.'

There was the slightest hint of irritation in Connie's voice and, for the first time since they'd met, Daisy felt a distance opening between them. 'How else am I to take it? I feel responsible.'

'That's ridiculous.'

'Is it? I knew she was unhappy. I knew she was being bullied. And what did I do about it?'

'What did any of us do? It's not just you.'

'No it's not, Driscoll.' Another voice had joined them. An unexpected voice. 'It's not your concern. It's mine, entirely mine. I did the bullying. I pushed her to her death.'

Looking up, they saw that it was Lydia Penrose who had come very quietly into the room, but her figure was no longer the Lydia they knew. The girl seemed to have shrunk overnight, and her face was tight and parched, the skin scoured across the bones.

Lydia planted her feet four square on the threadbare rug and looked down at them. 'I'm the one to blame,' she repeated, 'and I mean to make amends. Or, at least, to try.'

'But how?' Connie was frowning deeply.

'I can't bring Willa back, certainly,' Lydia said gruffly. 'But I can look after other dead people. A punishment to fit the crime.'

Daisy and Connie exchanged a speaking look. The tragedy had affected Lydia's mind, that was plain to see.

'Don't look like that.' Lydia had caught their glance. 'I know I sound mad, but I'm not. As a nurse I look after the living. I patch and mend and make better — or I'm supposed to. But I didn't, did I? I destroyed. I'm not worthy of the job any more, not after what I've done. So I'll look after the dead and the dying instead.'

The girls waited for an explanation. 'It's simple,' Lydia said. 'I'll train as ambulance crew. I understand they take on the most grisly of jobs.'

Daisy shuddered, remembering too vividly the sights she had seen only the other morning. Could Lydia really be intending to comb bomb sites for broken bodies and severed limbs?

'You do know what it entails?'

'I know. It's ghastly, but that's the point.'

'And you think that somehow it will help you?' Connie put in.

'It will help me pay back what I've taken away. It may even help others. Families that have seen their loved ones destroyed. Like Willa's family.'

Her decision, it seemed, was not for discussion. She turned abruptly and walked out of the room and they heard her thumping up the stairs, grief and determination marking her every step.

'Well!' Connie exclaimed.

'I suppose she must do what feels right for her.' Daisy envied the certainty. Lydia would go into action and gradually purge herself of this terrible stain, while she could only suffer a slow, gnawing remorse.

'It seems a bit extreme.'

Connie was still battling with the notion that anyone, even Lydia, would willingly embrace the horrors she was bound to encounter. Some of the injuries sustained by bomb victims had been devastating enough and made a lasting impression on her. She didn't want to imagine how much worse an ambulance crew might have to face.

'Everything is extreme at the moment.' Daisy sounded exhausted. 'And we haven't had the funeral yet.'

* * *

She went to bed that night, knowing she wouldn't sleep. Instead, she lay and tried to think her way out of the turmoil. Lydia had chosen renunciation. The girl was giving up a job she loved, a job she did well, in the hope of finding redemption. A cleansing, a purging, after what had happened. If only she could do the same. If only she could unlive the last few days.

Her mind kept coming back to Grayson. For all kinds of reasons, it had never been a good idea to get close to him. Even if he'd accepted the little she could offer, what kind of future would they have had? They were from wholly different worlds and Daisy would rather not imagine his mother's reaction, tucked away in her comfortable flat in Pimlico, to a girl who was the wrong class, the wrong background, even the wrong skin.

She had always felt as English as anyone around her, but what did she really know? Her mother had been English, that was certain, but her father? When she looked in the mirror, her dark hair and dark eyes, her almond skin, suggested a different story. None of that worried Grayson, she knew, but it would almost certainly worry his family. Her intense guilt over Willa had reinforced an older, deeper feeling, that Grayson and she were not meant for each other. Only bad things could come from a refusal to recognise it.

And there was no longer a need for them to meet. Gerald must have collected his papers by now and be readying himself to leave. His departure to a new world meant the death of their marriage. So why not the death, too, of this difficult relationship with Grayson? As long as Mrs Oliver's distraction worked, she would meet him tomorrow as arranged. Tuesday was the day before Willa's funeral, and that seemed entirely fitting.

CHAPTER TWENTY-FIVE

Every day when he woke to the realisation of where he was, Gerald felt physically sick, as though someone had punched him squarely in the chest. Everything about living in these rooms, this house, this district, was depressing. Deeply depressing. The maze of mean little streets, the grey soot, the dirt. Even if he hadn't been menaced by the fear of discovery, he would have had to get out of the place. He'd expected never to return to the East End, had believed he'd left his history far behind.

The day he'd joined the Indian Army as a raw recruit, the angels had sung. His parents had come to the station to see him on his way to Sandhurst, he remembered. He'd forbidden them to come any further than the London terminus and with good reason. He might be eighteen and wet behind the ears, but he was able to envisage only too well the reaction of senior officers to a Cockney tailor and his Cockney wife. He'd blenched at the thought of any meeting. Paddington was the nearest his parents would ever get to Sandhurst. Unbeknown to them, he'd already changed his name and was planning a final escape.

He'd written to them, of course, from time to time, but gradually as the weight of his studies increased and he'd felt the effort to succeed grow ever more difficult, his letters had dwindled to nothing. He'd paid them just one visit, a day that was forever engraved on his memory, the week before the posting to his first regiment in India. They'd splashed out on high tea and invited the neighbours into the 'best' room, a cold, dank, unused parlour, to partake in their reflected glory. That was how he'd seen it then and he'd winced with shame. Now, it looked very different. Now, after his years of pretence, of deceit, of wickedness — yes, wickedness — he could see they were merely proud. The costly ham tea was a way of saying they thought he was wonderful. They'd always thought he was wonderful, scrimping year after year to send him to Hanbury, listening attentively to any small remark he might vouchsafe during those wretched holidays spent in Spitalfields. He could never wait to get back to school, just as he couldn't wait that day to return to Sandhurst, to his newfound family of brother officers. And then to India, the final break with his embarrassing origins and the dreary streets in which he'd come of age.

It was another irony, poetic justice perhaps, that he'd ended back on those very same streets. He had become Jack Minns again. Only this time without the parents who had worked to give him his new life, a life that had collapsed irrevocably. In his trouble, he'd returned to them. Yet one more irony. He'd trudged across Europe, desperate for food and shelter, lying and stealing his way from country to country, taking any job that offered, anything that would buy bread, cheese, a drink of some kind to drown the misery. Then, at last, soaring white cliffs ahead and his heart lifting. At last, home. He was home, and soon he would walk the familiar pavements. But it was a dream that turned to nightmare, as so much of his life. Instead of the joyous homecoming, he'd faced a landscape laid to waste and two heaps of newly turned earth in Tower Hamlets Cemetery. Unmarked, unloved, pauper graves.

This morning, though, was different. The sun was shining and the wind had dropped. He peered through the streaked window at the street below. It was the first real day of spring, and the first of his new life. Striding over to the mantelpiece, he took down Daisy's letter. He must have done that a dozen times in the last few days, reading her note over and over again, checking that the words hadn't changed. He supposed it was because he couldn't quite believe his impossible quest had become possible. But it had, and the words he read were always the same. Whenever he thought of the liberty they promised, it was difficult to suppress a shout of elation, difficult to stop himself from dancing on the spot.

And today was the day. By now, Daisy would have done her stuff and the papers would be safely lodged at Rigby's. For a moment, he thought of his wife with fondness. He had to admit that she'd treated him decently. She'd been honest and loyal. And she was quite a looker. She always had been, of course, or else he would never have got himself tangled in the mess that was their marriage. He'd begun to think it a shame that she wasn't coming with him. She was his wife after all. But Grayson Harte would make sure the papers he'd authorised were for one person alone and, even if there had been tickets and a passport, he doubted she would have agreed to travel.

She was in training for a job she evidently enjoyed. And she didn't enjoy him, that was clear. It piqued him to know it, but he no longer held sway. Better, then, that she stay in England for however long this interminable war lasted, though he doubted it would be for much longer. A matter of months, in his estimation, before Hitler would be marching along Whitehall. Vaguely, he hoped Daisy would be all right when that day came, that she would survive the occupation. But he couldn't allow himself to worry too much about her; he had his own future to consider. He was about to become a citizen of a new country, a young and thrusting country, and it was better that he arrived there untrammelled by past attachments.

Gerald laced his shoes and readied himself to creep downstairs. These days, that was the way he moved in and out of the building. The men below had been unusually quiet the last day or so, but he didn't trust them or their plans, and he was always conscious of the need to remain as unnoticed as possible. As if on cue, he heard the first sound in days of a raised voice. Then another voice weighed in. He sighed. Couldn't they have kept their quarrel until he'd visited Rigby's and was back safely in his hideout? The journey to the shop wasn't going to be so easy, now that they'd woken from whatever torpor had kept them silent. Here and there he caught the odd word or phrase shouted or hissed with some violence. Hindi words.

One man, the one with the deeper voice, the one Gerald reckoned was Anglo-Indian and seemed to be in charge, was proposing something that the other was vehemently against. There were several *can't do it*s and *must do it*s. Then the phrase *only chance*. *Duty* was another word. He couldn't make much of the argument but whatever it was, it was stopping him from collecting his pass to safety.

Hopefully, the men would quarrel themselves into silence. But the row went on, escalating in noise as the minutes passed. They no longer seemed to care they might be overheard. This was serious. Before they'd always hushed each other, aware that he was living only a thin ceiling above and could understand their language. But this time, their argument was so fierce, they'd forgotten the possibility of an eavesdropper.

Perhaps he could slide past their front door while they were engaged in shouting at each other, and stay out until he saw at least one of them leave the house. There were plenty of places in Ellen Street he could conceal himself. And the men never left the house together. In fact, he didn't think the darker skinned man went out at all. With one of them absent, he could risk slinking back into the building.

He creaked across the floorboards to the far end of the room. The attic formed an L shape, the foot of the letter L jutting out over what must be a storeroom beneath, but because of the angle it made, it was possible to see into the room below. Just a few feet — if he pushed his face close up to the small window and looked sideways.

Gerald did just that and what he saw caused him to stagger backwards. The men were locked in combat, no longer shouting but uttering thick grunts mingled with the occasional rough curse. Their arms were around each other's necks, trying to wrestle one another to the floor, their fingers poking at unprotected eyes. Then one of them lunged and his kick sent the other man sprawling across the floor. Gerald was back at the window, pressing his forehead hard against the glass. The fallen man had dragged himself from sight, the other man, too. Presumably ready to follow with another kick. But no, the man was on his feet again and backing into Gerald's sight line and the other, the lighter skinned man, had followed and had his arm raised. There was a flash of silver. The flash of a blade? Gerald felt nauseous. He had no wish to look longer and dragged himself to the nearest chair. It was a while before his heart stopped jumping.

A strange quiet reigned, as though the house was holding its breath. He could hear nothing, not even a curse. What was he to do? He made a rapid decision — he would go. If the men were still engaged in a life and death struggle, they would be far too busy to pay him attention. And he had to get to the shop. He had to get those papers. But he would still be cautious, opening his door very, very slowly and then taking one step at a time, hoping against hope that the stairs remained silent beneath his soft soles. He had reached the landing below and was about to take the first step towards the ground floor, when the door to his left was suddenly flung open. It was the door to the men's apartment which meant they must have finished their quarrel — at just the wrong moment.

Their quarrel was certainly over. Gerald looked aghast when he realised what he was looking at. The man standing inches away was breathing heavily and his eyes were wild. But it was his shirt that held Gerald transfixed. A white shirt, at least it had once been white, but was now splattered an ominous red. And beyond the man, beyond the open door, Gerald's scared eyes took in the body of the second man, lying prone, lying in a pool of red that was inching a path through the floorboards.

Time slowed almost to a stop and for Gerald, it was as though the scene in front of him had been going on forever. In truth, it must have taken seconds before he jerked himself into full consciousness and took action. Taking flight, he jumped the stairs two at a time, desperate to get to the front door. But it was only seconds before the blood-spattered man moved, too, pounding after him in a frantic bid to block his escape. With every fibre of his body, Gerald strained to reach the door. If he could get there, lift the latch, flee along the road, he would be in reach of green space, in reach of bushes and trees that could conceal him from . . . a murderer. The word drummed through his brain, even as he pushed his legs to go faster.

All thought of collecting the papers had vanished. All he could think of was survival. He reached up and grasped the door latch. The footsteps behind him grew loud in his ears. Pulling up the latch, he twisted the brass knob, his hand shaking. The door opened an inch, two inches. He could feel the fresh air of the spring day. He could feel the man's breath on his neck.

* * *

For several minutes after it happened, Sweetman found himself in a state of panic. A double murder was something he hadn't foreseen, but he'd had no choice. He'd tried hard to persuade Mishra that his plan was the very best, better by far than the failed kidnapping. But his companion had been stubborn, had threatened to go to the police, give himself up, rather than be implicated in Chandan Patel's death.

He shouldn't have been surprised. For some time he'd fancied the man felt no real commitment to the cause, not in the way he did. And when it came to the crunch, his fellow conspirator had flunked it, as he'd always suspected. Sweetman had been left alone to carry out orders. Better alone, though, better than having Mishra alongside, constantly questioning, constantly squeamish.

But if the man wasn't with him, he was against him, and a danger that had to be stopped. He hadn't meant to kill, not really. But he'd been in a fury and the knife had been to hand and . . . it was better like that. It had a certainty about it and he liked certainty.

Hari Mishra wouldn't be missed. Since they'd been in England, the man had hardly gone out of the door. Just that one journey when they'd made the attempt to kidnap Patel. No one even knew he lived here, only the man above and he was in no position to squeal. Sweetman had been frantic, wondering how best to dispose of Hari's body, when Minns or whatever he called himself, had walked down the stairs and spoiled everything.

Why choose to arrive at just that moment? It was almost as though the man had been trying to catch Sweetman out. There'd been nothing for it but to silence him — thank God for the gun he'd rammed in his pocket at the last moment. And thank God the old lady in the basement flat had been moved to a nursing home last week. A gunshot at such close quarters might have pierced even her deafness.

It wasn't what Sweetman had wanted, but he couldn't have this Minns going to the police, any more than he could have allowed Mishra. He'd be a wanted man, watched for by every blue helmet in London. It was crucial to keep a low profile, if he was to do what he intended. Remain anonymous — until the day after tomorrow. But how, with two dead men on his hands? He had to get rid of them, cover his tracks, until he'd accomplished his mission. After that, he didn't care what happened to him.

Sweetman forced himself to be calm. His face was running with sweat, his hands shaking and sticky. But a few swigs from the whisky bottle he'd kept hidden set him straight. He slumped down in the chair and thought very hard. If only he could walk out of the house and leave the bodies behind a slammed door . . . At any other time, he could have done it but, by ill chance, tomorrow was the day the landlord collected his weekly rent. The man was meticulous in his timing, knocking at the door of each lodging at three in the afternoon and demanding his money. There was blood everywhere, in the room, on the stairs, by the front door. He couldn't risk the landlord seeing and going to the police before he'd had time to deal with Patel. Somehow, he had to stop him coming.

Then he knew what he had to do. He could always count on his brain to find the right solution. Really, he'd been wasted trying to train that idiot, Mishra. He would set off a bomb. There were hundreds of bombs all over London, dropped by the Luftwaffe but lying dormant until disturbed by some unfortunate. He would keep the landlord at bay with a bomb blast. For a while, it would cover up the murders, hopefully leaving the dead men in fragments and making identification difficult. The post-mortems would eventually show they'd been murdered, though post-mortems were sketchy these days when so many people were dying, but even if that happened, the bomb would confuse matters and the police enquiry would be delayed.

He took another swig of whisky. He'd do more. He'd make it look like the Minns chap had killed his fellow tenant by putting the knife in his hand, and then set off the bomb to cover the evidence. Eventually, they would discover there'd been a third tenant, but it would sow more confusion and more delay. And delay was what Sweetman needed.

It was lucky that he hadn't told Hari about the bomb. Each night, after his companion had gone to bed, he'd assembled it bit by bit from the instructions he'd been handed. He'd had an idea that if all else failed, they might use it to deal with the envoy. But he couldn't be sure that Patel would be near enough to the explosion to be injured, and he'd abandoned the idea in favour of a kidnapping. Now, the bomb could come into its own. He only hoped it was big enough to tear the house apart.

CHAPTER TWENTY-SIX

Daisy saw him almost immediately, walking towards her across Charterhouse Square, weaving a path through the newly leafing trees. As Grayson drew near, he held out his arms to her, but she didn't respond and he allowed them to fall slackly by his side.

'Daisy?' He seemed nonplussed.

'I'm afraid I can't talk for long. I've only a few minutes and then I'm due back on the ward.' Her voice was deliberately controlled and she stopped several feet away, looking past him and across the square.

'I don't pretend to know what's going on,' he said quietly, 'but at least look at me.'

That forced her to face him directly and his expression — stunned, hurt — made her stomach clench. 'Something has happened,' he said. 'Tell me.'

'It's nothing . . . no, it's everything.'

She couldn't tell him about Willa. He would say all the right things, of course. How sad, such a tragedy, so young, but he wouldn't understand. Not how despairing she felt. Not how, meeting again, she was riven with guilt at how much time she had lavished on him and how little on Willa.

'You're sounding cryptic. How about some explanation?'

'I don't mean to be. I've had time to think, that's all.'

'And what have you thought?' His expression was anxious, but the words were sharp-edged.

'I enjoyed our evening at the Ritz,' she began.

'Night,' he put in.

'Night, then.' She dug her toes into the grass. 'I'm truly grateful for what you've done for Gerald. And for me. With Gerald gone, I can get on with my life again.'

She stopped speaking and the silence was intense. Even the birds had ceased chattering to listen. 'I *am* grateful,' she repeated, and then in a rush, 'but I don't think we should see each other again.'

She was stumbling, she knew, acting blindly, but she had to find a way out. All the bad things that had ever happened to her were forcing her to walk away.

'You surely don't mean that.' His bafflement was complete.

'I do. I think it's best — for both of us. Please don't be angry or try to persuade me differently.'

'But why? Why this complete change? Two days ago I thought . . .' Grayson's voice trailed off. He was struggling to make sense of the situation and not doing very well.

'I thought so, too,' she said quietly. 'But I've decided otherwise. When I had time to think more clearly about the future, our being together didn't seem such a good idea.'

'But why, for God's sake?' He was still struggling. 'Is it because you're still married? I know there are difficulties, but they're not insurmountable. There is such a thing as divorce. It's not pleasant, I grant you, but sometimes it's the right thing to do.'

'It's not because of Gerald.'

Grayson deserved an explanation, but she couldn't give one, not one that he could understand. Not one, even, that she could understand. Taking a deep breath, she began again. 'I can't say more, but please accept my decision.'

'I should be able to, shouldn't I? After all, it's not the first time you've changed your mind.' There was the very slightest tinge of bitterness to his voice and she saw his lips tighten into a thin line. He was hurting, she knew, hurting badly, and her determination almost buckled.

'I know it's not what you want to hear,' she hurried on, 'but in time you'll come to see it's the right thing — for both of us.'

Grayson walked a few paces away, his hands thrust deep in his pockets. Then he turned and walked back to her. 'I really don't understand you.' His clear blue eyes were unreadable. 'I thought I did. I hoped I did. But this—'

'Goodbye.' She held out her hand, but he refused to take it. 'I hope you have a good war. Keep safe, Grayson.' There was nothing more she could say or do.

'That's it, is it?' His tone was cold and crisp as she turned to go.

'Yes, that's it,' she said, and walked back into the Home, her tears beginning in earnest as the door shut behind her.

* * *

Bertie Sandford looked up surprised when Grayson strode into their shared office the next morning wearing a thunderous expression.

'Lost half a crown and found sixpence?' he asked.

Grayson didn't answer, but sat down at his desk and began to thump through a pile of papers without reading a word.

'You met your girl, then?' Sandford sucked lazily at his pipe. When Grayson remained mute, he tried again. 'Don't tell me, she's given you the heave-ho. Well, what do you know?'

'What *do* you know?' Grayson asked belligerently.

Bertie leaned against the sludge-coloured wall, one hand opening a box of matches and the other waggling his pipe at Grayson. 'Only that you've been chasing a dream, old man, and one that was bound to end in disaster.'

Grayson's shoulders hunched. He didn't need this, particularly from a man who'd only ever felt love for himself.

'I told you,' Bertie went on unwisely, 'it's never a good thing to venture too far out of your circle. I'm sure this Dora—'

'Daisy,' he snarled.

'This Daisy, then, is a nice enough girl, a good looker, too, no doubt, but she's not right for you. Never has been.'

'Would you care to elaborate?' Grayson's tone suggested this was unlikely to be a sensible thing to do.

'I tried to tell you weeks ago. When she swanned into your life again, but you were so puffed with excitement at meeting her, you wouldn't listen. You've been a crazy man, getting involved in her schemes, risking your career, your future. Madness! If Carmichael hadn't given you *carte blanche*, you'd be stuffed good and proper.'

'But I've not been.'

'Luckily for you. My point is that you could have been. And still might be. And this girl, Daisy, now she's got what she wanted, is off. I'm right about that?'

When Grayson didn't answer, Bertie nodded sagely. 'I thought so. That type of girl always is.'

'What type of girl?' His voice was dangerously brittle.

Bertie got up from his desk and strolled across to his colleague. 'It's not her fault that she's used you.' His voice oozed unwanted sympathy. 'That's how her sort operate. Let's be frank, old man, she's not your class. She wouldn't fit in. You'd never be able to take her home to mother, would you?'

'You talk bullshit, Sandford. And you're a raging snob.'

'I'm just being realistic. Think about your home, your school, your career. It's not exactly on a par with hers, is it?'

Grayson had never given it much thought. Up until now it hadn't mattered. Now, suddenly it did. Was Sandford right? That he and Daisy were so far apart they could never make a good future together?

The thought stirred him to anger. 'What the hell has my background got to do with anything?' He jumped up from his desk and started towards his colleague.

Seeing the normally cool Grayson striding in his direction, murder on his face, Bertie abandoned his indolence. Hurriedly, he began to back out of the open doorway and cannoned into the man who was just then coming into the room.

'Mike, there you are,' he said, with obvious relief. 'Our friend has a little problem. Perhaps you can help.' And with that, he glided away.

Michael Corrigan tilted his head to one side. 'A problem?'

Grayson sighed and walked back to his desk. Slumping into the chair, he swung from side to side. 'She's dumped me,' he said baldly.

'Daisy?'

'Who else?'

'Phew. That's a cruncher.' Mike walked towards his friend and perched himself on the edge of his desk. 'I'm sorry, old chap. But how, why?'

'Will you believe me if I say I've no idea. All she'll say is that she's thought about the night we spent at the Ritz and no longer feels it's a good idea we're together.'

'Cold feet,' Corrigan proclaimed. 'That's cold feet. She's dipped her toes and liked the water, but now—'

'She's got cold feet. I don't think so, despite your entrancing metaphor.' For the first time since he'd left Daisy, Grayson's face wore a slight smile.

'So, why suddenly decide to give you the elbow?'

'I don't have an answer. Unless Bertie is right.'

'Highly unlikely. What does our beloved Bertie say?'

'That she's got what she wants from me — the papers for her appalling husband. I handed them over at the Ritz, remember. So . . . she doesn't need me anymore. I can be cast adrift.' The bitterness was back.

'That doesn't sound like the girl you've described to me.'

Grayson stopped his swinging. 'It doesn't, does it, but perhaps I don't really know her. She comes from a completely different background, as Bertie has been at pains to remark. I know he can never forget he's an Eton and Oxbridge man, but he may have a point. Daisy hasn't talked much about her early life, though quite enough for me to see that it was an "everyone for themselves" kind of set-up. You did what you had to, to survive. Maybe that's exactly what she's been doing this time. She needed Mortimer, Minns, out of the way or her life would be in pieces, and I was the only person who could rescue her. She came to me for help and, when she'd got what she wanted, she left.'

'But to — to sleep with you. That's pretty drastic.'

'It just happened,' Grayson said wearily. 'She probably didn't mean it to go that far, but we were caught in a huge air raid and she was genuinely scared, and . . .'

He stopped speaking for a moment as a thought caught at him. 'Of course, at that stage I hadn't handed over the papers. That wasn't until we left. Perhaps she thought sleeping with me would seal the deal.' There was another pause. 'I don't know what to think,' he finished miserably.

'You're suggesting that when she made love to you, she was pretending to care?'

'No.' Grayson almost shouted the word. Then repeated more quietly, 'No. I refuse to believe she was pretending. But whether she was or not, the end result is the same.'

He looked up with a set face. 'I can't do this anymore, Mike. I'm part of a team and I've a job to finish. I have to get on with that and forget her. I know I've tried to do it before — several times, in fact — but this time, I must mean it.'

His friend clasped him by the shoulder. 'It's lousy, I know, but you'll get through. It might not seem so now, but it could turn out for the best.'

Grayson nodded reluctantly. 'Maybe. And maybe she's right and we're not good for each other. There always seems trouble when we're together, that's for sure.'

'Talking of trouble, any further news on the Indian front? I don't suppose you've had time to follow up the info that's come in.'

'Not yet. But I did get something from Daisy. I would have passed it on to you, except we've been going in different directions these last few days, and I'm not sure it helps. It was something she told me that night at the Ritz. She witnessed the attempted kidnap.'

'She actually saw it?' Corrigan stared at him in surprise.

'It was after she'd met me at Lyons,' Grayson said a trifle sheepishly. 'She was walking back to Barts and crossing into Kingsway when the kidnap car nearly mowed her down. She saw it blocked by the fire engine and the police car and then saw it reverse — violently, she said. It passed her again on the other side of the road, travelling very fast, but she was certain there were two people in the car, and she had the feeling she'd seen one of them somewhere before.'

'That's pretty vague. She had no idea where she'd seen him?'

'No. There's something else, though. She thinks she might have been followed these last few weeks. Ever since Gerald Mortimer raised his slimy head, and *he* was convinced he was being spied on by the men who live in the flat below.'

Corrigan started to laugh.

'No, listen, Mike. That was my first reaction. But — remember I mentioned before that there were Indians living below Mortimer? Or at least one Indian, the other possibly Anglo. That could tally with our witness's description. And if the man in the kidnap car *is* the man who's been spying on Mortimer and following Daisy, then we should be able to get to him. All we need is to find where Mortimer lives.'

'But *is* he the same person?'

'That I don't know. Daisy never managed to see the stalker properly, if in fact he exists. But it might be worth following up, and I've an idea where to start, a shop called Rigby's. There's no real urgency — I doubt there's anything in it — but when we've finished up here this morning . . .'

Michael Corrigan slapped his friend on the back. 'Worth it, if only to keep your mind on other things. Will you go or shall I?'

'Why don't we go together?'

CHAPTER TWENTY-SEVEN

It was a raw morning, the weather in sympathy with the unhappy day that lay ahead. There were few mourners for Willa: a small band of nurses, Sister Phillips representing the management of St Barts and Willa's mother, a shrivelled, battered looking woman, who'd travelled alone from Cardiff. Mrs Jenkins was the sole member of her family in attendance and, from her few mumbled words, it seemed as though she'd had to fight hard to attend her eldest child's funeral. The bleak service in an empty church was soon over and the small group of mourners wandered outside, past a screen of dark ilex, following a gravelled path towards the open grave. Scattered headstones on either side glistened in the cold drizzle. A spiteful gust of wind caught the walkers unaware, chilling their faces with the faintest breath of ice. A freak snowstorm had been forecast, Daisy remembered. No April warmth for Willa.

Out of the corner of her eye, she saw another group of mourners at another graveside. They must have attended the funeral immediately before. Willa's service had been over so quickly that the two parties had almost coincided. Such a brief commemoration of a young life, she thought, brief and ultimately meaningless. Was that all that Willa's existence had amounted to? Was that all that any life amounted to? For days, Daisy had been in a dark place, plagued by the notion that her own life had come to a dead end. It was wrong of her, she knew, to succumb so easily to this black mood. She had everything to live for. She was doing a job she loved, Gerald was no longer a problem, and Grayson no longer a difficulty. But he was, of course.

Grayson haunted her every waking hour. She'd done the right thing, she kept telling herself. They were always destined to walk different paths and Willa's death had only precipitated the inevitable. He would fare so much better without her. It hadn't been *his* fault that she'd been distracted and thoughtless, and now felt so badly. It had been hers entirely. She'd allowed the girl's tragedy to unfold beneath her eyes.

The coffin was lowered into the gaping hole and she felt Connie's hand searching for hers. Nursing discipline prevailed and the two of them stood ramrod straight by the graveside, but neither girl was able to suppress her tears. Several of the nurses threw flowers onto the coffin and Daisy bent and placed a fragrant red rose across its shining wood. It was probably the first beautiful thing that Willa had ever been given. The boy she had mourned all those weeks ago, cut down before he was twenty, would have had little time to woo her with roses. She straightened up as the first shovels of earth were thrown into the grave.

We have entrusted our sister, Wilhelmina, to God's mercy, and we now commit her body to the ground, the Vicar intoned.

'It will soon be over,' Connie whispered.

'But not for Willa.'

Connie gripped her friend's hand more tightly. 'In a way, for Willa, too. Look at her mother. What kind of life have they both had?' Daisy could find no comfort in the thought.

Earth to earth, ashes to ashes, dust to dust: in sure and certain hope of the resurrection to eternal life . . .

A strangled gasp among the small circle of nurses who stood across the open grave made Daisy look up. Lydia's face, a white hollow of a face with huge, staring eyes, looked back at her. The girl seemed almost dead herself, slumped lifelessly against her colleagues while the Vicar's chant went remorselessly on.

. . . through our Lord Jesus Christ who will transform our frail bodies that they may be conformed to His glorious body . . .

Daisy had heard enough. She tugged at Connie's arm and, tears streaming, they turned to go. A stumbling Lydia had preceded them, supported on either side by a fellow nurse. Behind, the final shovels of earth fell with a dull thud and voices sounded the communal *Amen*. For a moment, they paused in their walk. The deed was done. Willa was buried. Connie blew her nose loudly, while Daisy dragged another handkerchief from her pocket and dabbed her face dry.

Blearily, she looked around. The mourners from the second funeral party had spread themselves across the graveyard and were making their individual ways back to the church's lychgate. Except one, she noticed.

Connie blew her nose again. 'Did I tell you that Colin's parents are in London tomorrow?' Her friend was trying for a veneer of normality.

Daisy shook her head. She had lost any interest in Connie's love life.

'They're travelling up from Portsmouth for the day. Colin's got a twenty-four-hour pass. He wants me to meet them.'

'How are you going to manage that?' All the nurses' free time had been cancelled that week. Despite her slowness, Willa would be missed on the ward.

'Sister has given me special permission.' And when Daisy seemed unlikely to respond, Connie held up her left hand and waved it in front of her friend. 'Look.'

A small diamond sparkled out of the thin band of gold she wore on her fourth finger.

'You're engaged! And you never said.' Daisy's tears had dried and she couldn't stop herself from sounding reproachful. 'How long have you been engaged?'

'Only a few days and I didn't feel I could . . . you know,' and she turned her head towards the grave they had just left. 'It didn't seem right to be celebrating.'

'Not celebrating — but you could have told me.'

'I couldn't reach you,' Connie said simply. 'You've been somewhere else since Willa died. It's only now that the funeral is over, I thought you might want to know.'

It was true. She had been too self-absorbed to notice what was happening to her best friend. And what was happening would change Connie's life.

'Dear Connie, congratulations.' She put her arms around the girl and hugged her fiercely. 'I'm sure you and Colin will be very happy together. You were made for each other.' It was trite but true.

'Like you and Grayson.'

Daisy said nothing. There would be plenty of time to let her friend down gradually. In the meantime, she must snap out of the depression that was taking hold of her. She had a job to do and a war to win, along with everyone else.

They had reached the lychgate now and stood waiting for the remaining nurses to catch them up. The lone man Daisy had thought a mourner at the earlier funeral began to walk towards them. His solitude made him conspicuous. That and his clothes — he was dressed completely in black. But then why wouldn't he be, when he'd been attending a funeral? A black trilby was pulled down over much of his face.

For a moment, he was outlined against the gunmetal sky and something about his figure tugged at Daisy with its familiarity. He was walking very slowly as though hoping they might leave first but, when they made no move, he was forced to inch past them. As he did so, she looked him full in the face. Unwillingly, he caught her eye from beneath the brim of his trilby, and she knew she'd been right. He *was* familiar. She had seen him before or at least the suggestion of him — Baker Street, the underground. He must be the man who had cannoned into her. The man who had pushed her dangerously close to the electrified rail line.

And a man she'd seen somewhere else. Her mind struggled to remember and then gave up. But what was he doing here? Was it a coincidence that they'd met today in this churchyard or was he here for another reason? It was conceivable that he'd buried someone he knew but, if he hadn't, he must have come because she was here. He'd come to find her, to spy on her. So, she *had* been followed these last few weeks. The shadowy figure she'd glimpsed hadn't been imagination.

Was he one of Gerald's Indians, perhaps, as interested in her as her husband? If that were so, his being here made little sense. Why would the man continue to watch her when there was no longer a need. Whatever his suspicions of Gerald and herself, they were pointless. The bird had flown. Gerald would have left his rooms by now and jumped free of any danger this man could pose.

It was then, for the first time, that Daisy wondered why she'd heard nothing from her husband. She'd been so caught up in grief that it hadn't occurred to her there had been no word from him. No word of thanks, no word of goodbye. Would he really have gone without even a brief note to say he was leaving? She supposed it was possible, but it didn't seem likely. He was about to travel thousands of miles across the sea, never to return. And he *was* still her husband, whatever bad things had happened between them. There was something odd about Gerald's silence. And, suddenly, she was filled with fear for him.

* * *

It was no use, she must find out what had happened. She had to go to Rigby's. No doubt she was worrying over nothing: Gerald had simply collected the envelope from the shop and disappeared without a word. But, then, why was this man still following her? He must realise there was no longer any point to his spying.

There was only one way to settle her mind. She would go to Rigby's and check on the papers. If they were still in the shop, she would know something was very wrong. And now was the time to do it. Every nurse at the funeral had been given an additional hour's free time before they needed to be back on the ward. From St Anne's Church, she could reach Gower's Walk in twenty minutes and be back at Barts on time.

'I need to go on a small errand, Connie,' she said, as they turned the corner into the main road.

'What now? Don't you want a cuppa before we're on the go again? I'm gasping for one.'

'It's just something I must do.' She was sounding annoyingly vague, she knew, but Daisy didn't want to spell out her fears, just in case that made them real. 'I won't be long,' she promised.

'I'll come with you   I don't trust you on your own, not in your present frame of mind.'

'I'll be fine, really.' And to prove it, she gave an imitation of a smile. 'Go and get your tea and I'll be back at Barts before you've finished the first cup.'

Connie pulled a face. 'Not with the thirst I've got! But if you're sure . . .'

'I'm sure,' she said firmly. 'If you run, you'll catch the others up.'

Once she'd watched her friend disappear, she set out briskly in the opposite direction towards Gower's Walk.

Mr Rigby was closing for lunch as she reached the shop. When he saw Daisy appear in the doorway, his face turned even sourer than on her previous visit.

'I'm closed,' he said, completely disregarding the Open sign which still swung at the glass door.

'This won't take a minute, Mr Rigby.' Daisy was determined.

'It better not.' He came out from behind the counter and stood with one hand on the door, ready to slam it once she left.

'Do you remember that I delivered an envelope here a few days ago? It was addressed to a Mr Jack Minns.'

The shopkeeper spat onto the pavement beyond. 'Oh, 'im.'

'Yes, him. Do you know if he collected it?'

'No idea.'

'But you would have served him?' she persisted.

'Maybe. Maybe not. I'm not chained to the counter, yer know. There's others. I'm quite able to employ others.' His mouth twisted into a smirk.

'I'm sure you are.' It went against the grain, but she needed to be conciliatory. If she upset him, he was quite capable of pushing her out of the door without the answers she needed. 'But would you do me a great favour and check whether or not Mr Minns collected the envelope?'

'Envelope,' he sniffed, shuffling reluctantly away from the door. 'He don't need to collect no envelopes. White feathers is more his line. He should have quite a collection by now.'

'White feathers?' She was fazed by the turn the conversation had taken.

'Yer know what a white feather means, I take it.'

Daisy flushed, but her dislike made her bold. 'Of course, I do. Was it you who sent one to Mr Minns?'

'What if I did?'

She thought rapidly. Gerald had been convinced that the feather pushed beneath his door had come from the men in the flat below, convinced they were gathering evidence against him. But what if it had been Rigby who'd delivered the feather or paid a boy to deliver it for him? It was possible, after all, that the men hadn't suspected Gerald and hadn't been spying on him. For a moment, she experienced a ripple of relief, the lifting of a great burden. But only for a moment, until she remembered that white feather or not, she, too, had been spied on, and just minutes earlier.

'No reason,' she said. That was cowardly of her. She should have defended Gerald as a brave soldier, but she hadn't. She was desperate for this unpleasant man to go in search of the envelope. 'Could you look, please?'

His glare was accompanied by another angry sniff before he shambled towards the rear of the premises. Within a very short time, he was back again, a brown envelope in his hand. The very envelope that Grayson had passed to her at the Ritz Hotel and that she'd left in this shop just a few short days ago. Daisy looked at the name written in bold, black ink. There was no mistake. Something had gone very wrong. In a daze, she stuffed it back into her handbag, not knowing what she should do next. The decision was made for her.

CHAPTER TWENTY-EIGHT

Out of nowhere, a huge explosion shook the building and Daisy had to grab the shop counter to stay upright, Rigby holding fast to the other side. For seconds afterwards, the shop seemed to rock back and forth but, once the walls stopped moving, she rushed to the door. The shopkeeper was only a few paces behind.

She stumbled out on to the pavement. The sky above was an empty blue. Not a plane in sight, yet smoke was rising in great plumes from an adjoining street, smoke that looked a mile high. The sound of falling masonry crowded out her ears.

'Unexploded bomb,' Rigby said with some satisfaction. 'They keep yer on yer toes.'

But Daisy wasn't listening; she was filled with a terrible premonition. This was Gerald's local shop and he must live nearby, in a road where a house was nothing but rubble. He'd been sick and confined to his rooms, she decided, that's why he hadn't collected the envelope. Why hadn't she thought of that before? And, now, he might be grossly injured or worse. She must go, offer what help she could.

She began to run towards the plumes of smoke and, as soon as she rounded the corner of Ellen Street, the devastation was clear to see. A group of confused people were wandering aimlessly along the cratered road and Daisy weaved a path through them as quickly as she could. Rubble had spilled across the street making it almost impassable, but an ambulance was already inching its way through the debris. Close by, she heard the loud clang of a fire engine.

Drawing opposite the ruined building, she could see that, unlike the dolls' house dwellings on either side, this house had been three storeys high. Fragments of each of the floors teetered crazily against the sky, furniture scattered and upended, and scraps of cloth fanning in and out of pockets of fire. The firemen had arrived and were running hoses towards each of the small conflagrations.

'Not too bad, Jim,' she heard one of them say.

'Could have been worse,' was the cheerful reply.

Could it, she wondered? Did Gerald lie somewhere amid this desolation? She must find out. Picking her way across the cracked flagstones, she approached the fireman who had been giving directions to his men.

'I was passing by, officer, but I'm a nurse. Is there any way I can help?'

He shook his head. 'I doubt it. No one in the middle of that is going to need much nursing. We'll have the fire under control in a jiffy, then the ambulance crew can move in. They might need your help, I suppose. Some poor blighter might have survived — you never know.'

The flames were soon doused, and the ruins smouldering quietly, as the ambulance men began to carve a path through the shattered brickwork. It might have been a large house, Daisy reflected, but it had been a poor one, too, and it was hard to imagine Gerald spending his days in such a wretched place. Finishing his days, perhaps. She pushed the dreadful thought from her mind.

There was a shout from one of the ambulance crew and his colleagues went running towards him. They began digging, bricks flying and lumps of plaster cast aside. Then they were heaving a body on to a stretcher and Daisy felt her stomach clench. The body was Gerald's, she was sure.

She hugged the pavement, standing in the shadow of the ambulance as the crew pushed past her with their burden. As they lifted the stretcher into the vehicle, the rough blanket covering the body fell open and she saw the man's face. Not Gerald's. A darker skin, an Indian skin. Anish's face came suddenly to her, Anish lying dead on the ground amid a rain that was drowning the whole world. She shook her head to dispel the bad memories.

If there had been any doubt in Daisy's mind that this ruin was Gerald's house, the dead man confirmed it. No one else was likely to have Indians as neighbours. But if so, where was he? It seemed he hadn't been at home, yet he hadn't collected the precious documents. So, what had happened?

One of the firemen came up to her. 'Unexploded bomb,' he said, echoing Rigby's words. 'They're the devil.'

'Was it from the last raid?' The raid from which she sheltered in Grayson's arms.

'More than likely. That's been the worst by far. There'll be bombs lying asleep all over London. This one won't be the last to go up, that's for sure.'

Daisy gave him a sad nod. If she was to get back to the ward on time, she must start walking. She'd gone no more than a few paces, however, when a second shout made her stop, her body stiffening in sudden panic.

'There's another of 'em here.'

Running back to the bombed house, she saw the ambulance crew dragging another body to the surface. Before they could stop her, she'd clambered on to one of the piles of fallen masonry and was jumping from one tottering mound to the next, desperate to get to their side.

'Miss! Nurse! You can't do that!'

But she had. She had reached them. She had reached the body. And just as she'd always known, it was Gerald. Gerald caked in grime, his clothes torn to pieces by the blast. And with an unmistakeable hole in his temple.

The man nearest her gave a low whistle. 'Well, what do you know. He killed hisself.' And he pointed to the pistol which lay at an angle a few inches from Gerald's outstretched hand. 'He killed hisself,' he repeated, wonderingly.

'No! He couldn't! He wouldn't.'

Daisy's cry made the men stare, but she hardly noticed. She knew Gerald would never have committed suicide. It was not in his nature. And not now, not when he had everything to live for.

'Do you know this person, Miss?' the ambulance man asked respectfully.

'Yes.' Her voice came as barely a whisper. 'But the bomb . . .'

The man scratched his head. 'Must have gone off by accident. After he killed hisself, that's what I'm thinking. Bit of a strange coincidence, wouldn't you say? It killed the other poor blighter at the same time.'

'No, it didn't.' The driver of the ambulance had joined them.

'What d'you mean, Ted?'

'I mean it wasn't the bomb that killed the Indian fella. He was already dead. We missed it earlier on — he was covered in so much dust — but there's a knife wound in his chest. Clear as daylight. He was killed before the bomb went off, that's what I'm thinking.'

'So this bloke—' and the two men looked down at the broken body lying between them — 'must have killed the Indian fella, then decided to kill hisself. Because of what he'd done, begging your pardon, Miss.'

Daisy felt numb, her body frozen. But her mind was still working and none of this made sense.

'Why would he have done such a thing?' she demanded.

'Search me. Probably got into some kind of quarrel, the pair of 'em. Not that unusual these days.'

'But the bomb,' she insisted. 'It can't have been a coincidence. How do you explain the bomb?'

'Easy enough. He set it off hisself. I reckon if we search, we'll find a timer somewhere in this load of debris. He primed it before he put the gun to his head.'

'But for what reason?'

'I don't rightly know, Miss. A cover up, maybe. He didn't want people to know he was a murderer, so he tried to cover up the evidence.'

'He didn't do a very good job then, did he?' Ted muttered.

Daisy had heard enough, heard too much. She must blank this from her mind, get back to the hospital and work. Just work and it would go away. She heard the firemen start their engine and she turned to leave, but the ambulance driver put out a hand to stop her.

'You can't go, Miss. This is murder and you're a witness. We'll need to call the police and you'll have to give a statement.'

'I have to go.'

She must get back to Barts, back to her patients, lose herself in the comforting routine of the ward — until she'd had time to come to terms with what she'd seen, if she ever did.

Daisy stumbled her way back to the pavement. These men were wrong. Gerald was no murderer. He was capable of bad things, she knew only too well, but not murder. Yet he'd shot Anish, her mind was telling her. But that was to save her. That was different.

And this Indian hadn't been shot. He'd been killed by a knife wound to the chest. A knife was close, personal, bloody. Gerald would never have done that. And if he'd killed one of the men he thought were spies, why not the other? The second man was still out there, walking the streets untouched. And still watching her. She shivered at the thought and turned instinctively, thinking she would see his black trilby, his black mourning suit.

Instead, she saw Grayson Harte coming towards them, accompanied by a pale, red-haired man. He looked stunned to see her, then masked his astonishment with a curt nod in her direction. Clambering across the pile of debris, he joined the group of men. They were still gathered around the body which lay where they'd found it.

Immediately he saw Grayson, the driver of the ambulance began talking, his hands gesticulating first towards the dead man and then to the vehicle waiting by the roadside. Daisy tried to close her ears to the driver's words. She didn't want to hear him repeat what he had to say about Gerald's death.

Grayson looked down at the body. 'I know this man,' she heard him say. 'And I don't think that's what happened. It's far more likely that someone else was involved in the killings — a third man.'

The third man who had come to the graveyard, she thought, and felt her hands go clammy.

'I would say he killed both these men and set the bomb to cover his tracks,' Grayson continued, 'but the police will need to come to their own conclusions. Take the bodies to the morgue and my colleague and I will inform the authorities.'

The driver grunted, unhappy it seemed with this turn of events. But Grayson flipped open a wallet and pushed it beneath the man's nose. His credentials, Daisy presumed. The red-haired man did the same. Shrugging his shoulders, the driver ordered one of the crew to bring up a stretcher. The Secret Intelligence Service was a law unto themselves and it wasn't his job to argue. His job was to get the bodies into cold storage as soon as possible.

Satisfied, Grayson made his way over to where she was standing. As always, his clothes were immaculate, but it seemed to Daisy that since yesterday he'd aged. There were tired lines around his mouth and the slightest sprinkling of grey in his hair that she'd never noticed before.

'It's fortunate we were in the area,' he said. 'We'll try to keep this business quiet, and it would be best if you say as little as possible. The police will have to be informed, but they'll treat it as a simple murder.'

'It is murder,' she retorted.

'But hardly simple. My guess is that Gerald was killed because he knew too much, or the murderer thought he did. It's likely the other man was killed for the same reason. Bearing in mind the kidnap attempt, it looks as though we have a determined spy on our hands and the less all of us say publicly, the better.'

Her mind was working furiously. That was it! That's where she'd seen the third man. Or, at least, she'd seen his eyes. He was the kidnapper on Kingsway. He'd had a companion with him in the car, a companion who would soon be on his way to the morgue. Grayson had guessed correctly. Should she tell him so? Every minute he'd been talking, she'd felt his hostility and she had no wish to prolong the encounter. It was better to say nothing, better to leave the affair to him. He was smart enough.

And she had more than enough to think about — another person to grieve for. Gerald had been trouble from the moment they'd married, but she had never wished him dead. She had stopped loving him a long time ago, but to see him die for the second time . . .

His body was being moved onto a stretcher and she noticed how easily the crew picked him up. He must have lost weight, a lot of weight. He couldn't have been eating properly, she thought. She felt an overwhelming sadness, then anger, then guilt, a cocktail of emotions rolled into one.

'This is my colleague, Michael Corrigan,' Grayson was saying.

Corrigan shook her hand and a pair of hazel eyes smiled at her. She liked him straightaway and felt ashamed of her decision to say nothing of the morning's events. The intelligence service was working for the country. They needed all the assistance they could get and her information might help track the other man, the man who was the real murderer.

'The second Indian,' she asked, 'do you know anything about him?' The stretcher party was passing on its way to the ambulance and she lowered her voice.

Corrigan looked uneasy. 'At the moment, we don't know who he is or what he plans, though we have our suspicions.'

'What we do know,' Grayson put in, 'is that he's extremely dangerous. He's on the loose and has to be found.'

'He was at the funeral,' she blurted out, 'or rather at the graveyard.'

Both men stared at her. 'Whose funeral?' Grayson asked. 'When?'

'It doesn't matter whose — but he was in St Anne's churchyard an hour ago. I saw him.'

Grayson looked astounded. 'He was a mourner?'

'I doubt it. I think he was watching me.'

'Then he will have followed you here, or he'll be on his way. He must believe you can identify him — you're a threat to whatever he's planning.'

'But I'm not.'

'As long as he believes you are, you're in danger. You can't go back to Barts,' Corrigan said with decision.

'No,' Grayson echoed, 'nor back to Charterhouse Square.'

'But—'

'No buts.' Grayson was at his most peremptory.

'I've nowhere else to go.'

'But I have and that's where you'll go.'

'If you mean your flat, Grayson, I'm not—'

'I don't mean my flat,' he interrupted. 'Is that likely?' She flushed at his tone.

'We'll take you to a safe house,' his comrade said quietly.

'A safe house is what it sounds. Mike here will drive you. Once you're there, you'll have a man to guard you. Just until we catch this joker, which shouldn't be long.'

Daisy felt control sliding out of her hands. 'My work,' she exclaimed, trying to wrest back authority. 'I'm due back at the hospital — now.'

'You can't go. It's too dangerous.' Grayson was terse. 'I'll go to Barts immediately and speak to Matron. Explain the situation. Under the circumstances, I'm sure she'll grant you indefinite leave.'

Before she could protest further, he'd turned to speak to his colleague. 'I'll walk to the hospital from here, Mike. It's not far. You take the car but, whatever you do, don't drive straight there.'

'Don't worry. I know the drill.' Corrigan smiled his reassurance.

Without another word, Grayson turned and strode along Ellen Street, heading towards the City. Daisy had never felt more alone.

CHAPTER TWENTY-NINE

Grayson's encounter with the matron of St Barts was short and sharp. Her expression made it clear she thought it stupid, reprehensible even, to have involved one of her nurses in some ridiculous cloak and dagger enterprise when her staff was already stretched to breaking. At one point, Grayson thought he heard her mutter *Boys Own Paper*, though he could have been wrong. It was certainly how she made him feel, an irresponsible schoolboy wallowing in fantasy. He found himself metaphorically pulling up his knee socks.

Leaving her stately presence with a silent sigh of relief, he walked down the staircase to the hospital entrance. Fresh air was what he sought. Instead, a nurse flying down the stairs behind him, bundled him to the ground and landed on top of him. She was a substantial girl and, for a moment, he was winded. Scrambling to her feet, her face was scarlet with embarrassment.

'I'm so sorry.' She held out a hand to help him to his feet. 'I was rushing, I'm afraid. I didn't see you there.'

'I've obviously shrunk in the last half hour,' he said easily. 'That must be your matron's doing.'

'You've been to see Matron? Gosh.'

'Gosh, indeed.'

They were both upright now and he found her examining him closely.

'I suppose . . .' she began, 'I suppose you wouldn't be . . . you aren't by any chance . . .'

'Grayson Harte.' He held out his hand and she shook it vigorously. 'Daisy was right,' she said cryptically.

'And you are?'

'Connie, Connie Telford. I'm her best friend. I was rushing because she's gone missing and I was trying to find her. She promised she'd be back, but she hasn't turned up and Sister is in a steam over it. I wanted to warn her.'

'I think you'll find that Daisy's absence has been accounted for,' he said gently.

Connie looked perplexed. 'But what's happened? She said she had something to do, that was all, then she'd be back. So where is she?'

'I can't tell you that, Miss Telford,' he said regretfully. 'But you can be sure that Daisy is safe. She won't be returning to work for a short while, that's all.'

'But why ever not?'

He took her by the arm and led her down the remaining stairs. The entrance hall was buzzing: doctors dashing in and out of doors, orderlies wheeling patients, visitors delivering gifts at the porter's desk. He guided her towards a small alcove where they could speak without being overheard.

'I can't say much, but you can trust what I say. If Daisy were to return, either here or to Charterhouse Square, she would be in danger.'

Connie's mouth fell open, and Grayson kept silent while she thought over what he'd said. At length, she asked, 'When will she be coming back?' She sounded unhappy.

'That's something else I can't say. She'll be back when we're confident the danger is over.'

'And who is this "we"?'

'That's—'

'Something you can't say,' she finished for him. She took a few agitated paces back and forth. 'You will look after her?'

'We'll return her safely, I promise.'

'But you, you, Mr Harte,' she insisted. '*You'll* make sure she's okay?'

It was evident that Connie had no idea her friend had decided against him. 'I'll do all I can,' he said a trifle grimly, 'but you should know that Daisy and I are not on the best of terms.'

The girl gave him a startled look. 'But how come? Last time I spoke to her she was so happy. She was over the moon — and that was because of you.'

'I wish she was still over the moon. But something happened to change her mind, though I've no idea what.'

Connie stopped her pacing and looked thoughtful. 'Willa happened,' she said flatly.

'What or who is Willa?' It was his turn to look puzzled.

'She isn't — not any more, I'm afraid. She died last week and today was her funeral.'

'Daisy said she'd been to a funeral.' He was still puzzled. 'But how does that affect anything?'

'She thought it was her fault — that Willa died,' Connie said in the quietest of voices. 'You see, Willa committed suicide and Daisy hasn't forgiven herself for that.'

He felt he was grappling through a dark fog. 'But why? I don't understand.'

'Neither do I, Grayson. I hope you don't mind me calling you Grayson. That's how I always think of you. I don't understand it at all, but Daisy seems to have got it into her head that if she'd paid Willa more attention, the girl would never have hung herself.'

'And what has that to do with me, with us?' The fog had just become impenetrable.

'You were the reason she didn't look after Willa. You distracted her.' His expression was one of bewilderment, and Connie grasped his hand. 'I know that it sounds utterly crazy, but I think Daisy *has* been slightly crazy these last few weeks. First of all that husband of hers — that Gerald — and then the man who was following her. Then seeing you again and . . . well, you know.'

He did know or he was beginning to. It was crazy, as her friend had said, but he could see how the suicide might have pushed Daisy that little bit too far. Her resources were exhausted and their future together had become the payment.

He held out his hand again. 'You've been a great help, Connie. Thank you.'

'I'm not sure how,' she confessed, 'but bring her back safely, please.'

* * *

That morning, Sweetman had woken newly energised. He'd slept surprisingly well which could only be good news — he'd be sleeping rough tonight. In a few hours' time, these hateful rooms in the hateful house would be no more. Stuffing his few possessions into a small suitcase — nothing of his must be found in the debris — he set the timer for several hours ahead. That would ensure he was miles away when the bomb went off. He'd take the suitcase to Charing Cross and leave it in the Left Luggage and if, by any chance, he survived tomorrow's bloodbath, collect it before he made his way to the Kent coast within the hour. A French fishing boat under German orders would be waiting for him.

There was just one more thing he had to do. Find the nurse. She couldn't know what had happened, since her fellow spy had had no time to alert her before he died. But Sweetman couldn't be sure just how much she did know, and it was possible that the two of them had an arrangement to contact each other daily and, when Minns stayed silent, she would decide to raise the alarm.

He should have dealt with her before, that much was clear. He'd allowed things to run on too long, allowed her and her confederate upstairs a freedom they didn't deserve. And look what had happened. He would sort out this mess, but he couldn't afford another botch. He had to have a clear run for tomorrow's meeting and she was the only obstacle left. She was an uncertain commodity and that was what Sweetman hated.

The early morning sky had promised well, but when he slammed shut the front door of Ellen Street for the last time, the sun had disappeared and the wind was raw. He turned up his coat collar and pulled down the black trilby that worked brilliantly to disguise his features. He would walk to Barts and wait for her to finish her shift. Hopefully, she would leave the hospital alone. But when he'd waited on the pavement opposite for some time, his quarry appeared with a gaggle of fellow nurses. All were in uniform, their deep blue capes a sombre gathering beneath the dark sky.

He followed them, road by road, keeping a careful distance, until finally they entered a church. St Anne's, he noticed. Lingering in the porch, he heard the beginnings of a funeral service and retreated to the graveyard. A short distance away, another party of mourners were gathered beside an open grave and he sauntered casually towards them, taking up a position at the edge of the group. No one spoke to him, no one even noticed him. That was the good thing about English funerals, he thought. The people who attended came from all locations and all walks of life. Many were complete strangers to each other and hardly anyone spoke.

His satisfaction was short-lived. He realised too late that he'd made a mistake in staying in the cemetery. He was far too conspicuous. The church service had been briefer than he'd expected, the committal proceedings even briefer, and quite suddenly the bustle of nurses were following on the heels of the group he'd adopted. He'd been caught out. He should have hung back, pretended to tie his shoelace or something equally commonplace, but instead had found himself walking past the woman he was hunting.

She'd looked at him hard. He'd pulled the trilby over his face as far as he dared, but she'd known him, he was sure. That was an added reason, if he needed one, to eliminate the threat she posed. There were still twenty-four hours to go before Patel's meeting and she was a danger. He hadn't much hope of surviving tomorrow, but he was determined that his plan would, determined he'd scupper any possibility that India would enter the war on Britain's side.

He had to get to her before she had the chance to speak. She had recognised him, possibly as the man who'd been following her, maybe even the man who'd pushed her at Baker Street. Neither possibility was serious enough to make him lose sleep. But, if she realised he'd been the man driving the kidnap car, that could sink him. She would tell the SIS and they would be on to him in a flash. They must already be highly suspicious, but so far all they had was an unknown threat to Patel and no idea where the threat came from.

She was the one who could furnish them with a detailed description and, in hours, he would be the object of a manhunt. If he knew anything about the SIS, they would find him. The evidence against him was flimsy. It was only her word, her description, that implicated him in the kidnapping, but once they started digging, they would trace him back to Ellen Street and find what was left of the dead men. He would be detained for murder. The bomb might confuse the police, but not the SIS. He would be locked up and his plan wrecked, his mission failed.

He needed to get her alone. He would walk back to the hospital, keeping well to the rear of the group, and hope for a chance to separate her from her friends. But he lost sight of the girls as he negotiated a series of twists and turns in the road and, when he caught up with them again, he could see at once that she was no longer with them. Had she for some reason run ahead to the hospital? He veered off the main route and turned into a back street, then into the next, racing through one road after another, trying to get ahead. If she'd returned before her friends, someone at the hospital would notice. He'd spent time familiarising himself with Barts and early on had discovered the main ward she worked on. At the front entrance, a postman was delivering packages and the duty porter was temporarily distracted while he signed for them. Sweetman slipped past and dashed for the stairs. At the door of Daisy's ward, he collided with a nurse and her trolley.

'I'm so sorry,' he said, sweeping off his hat in an extravagant gesture.

She looked at him distrustfully. 'Can I help you? You do know that visiting time isn't until four this afternoon.'

'I'm so sorry,' he said again. 'I hadn't realised. I'll come back later. But I wonder, Nurse — a personal matter only — do you happen to know if any of your colleagues are back from the funeral?'

She looked even more distrustful. 'No, they're not, Mr . . . ?'

'So sorry to have bothered you,' he said, stuffing his hat back on his head and jumping down the stairs two at a time. He felt the nurse's disapproving eyes watching him, but even if she were to raise the alarm, he would be long gone.

If the girl was not at the hospital, then maybe she'd returned to the Nurses' Home. It would be unusual, he thought, but then his knowledge of hospital routine was sparse. Hurrying towards Charterhouse Square, he was fortunate to meet one of its inmates coming down the front steps. Another nurse and another potential source of information.

'Is Nurse Blenkinsop in?' he asked, startling himself with the stupid English name that had come out of nowhere. He must be in a higher state of tension than he'd realised.

She looked bewildered. 'I don't believe we have a Blenkinsop.'

'I'm sure she lives here,' he persisted. 'Could you go and see?' He intended to creep in behind her and scour the building for himself.

But she closed the door with a firm thud. 'You must be mistaken. In any case, the only nurses here are sleeping and after twelve hours of night duty, I think they deserve to, don't you?' And with a saucy smile, she walked off down the road.

The woman he sought hadn't been on night duty. She wouldn't be sleeping. She'd been at that accursed funeral, so where had she vanished to? Then he knew. She'd recognised him, hadn't she, so of course she'd gone to tell her fellow spy — gone to Ellen Street. Except there was no longer a house to visit and no longer a spy to tell. His heart raced with excitement. He knew he'd find her there. First, though, he needed to steal a car. That shouldn't prove a problem. People were so careless with their property, particularly in wartime.

In half an hour, he had parked around the corner from Ellen Street and was walking slowly towards the damaged building. It was an incredible sight. To cause such chaos, and with such a small bomb. He'd seen an ambulance a few streets away. It must have been on its way to the morgue, though post-mortems wouldn't be done today and there would be no report for a while. He was safe from that. But not from her. He'd been right — she was here. She'd come straight to her contact and found him dead. Now, Sweetman reckoned, she was bound to go straight to the SIS at Baker Street.

He took shelter behind a large van parked at the bottom of the road. A red-haired man he'd never seen before was by her side. Was he a friend? He didn't seem it. The way they were standing suggested a more formal relationship, but he saw the man bend his head towards her as though in sympathy. He was a passer-by perhaps, listening to her tale and feeling sorry for her. He could just about catch a glimpse of her face from where he crouched. She was very pale and it looked as though she might have been crying. Perhaps the spy in the attic had been more than just a colleague. Too bad. The SIS officer he'd seen her with before was nowhere around, but if he'd judged correctly, she would soon be on her way to Baker Street. He'd got to her in time.

The red-haired man was escorting her to a black saloon parked to one side. The man must have offered her a lift, and Sweetman would stake his life on it that they'd head immediately to the West End. He walked swiftly back to the stolen car and slid behind the wheel, waiting for the saloon to edge out of Ellen Street. It should be simple enough to follow at a distance.

It turned out, though, to be far more difficult than he'd expected. The driver seemed to be choosing the most complicated route he could. Why that was so, Sweetman had no idea. All his concentration was focussed on the saloon in front, following it on its tortuous journey down narrow streets and across back alleys. At first, he'd thought the car was travelling westwards and knew a glimmer of satisfaction. Baker Street it was. The driver would have to drop her near number 64 and, once she was alone, he would strike. But then the car in front swung suddenly east, then north. Every point of the compass, he muttered to himself. And the man kept on driving. Where the hell were they going?

Gradually, though, he could feel the journey settling into one direction. Northwards, now always northwards. He was baffled but pleased. If he could have chosen an ideal direction for the girl to be driven, it would have been north. Yet another plan he'd been hatching! Everything was falling into place, he thought with satisfaction. It was clear his mission was blessed.

CHAPTER THIRTY

It was a long walk back to Baker Street from Barts, but it gave Grayson time to digest what Connie Telford had told him. When he'd seen Daisy at Ellen Street a short while ago, he'd been pulled apart by a clash of emotions. Her small, upright figure looking down at her murdered husband, was something that tugged ferociously at his heart. Yet, at the same time he'd been angry with her, angry that once more he'd been dismissed on what seemed mere caprice. But her friend's words had given him pause.

On the surface, it still made no sense. This poor girl who'd died, whoever she was, had not committed suicide because of Daisy, but that hadn't stopped Daisy from feeling responsible. The death hadn't happened on her watch alone; the girl must have met and mixed with dozens of people every day. If you wanted to lay the blame somewhere, then surely it was the hospital itself that might have done more to prevent the tragedy. But that was not how Daisy saw it, and Connie was right. These past few weeks she'd been forced to deal with more than anyone should, not least the reappearance of a dead husband. That was the key, of course. Old experience, painful experience, had reared its head. She'd never shaken herself free of India and what had happened there; she still felt a responsibility for the terrible events, though there was no earthly reason why she should. She hadn't killed Anish nor sent Gerald to a watery grave. Just the opposite. She'd almost perished herself.

But crazy or not, her desolation at the girl's death was closely linked with earlier disasters. Grayson tried to think it through, to put himself in her shoes. Maybe it wasn't that remarkable that she'd reacted as she had. While war had pushed the world into a frantic merry-go-round — breaking old connections, making unlikely friends, falling in love with strangers — Daisy had anchored herself to the safety of her nurse's world. She'd used its protection to build a shield, or rather rebuild the one she'd carried with her since her orphaned childhood. He couldn't really know, couldn't really understand, what that had been like.

His life had been happy. His father had died when he was small, it was true, but he'd been too young for it ever to have had a lasting effect. Reared by a doting mother who'd done everything in her power to make his life easy, he'd been set on the path to success. He'd made one or two mistakes, found himself up one or two blind alleys, but eventually settled in a job he loved, a life he loved. And always he'd had the reassurance of a loving family.

Daisy had not been so blessed, and he could see that the defensive wall she'd built had been necessary. Since she returned from India, she'd hidden behind it until, that is, Gerald had resurfaced — the dead made living — and did what he was so good at, Grayson thought sourly, destroyed her peace of mind and destroyed her happiness. With her husband's resurrection, past and present had coalesced for her, and old and new tragedies become one.

And whether he liked it or not, he was part of that tragedy. Whenever he got too close, she ran from him, thinking to escape back into safety. But there was no escape: recent events had proved that. Sooner or later, she would have to face her demons, face what had happened in India and what was happening right now, here in this injured city. Grayson hoped it would be with him by her side. Surely the love they'd shared had to mean something? But even if it didn't, even if he never managed to change her mind, he would move heaven and earth to keep her safe. He quickened his pace. He must get to Baker Street and see Mike. His colleague would be returning soon with news of Daisy and the small house in Highgate.

* * *

Daisy was relieved when the car finally slowed and pulled in to the kerbside. It had been a hazardous journey, racing down the narrowest of roads, charging up one-way streets, constantly changing direction, constantly doubling back on the way they had come. And always travelling at speed. It was the stuff of every spy story she had ever read but, when they finally came to a halt, she felt an odd disappointment. She didn't know what she'd expected, but the street they were in was at best unprepossessing, one of the many anonymous residential roads dotted across the north of London. A curtain twitched to her left but, other than that, there was no sign of life. She stared up at the house she imagined was their destination and its blank windows stared back.

Corrigan was helping her from the car, her legs feeling frail, as though at any moment they would fold beneath her. Was that reaction to a terrifying journey or simple exhaustion from the events of the day? Daisy could hardly believe it was only this morning that she'd attended Willa's funeral, only this morning that she'd seen the face of the man who'd stalked her, the man from whom she must be kept safe.

'The police will want to talk to you,' Mike said, leading the way into a hall papered from top to bottom with cabbage roses. Their feet slapped against the bare linoleum. 'They'll send an officer quite shortly. I imagine he'll be accompanied by a police artist. They'll hope to get a reasonable description of the man.'

She felt flustered. 'I'm not sure I'm going to be much help. I would know his eyes, but the rest of him was so thoroughly muffled. The trilby, you see . . .'

'But you could describe his eyes, his face shape? And his height, weight, that kind of thing.'

She felt heavy and tired. She wanted to sleep. 'I think so. I'm sorry if I sound useless, but today was the first time I saw him at all properly.'

'You'll do your best, I'm sure.' Corrigan was upbeat. 'It will probably be enough. These artist chaps are pretty good.'

He ushered her into the sitting room and her first impressions of the house were confirmed. She hoped she wouldn't have to make a lengthy stay. Here and there the carpet wore bare patches and the chairs looked uncomfortable. She wished Connie was with her and wondered what her friend was doing right now, and what she was making of Daisy's absence. She'd promised to be back at Barts in a matter of minutes but, instead, was likely to be away for days — unless, until, the man was apprehended.

'Shall I make some tea?'

'Not for me, thank you,' she assured him. She had an immense longing for quiet, a need to be on her own.

'Then I'll take you round the house and be off. There's not a lot to see, but that's the whole point. Nothing showy, nothing to stand out. You'll be perfectly safe here.'

'Where are we exactly?'

'Highgate. Well, to be honest, not quite Highgate. The less salubrious bit, I'm afraid. But it's convenient.'

She wondered at the adjective.

'Grayson and I will be just next door — in Hampstead,' he explained. 'We've been designated the welcoming committee at Pitt House when Chandan Patel arrives tonight.'

'He's the envoy from Congress, isn't he?'

'I see you've been doing your homework,' he joked. 'The meeting was set for tomorrow, but it's been advanced — it's become crucial we don't wait longer. The Foreign Secretary will be present. It's very hush hush but your knowing won't hurt. It will be over in hours.'

'Why at night, though?'

'At midnight, in fact. The witching hour!'

'Then it must be "hush hush". I can't imagine the Foreign Secretary would be willing to travel so late otherwise.'

'A lot's at stake, Daisy,' he said seriously. 'The government needs to get an agreement as soon as possible and it's very important for us, for Britain, that they do.'

'And you'll be at the centre of things.' And Grayson, too, she thought. No wonder he loved his job.

'Only a very few of us know what's happening. It's had to be kept top secret — there's already been an attempt on Patel. A kidnapping that failed. I believe you saw it.'

The heaviness returned. 'I did. It was the man I saw today, I'm almost sure.'

'Quite likely, but we're not closing any avenues just yet. Someone is out to get the envoy and whoever he is, we need to make sure he doesn't succeed. Patel will have an armed guard to Pitt House and there will be soldiers on the gate.'

'I'll let you get on with your adventure then.'

He ignored the mild mockery and waved his hand towards the hall. 'The kitchen's through there by the way. There's tea and milk and a small amount of food, though not much. Grayson will send one of our junior officers as soon as he can. The man should be here in a while and he'll bring fresh supplies with him.'

'He'll be staying in the house?'

'Until we're sure you're no longer in danger. And that shouldn't be long. Once the meeting is over, Patel will be driven under escort to Southampton and put on a P and O back to Bombay. That will be one of our problems out of the way. Maybe more than one. If your villain is after Patel, as we suspect, there'll be nothing to keep him here once the Congressman has sailed. He'll want to get out of the country as soon as he can. Probably back to India, and we can nab him at the port.'

'And if you don't? If he doesn't try to leave England?'

'He'll be hunted down and arrested. Then he'll stand trial for kidnapping. Possibly murder.'

'And I'll be an important witness?'

'I'm afraid you will. But he'll be banged up for years — if he's lucky. And executed, if he's not. So no need for you to worry.' His voice was full of cheer and Daisy wished she could feel as sanguine.

'By the way, there are two bedrooms upstairs. One of them has the bed made up. Briant, if he's the man Grayson sends, will sleep on the sofa.'

She wasn't looking forward to her captivity and with a man she'd never met, but she thanked him dutifully. 'You will keep in touch, Mr Corrigan?'

'Mike, call me Mike. I will or Grayson will. Like I said, we're only a few miles away. We'll let you grab some sleep tonight, but one of us will be round in the morning to see how you're doing. Probably Grayson.'

She found herself flushing and she knew that he'd noticed. 'It's not my place to say this,' he said diffidently, 'but you should know that he's very cut up about this whole business.' Her flush deepened. 'I realise it's been difficult for you these last few weeks, pretty bloody awful as far as I can make out, but Grayson has done his best to protect you. He risked his career to get those papers.' There was an uncomfortable silence. 'I didn't know if you knew that.'

Daisy hadn't known, but if she'd thought sensibly for one moment, she would have realised the risk Grayson must have run. She felt ashamed and had no answer for his friend.

'Anyway, I'll be off.' He held out his hand before walking to the door. Stepping out on to the pavement, he said, 'Keep this door locked until Briant comes — I think it will be Briant. He'll give one long and two short rings on the bell and you'll know it's him. And remember, he's just there to make sure you feel safe. There's no real danger, so don't be worried.'

She smiled faintly and watched him walk to his car, then shut the door and locked it behind her. She didn't see the second vehicle that had pulled out a hundred yards up the road and was following on Corrigan's tail.

Back in the sitting room, Daisy slumped onto the stiff sofa and stared at the floral wallpaper. Peonies in this room, she noticed. At least they were a change from the ever-present roses, but the furniture was every bit as uncomfortable as she'd imagined. Several sad pictures drooped from their hanging chains: *The Monarch of the Glen, The Stag at Bay*. Someone had had a taste for Landseer and Scottish landscape.

Her mind wandered over the conversation she'd just had. Corrigan was Grayson's friend, so of course he was going to defend him. But he was right, nonetheless. Grayson had proved the best of friends to her and none of this — Willa, Gerald — was his fault. She was the one who'd chosen to see it that way. She was the one who'd chosen to involve Grayson in the first place. If she hadn't gone to Baker Street that day, they would never have met again. If she hadn't asked him for help, he wouldn't have put his career on the line to get those papers. And Gerald? Would he be dead? The man who'd killed him had done so, not because of the papers, but because he suspected Gerald would disrupt whatever hideous plan he was concocting. So, yes, her husband would probably have died still.

Gerald's face, as she'd last seen it, came clearly to mind. Pale, calm, stripped bare of its worry lines. Just that one round hole in the side of his head to suggest that all was not well. The bomb had torn his clothes to rags, but left him whole. That, at least, had been a mercy. Her husband had been dead before but had somehow returned from the grave. No possibility of a return this time, though. Her marriage was finally over, yet no matter how many times Daisy said the words, they seemed to have no meaning.

These last few days, she had been rubbed raw, her heart chewed to pieces and her emotions made so sharp they seemed to stab through her skin. Peace was what she craved, peace to go back to the hospital, back to the ward and her patients. She wondered when that would be, and hoped against hope she would not be long in this bleak house. Her thoughts were her only distraction and they were far from happy. She swung her legs up on the sofa and waited for the bell to ring.

CHAPTER THIRTY-ONE

It was several hours before Daisy heard it. She must have fallen into an uneasy doze and felt anything but rested. Mind and body ached in unison — the sleep had done nothing to make her feel better. The bell rang out and she counted. One long, two short peals. Staggering to her feet, she tugged on the shoes she'd abandoned. She was cold, she realised, and wrapped her nurse's cape tightly around her as she padded across the lino of the hall. The bolts had been a little stiff when she'd closed the door and, opening it, she had almost to wrench them free.

There was just the key to turn. 'I'm getting there,' she said loudly, in case Briant thought she'd gone back to sleep.

With a loud puff of air, the door slammed back towards her. A man stood on the threshold. Not Briant, not Briant, her mind drummed. Momentarily dazed, she stepped back and tried to shut the door in his face, but the man's shoulders had already barricaded her in. She turned to run — to the bedroom, to the bathroom, anywhere with a lock. One black gloved hand reached for her arm and yanked her back. Another circled her head and held her painfully close. She kicked out at her assailant, but it was useless. She was locked in his grasp. She saw him raise a hand, then felt a sharp tingle in her neck. The prick of a needle, she thought, and her eyes closed.

* * *

It was a pity about the girl, Sweetman reflected, as he loaded her body into the boot of his car. Up close she was pretty, very pretty, a sweet, delicate looking woman. But he couldn't think like that. He couldn't allow himself to have qualms, not at this late stage. In the last few hours, the future he'd imagined for himself had changed dramatically. He no longer needed to die for the cause. No martyr's death after all — he would do what he had to, and flee. But while the girl lived, there would always be danger since her evidence could hang him. He had to get her out of the way, somewhere so secure that no one could ride to her rescue. He'd fixed on the very place and it had the touch of genius about it. He wouldn't need to kill her. Something in him baulked at that. He could just leave her there and time would do the necessary. She would probably never be found.

It was a stroke of luck that the red-haired man had taken her to this shabby house in Highgate. More than luck; it could not have been more fortuitous. By following them, he'd learned exactly where the crucial meeting with Patel was to take place. And when. He'd believed it would be tomorrow at Baker Street and, once he'd dealt with the girl, had intended to keep watch there. If he had, he would have been badly wrong-footed.

They had panicked. They'd changed the timing of the meeting and the location. Intercepting her protector had proved a master stroke, and now Sweetman had all the information he needed. Of course, when he'd followed the car, he'd no idea who the driver was or where he was going, but when they'd drawn up outside the house, he'd seen the man look this way and that, checking on the neighbourhood before he produced a key from his pocket. The red-haired man was no sympathetic passer-by, as he'd first thought. And he was no friend either. Sweetman had established that from the start. In which case, he had to be an intelligence officer, not the one he'd seen her meet before, but a colleague. And this was a safe house.

It had been this man's bad luck to be chosen to drive her, but whatever the woman had told him, it would be going no further. As soon as the SIS man left, he'd followed him from a distance. It hadn't taken long to catch him alone on a road and ram him into an obliging lamp post. That had been an excellent move. The man was disabled, possibly dead by now, but what was certain was that he wouldn't be contacting Baker Street any time soon to pass on information.

And, when he'd slipped from his car and walked over to the still steaming vehicle, he'd had even more luck. If anyone turned into the road inopportunely, he had his excuse ready. He'd stopped to help. But no one came and he was able to search uninterrupted. A security badge was the first treasure he found and then an encrypted message. It had to be about the meeting and it hadn't taken long to work out. Code breaking was his speciality and he soon had the time and the place.

Midnight! They must be taking the threat from him seriously, and so they should. He would take the man's jacket, too — that was the icing on the cake. It would allow him to survive and return to India a hero. It was a pity the man had red hair, but if Sweetman wore his trilby pulled low, what guard would know the difference in the pitch black? In no time, he would be on his way to the coast and to freedom.

* * *

Daisy lifted her head and retched. The side of her neck felt sore and swollen, and whatever she'd had pumped into her was making her nauseous. She tried to prop herself into a sitting position, her hands grappling against icy flagstones. A sheet of steel cut through her forehead and her stomach was heaving. She knew she was going to be very sick. A hand came out of nowhere and shoved her roughly against a wall and she felt its dank plaster seep into her back. She tried to prise her eyelids open, but there was nothing to see; the world was coloured black.

Gradually, though, her eyes began to pick out shapes and she realised that the faintest sliver of light was percolating from the very top of the wall opposite. It hurt to move her head, but she tried very slowly. First left, then right. She made out two, three, large shapes squatting immobile in this cold, cold room. Large stone shapes, coffin shapes. They *were* coffins. Or, at least tombs of some kind. She was lying in a morgue.

'You are in a mausoleum,' a voice said, half flint, half amused.

She tried to fathom where the voice had come from and felt, rather than saw, a figure moving. Then, out of the blackness, a man's face was hanging over her. She could make nothing of his features but she knew him, nevertheless.

'Who are you?'

'My name is Rohan Sweetman, as I'm sure you know.'

'I don't know. How could I? And what do you want with me?' She tried to sound braver than she felt.

The man said nothing. 'Why am I here?' she repeated. 'I've done nothing to harm you.'

'I will be the judge of that, Miss Driscoll. It is Miss Driscoll, isn't it? I think I heard the name from one of your companions.' He spoke with the very slightest trace of an accent, but it was one she couldn't place. 'You are here because you recognised me today. Need I remind you? You know far too much about me, and you cannot be so foolish as to think I would allow you to roam free and tell your tales.'

What tales, she thought? That she might be able to identify him as the man she'd seen in Kingsway? Is that why he'd snatched her and made her so ill? There was no point in assuring him that she'd hardly seen the kidnapper, and any description had been flimsy. He wouldn't believe her.

She steeled herself to fight. 'What if I've already told my tale?' she taunted. 'Isn't it a little late to imprison me?'

‘That has been dealt with. Whatever information you passed to the man, he will bother us no more. And my plan will go ahead.’

What man was he talking of? Grayson? Mike Corrigan? They knew no more than she, but in her captor’s twisted mind, they were a threat to be destroyed. Daisy felt even sicker. ‘What have you done?’

‘We will not discuss it. In fact, we will discuss nothing. I intend to remain here a while and silence is necessary.’

His voice mesmerised her. She tried to work out where she’d heard a similar inflection. It wasn’t a true Indian accent. No, not Indian, she thought, but Anglo-Indian. When she’d lived in Jasirapur, she’d had few dealings with Anglo-Indians — she’d been strongly advised to keep her distance. The British refused to consider them social equals and the Indians despised them for not being sufficiently Indian. Unenviably, they were a group caught in the middle.

Daisy decided to disobey his injunction. ‘You’re Anglo-Indian, aren’t you?’

‘I’m an Indian,’ he said harshly.

‘I don’t think so.’

His hand shot out and grabbed her arm, twisting it until she cried out. ‘You would do well not to anger me, Miss Driscoll. No one will hear your cries.’

Her bravado collapsed under his assault. ‘Where are we?’ Her voice faltered a little. ‘And what have I ever done to hurt you?’

‘We are in a cemetery, a very large cemetery. And you are here because you have chosen to involve yourself in business that is not yours.’

‘You’re wrong. I haven’t.’ Her arm was still throbbing, but her stomach had settled a little and the pain in her head was gradually clearing.

‘Dear me, you do have a tendency to contradict. Really, you would do well not to annoy me further.’

‘I’m speaking the truth.’ Her voice had grown stronger. ‘I have no notion what your business might be.’ It wasn’t strictly true, but if the SIS had no clear idea of what this man was planning, how could she?

'You were intimate with the man who lived in Ellen Street. You were seen talking to him on a number of occasions.'

'That's hardly unexpected since he was my husband.'

'Your husband?' he sounded incredulous.

'Yes, my husband. I was helping him to leave the country.'

'He was a spy.'

'That's ridiculous.'

Daisy no longer cared how much she upset him since it was plain that she had nothing to lose. His plan was becoming clearer and it was horrible. He had brought her to this place of the dead where, she thought, nobody visited. Where nobody would think to search. And he would leave her here to die — unless he killed her first. That would almost be preferable.

'Ridiculous,' she repeated. 'Gerald was no spy.'

She heard the man moving around a few feet away. He seemed agitated, but she had no idea why. She couldn't think he felt any remorse for the murders he'd committed. It was probably that having decided Gerald was a spy, he didn't like to be proved wrong. Fanatics, she imagined, rarely did.

'I'm sure he knew the Special Intelligence Officer,' he was insisting. 'And you knew him, too.'

'The officer is an old acquaintance of ours from India. He was helping Gerald to get papers that would allow my husband to travel. The papers had just arrived when you killed him. There was no need to kill him. No need at all. He was on his way to America.'

Her abductor stopped pacing. 'That is what you English call *water under the bridge*. Your husband had to die,' he said with decision. 'He saw something he shouldn't, something that would have endangered my mission.'

'You killed your friend, too.' Daisy continued to needle. 'Did he endanger your mission as well?' She couldn't see how angering this man might help her escape, but she had no other weapon.

'He was no friend.'

'Your fellow spy then.'

'He was useless.'

'You mean, he didn't like your plan.'

'How would you know? You have no inkling of what I plan — or so you claim.' He had come closer now, and bent his face to peer down at her.

'I haven't, but I imagine you don't take too well to people who disagree with you.'

'He would have ruined everything.' The man had forgotten his vow of silence. He was glad of an audience, it seemed. 'He had to go. He was mediocre.'

'And you are brilliant? Is that what you're saying?'

'I am a patriot. That's all you need to know.' He straightened up and began to walk away. 'We will stop talking now.'

But she refused. 'If you're a patriot, why aren't you in India, helping to defend your homeland from the Japanese?'

'The Japanese are our friends.' He'd been stung by her remark. 'They will help us to independence.'

'If you think that, you're really not as brilliant as you claim. The Japanese aren't your friends. They will treat India as a pawn.'

'As the British have done for centuries, you mean.'

It was her turn to fall silent. Her last conversation with Anish, her very last, sprang painfully alive. He, too, had been convinced the Japanese would bring freedom to his country. It seemed strange, though, that someone from his background was so committed to the same cause. Unless his real purpose was something quite different. Revenge possibly? Retribution? Unsurprisingly, Anglo-Indians could bear a personal grudge against the Raj, but such a motive was a far cry from Anish's clarion call to freedom.

'The Japanese will be your conquerors, too. And far worse,' she retorted.

'You are a stupid little girl, very stupid. The British will be humbled, their arrogance brought low. The Indians in Congress will be humbled, too.'

Anish had been frustrated by the slowness of Congress to act, she remembered, but he would not have wanted them humbled.

'Japan is Germany's staunchest ally,' Sweetman was continuing, 'and Germany is the greatest power on earth. Together, they will free India. And those who have helped in the struggle will be rewarded. We shall come into our own at last.'

'In that case, shouldn't you go back to India and help in the struggle?'

'I intend to. My leaving cannot come a minute too soon. In a matter of days, I shall be far from this dark and dreary country. Once Chandan Patel is dealt with.'

'But do you think you *can* deal with Patel? Your last effort was hardly a roaring success.' If she could provoke him into revealing the details of his plan, and then escape . . . a daydream, she feared.

'This time, there will be no mistake. He will be dealt with.' The cold force of his words made her draw her cape tightly around her.

CHAPTER THIRTY-TWO

'So, you mean to kill him. That will be three people dead at your hands. Why do you feel such a need to kill?'

'This is war and people get killed. As a nurse, you should have no difficulty in understanding. Patel must be stopped from signing any treaty with the British.'

'But if you kill him, Congress will simply send another envoy.'

'You are being stupid again. The British will be implicated in Patel's death, I will see to that. There will be mystery, rumours, and they will be suspected of double dealing, which will not be difficult, given their history. They will shoulder the blame for Patel and Congress will be outraged. One of their own murdered on British property while in the hands of the Special Intelligence Service! Congress will cut off all negotiations. Even better, they will be persuaded to bargain with Germany.' He sounded immensely pleased with himself. 'So you see, killing Patel is a masterstroke. Far better than any kidnapping.'

'And you think you'll be offered the opportunity?'

'I will make the opportunity. I know where he is to be taken and I know when. I will arrive at precisely eleven thirty. Patel will be waiting, alone but for the SIS man who escorts him. It will be easy enough to shoot him and anyone else who tries to stop me.'

Daisy thought about his words. Could he really shoot his way in and out of a house that must be guarded like a fortress? She could hardly believe it possible.

'There will be soldiers, armed guards on the gate. You don't honestly think they'll let you walk into wherever the meeting is being held.' She knew where. Corrigan had told her, but she would not disclose the name, just in case this man was bluffing. Her hope was short-lived.

'Patel's armed escort will almost certainly be stood down. This is a very sensitive meeting and they will want to keep the participants as secret as possible. And, as for the guards at Pitt House — they present no problem. You see, I shall be Michael Corrigan and they will welcome me with open arms.' He sounded smugger than ever.

'What do you mean, you'll be Michael Corrigan?' Then, as she realised the full meaning of his words, 'What have you done to him?' Her voice rose in alarm.

'I have not touched him. Not a finger. He was simply unfortunate enough to meet a lamp post a short way from here.'

'You've killed him!'

'Possibly, possibly not — I have no idea. But Mr Corrigan will not be taking an active part in tonight's events.'

Daisy thought about the gentle, red-haired man, so concerned for her safety, and felt anger flood through her.

'You are no patriot,' she spat out. 'You are nothing more than a cold-blooded killer.'

'Your opinions are immaterial, Miss Driscoll. I have no use for them or for you. Fortunately, it is time I was gone. I have a small errand at Charing Cross — my luggage, the last trace that I was ever here — but then the real work begins.'

She saw the faint outline of his figure move towards what she imagined was a door. A heavy iron slab crunched open a fraction and a shaft of light cut its thin path through the gloom. She saw him turn and face her. Without doubt, his eyes were those of the man who had jostled her at Baker Street station. Not an accident then. They were the eyes of the man who'd driven the kidnap car, and the man who'd watched her from the shadows.

'Do enjoy the company you find yourself in,' he taunted. 'After all, it will not be too long before you are joining them.'

The man's black trilby and leather patched jacket slid through the opening. The door clanged shut, the key grated in the lock. He had been wearing Mike Corrigan's jacket, she realised, and he was on his way to Pitt House to slaughter Chandan Patel and anyone unlucky enough to be in his company. Grayson. He would kill Grayson.

Her heart wept. He would kill Grayson and there was nothing she could do. Grayson, who had been her friend from the moment they'd met, her more than friend in those difficult months in India and, just days ago, had become her lover. Was it possible she would never see him again? In a moment of clarity, she realised she had no wish to be in a world he didn't share. When yesterday she'd told him goodbye, she'd been distraught, hardly in her right mind. But even in that half mad state, she'd cherished the knowledge that he was not far away. How stupid she'd been. Why hadn't she grabbed life with both hands when she had the chance?

At the very moment she'd become a widow again, she'd lost the man she loved. The irony almost choked her. And *she* had been the one to lead him to his death. If she had never gone to Baker Street that day, never demanded papers, everything would have been different. For Grayson, for Michael Corrigan. Poor Michael, who had done nothing but escort her and was now lying crumpled in his car, unconscious, perhaps already dead. She was riven with guilt. Again.

Guilt had permeated Daisy's life from its illegitimate beginnings to this moment as an impotent prisoner, but familiarity with the feeling did not stop it eating away at her. Without her intervention, Grayson and Mike would have been targets for Sweetman; without her, Sweetman might still have tracked Patel and the men who protected him, determined on shooting every last person. The difference was that she'd made it easy for him. Very easy.

He would wear Corrigan's jacket and wave Corrigan's security pass. He would dupe the guards and march into the house unchallenged. If she'd never gone to Rigby's to check on Gerald, if she'd returned with Connie after the funeral and kept herself safe in company, there would have been no Highgate house, no car accident and Grayson and his friend would have had at least a chance of escape. Sweetman would have been picked off by the guards before he could get a foot over the threshold. She had put them in extreme danger, she realised, and she must do something. But what could she do, trapped in this place of decay?

For a moment, she brightened. Perhaps the alarm had already been raised. Corrigan and the wrecked car could have been found and Baker Street alerted. Briant would have rung her doorbell and, getting no reply, would know there was something badly wrong.

But Corrigan had had his identity stolen, the dark voice in her head intoned. How long would it take the police to establish who the injured man was? And what would happen when Briant got no response to his ringing? There would be no suggestion of anything amiss. The house would be dozing, its door shut, its curtains closed. Briant might not have a key since he would be expecting her to answer. What would he do when no one came to the door? Communications were almost impossible in the city these days. If Briant shrugged his shoulders and made a leisurely return to Baker Street to report his failure, it would be a long while before Grayson knew there was trouble. Too long, far too long.

* * *

It had taken Grayson a long time to track Briant down. The man had been out of town on an errand and it was only as Grayson was gathering his papers together for the Pitt House meeting, that his quarry finally walked into the office. He would have asked one of Briant's colleagues to go to Highgate if the team had not been several men short. He didn't like Daisy to be alone in the house, though she was perfectly safe. No one would ever find her, tucked away in that network of anonymous streets. But she needed reassurance, company even, after what she'd been through today. The funeral of the girl she'd been mourning so badly. The final demise of her once dead husband.

Grayson had felt little sorrow when he'd looked down on the face of the dead man. It was an unpleasant way to die but Mortimer was a wretch, a deserter tainted by dishonour, though few would ever know it. His regiment thought him already dead, thought him a man who'd died a hero. What Daisy thought, Grayson had no idea. He had never been certain of her feelings for the man she had once loved so passionately. For all he knew, she might be grieving badly. He hoped not. He hoped that a small part of her might be rejoicing, tasteless though that might be. Today she had gained a new freedom. Mortimer had always been her millstone, and a journey across the Atlantic was no guarantee that things would change. Grayson had never been confident that if the man reached America, Daisy would hear the last of him. Mortimer was the proverbial bad penny. At least, now, she had most definitely heard the last of him.

After he'd seen Briant off, he sat down at his desk and waited for Michael Corrigan to join him. His colleague knew the importance of tonight's meeting at Pitt House since the mission had been given the highest priority, so where was he? It was possible, he supposed, that Mike had waited for Briant to turn up at the house. If so, at least Daisy would have had company and Briant would soon be there. She could go to bed and sleep soundly. He looked at the clock. It was ten thirty and time to go. It could be that Corrigan had decided to travel straight to Hampstead and been unable to let him know, communications being what they were. He would leave now and hopefully meet Mike at Pitt House; together they were to form Patel's welcoming committee.

His protection, too, since discretion was vital and, for several hours, the armed escort would be stood down.

Driving rain accompanied him on his journey, the windscreen wipers working at full tilt. At the best of times, it was hazardous driving after sunset and this night was certainly not the best of times. Since the blackout, street lights had been switched off, traffic lights wore slotted covers to deflect their beams downwards, and cars had their lights obscured. It all made for a very difficult journey and road accidents were frequent, even with the low speed limit recently imposed. Despite the confusion and potential danger, people had somehow become used to it — amazing, really, how well your eyes adjusted, and you found yourself able to follow the road, even beneath a clouded sky like tonight's.

It was slow going, though, and well past eleven o'clock by the time he pulled up at the entrance to Pitt House. He looked for Corrigan's car and was bemused not to see it. What on earth had happened to the man? It was beginning to look very much as though he would be Patel's sole escort for this important meeting. Not that he had much time to worry over the change of plan, for almost immediately a sleek, black saloon pulled up alongside, accompanied by a bevy of armed motorcyclists. He jumped out of his car to greet the man who could hold all their futures in his hands.

Patel was small and lithe, with an engaging smile and a warm handshake. The rain was continuing to pelt and Grayson hurriedly escorted him inside the building, leading the way to an inner chamber that had been set up hours before. Five or six chairs around a polished table, paper and pens, a carafe of water, and a glorious fire roaring in the grate. Patel warmed his hands at it and smilingly accepted the tea that had materialised. Now, all they had to do was wait. The minister was certain to arrive promptly, Grayson thought. This meeting was far too crucial for any dawdling.

But he wished Mike was here. He couldn't understand his colleague's absence and his mind began to worry at the problem as the minutes ticked by. Had Corrigan's car broken down? Had he been unable to get into the Highgate house? Had there been a problem with Daisy? He hadn't thought of it before, but she might have fallen ill, collapsed from the stress of the day. No, not Daisy. He dismissed the idea as soon as it occurred. She might look as fragile as a flower, but she had a core of steel.

CHAPTER THIRTY-THREE

For the past hour, Daisy had been growing cold — colder and ever more lethargic. She felt suspended in a nothingness, trapped in an underworld with only the dead for company. Since Sweetman disappeared, the living world had all but faded from sight. She had to keep moving, she told herself, had to stay awake. Resist the impulse to lay herself down and sleep. A drift into death.

That was not her way. She was a fighter, she always had been, and she would fight now. If not for herself, for Grayson. She had to escape this grand tomb and warn him that Sweetman was on his way. Tell him, if he didn't already know, that his friend had met with disaster.

She glanced towards the place where Sweetman had skulked out into the world. For an instant, while the door had opened a fraction, Daisy had seen the full extent of the mausoleum. It wasn't as large as she'd imagined, and it was hexagonal in shape, eroding space even further. No wonder the three tombs appeared so dominant. The door Sweetman had used was unusually narrow, she remembered, perhaps because of the room's shape, and she began to speculate on how the builders had managed to move immense stone sarcophagi through such a restricted opening. At least, it kept her mind active.

But she needed her body active, too. Scrambling up, she stamped her feet fiercely, beating a tattoo on the flagstones, then pummelled the air with her arms, trying to warm herself, trying to get the blood flowing. She shuffled forward, finding her way to the middle of the room and to one of the three shapes, darker than the dark that surrounded them. They must have built the tombs *in situ*, she thought, there was no other explanation. She ran a hand along the top of the coffin lid, then down the sides. Virtually the entire surface was heavily ornamented. A stonemason, a master craftsman at that, had chipped away at this stone and fashioned an intricate pattern. Flowers, she traced with her fingers, and there was a bird and was this bolder relief a group of trees? How could a craftsman have done such beautiful tracery in this cramped space and with the minimum of light? Even with the door open and with lamps strategically positioned, he would have worked in gloom. No, he couldn't have done it.

Bending over, Daisy rubbed at her legs. They were in danger of sleeping from the knees down, since her cape finished short and she wore only thinnish stockings. It was in another world that she'd donned her uniform in preparation for the funeral and the day of nursing to follow. What were they doing on the ward at this moment? What was Connie doing? She longed to be back in a normal world, a mundane world of patching and bathing and soothing.

Walking back from the tombs to her position by the wall, she was about to sit down once more when the thought crossed her mind that if the tombs hadn't come through the door, and hadn't been constructed on site, they must have been built and ornamented elsewhere and in some way lowered into the chamber. But how? She stepped carefully back to the centre of the room and looked up. Blank darkness met her stare. A small trickle of light came from the narrow window high up on the left-hand side of the wall, but this far down, it was of little help. She hitched up her skirts and managed to clamber on to the middle and largest of the tombs. Steadying herself by planting her feet as firmly as she could astride the stone coffin lid, she looked up again. From here, she could see a little better. She continued to stare upwards and, just as she felt she was giddy enough to fall, she brought into focus a wooden beam which ran crossways from wall to wall of the mausoleum. In the middle of the beam and immediately above the tomb on which she stood, there appeared to be a hook. A large iron hook.

Daisy was sure of it. They had used a pulley system to lower the sarcophagi into place. In which case . . . a part of the ceiling must have been left open to the sky while the operation took place. And then plastered over. She felt excitement spurt through her. If she could get to the beam, discover that opening, she might perhaps be able to punch her way through the plaster into the roof space. Then it would be a simple matter of dislodging roof tiles, a sufficient number to make a hole large enough to climb out of. She could escape. She could save Grayson.

But her excitement shrivelled as quickly as it had sprung to life. How on earth was she to reach the beam? It was at least fifteen feet above her head, even while standing on the tomb. She needed a rope, a rope that would catch on to the hook. Was she still agile enough to climb a rope? If practice was all, she would shin to the top in seconds — how many times had she done that as a child? A rope had been their escape route from the orphanage at Eden House. One of them keeping cavey, while the other threw a rope into the branches of a tree which grew on Cobb Street just outside the building's perimeter. They would haul themselves up and over the wall. It was one of the few occasions as a child that she'd felt any sense of camaraderie. Whoever went over the wall would come back with food for those left behind — food that had been thrown out, food that had been begged, sometimes food stolen from an unwary stallholder. But she'd been ten years old at the time and there had been a solid brick wall to guide her feet.

She scolded herself for her silliness. Here she was fantasising about climbing a rope when there was not even a rope.

Unless . . . she peeled off her cape, then her starched pinafore and, after a few minutes' hesitation, her dress and petticoat. Her skin was stiff with cold and she found herself shivering uncontrollably in her thin cotton underwear. Get on with it, she urged herself, or you'll freeze to the spot.

Swiftly, she made each item of clothing into a roll, then twisted them into long sausages, tying each sausage one to another. Standing back, Daisy surveyed what she could see of her handiwork. She had her makeshift rope, though whether it would reach far enough, she had no idea. The only way she'd find out was to try. The rope had to catch on to the hook, so she tied a large loop in the top of the petticoat and clambered back onto the tomb. Experimentally, she threw the rope upwards. It fell to her feet. She tried again, and then again and again, for minutes on end, until her arms throbbed and her shoulders were contorted with pain. It wasn't going to work, she thought dejectedly. The loop she'd tied could get no purchase on the hook. Idly, she turned the rope upside down. Before she gave in, she would try throwing it, cape upwards. Her first throw and she heard a clinking sound. She tugged. The rope was firm! The chain that fastened her cape, she realised, had miraculously fallen over the hook and was keeping the rope in the air.

Would it hold her weight, though? She was light, very light, but she was taking a dreadful risk. She could almost hear the cloth splitting as the chain was torn from its surrounding cape. She would fall, straight down on to the sarcophagus or plummet beyond to the stone floor. It might mean a quick death but equally an agonising injury. She had to try, though. Taking off her shoes and stockings, she tied one shoe to each end of the hosiery and hung them round her neck. She needed her feet bare if she were to have any chance of getting to the top of the rope. Reaching up, she took a small jump, her hands clutching at the material she had rolled and twisted. Then her naked feet clamped themselves around the flimsy petticoat and she began to haul herself up towards the stripes of her nurses' frock. One hand after another, knees bending and straightening, feet following, as she inched her way upwards. She must be over halfway now, she thought, and paused before she once more reached up. This time she felt the wool of her cape and knew there could only be a few feet to go.

Then she heard the noise, very close, just above her head. A splitting noise. It was the chain pulling away from the cloth. It had had enough. As she'd climbed higher, the strain on it had grown greater and it was now shredding. She dared not look down at what awaited her, but fixed her eyes above. In the dim light coming from the window, she could see the hook and the bar which supported it. Just one, two more lunges and she should be there.

The splitting sounded louder. Daisy was exhausted, her arms numb, her legs in pain, her feet twinging with cramp and cold. With a huge effort, she grabbed another piece of cape and again heaved herself upwards. In desperation, one of her hands shot out and grabbed for the beam. Then, she was clasping it with both hands, suspended in mid-air, the cloak hanging by a thread beside her. The breath had been knocked out of her, but she dared not pause. There was no time to recover, no way she would feel better until she was sitting on that beam. Again, she pushed herself up, the sinews in her arms rigid and tearing. One knee was on the wood — the beam was wider than she'd thought, wide enough to kneel comfortably. And then she was there, her head bent, her breath coming in short gasps. Beneath her, the tomb was barely distinguishable and the floor had vanished into obscurity. Had she really climbed that distance? Euphoric barely described how she felt.

But hard reality soon replaced euphoria. As soon as her breathing returned to normal, she manoeuvred herself into a standing position and forced her tired arms to reach up again, this time to the ceiling. Its central section was shaped like a dome and she was sure there would be a patch that would have only a light covering of plaster. That was the spot she must find. Her knuckles knocked at the plasterwork. It sounded ominously solid. Inch by inch, she knocked a circle around the dome, but always with the same result. There was no place that was hollow. The roof must have been concreted over from the outside and there was no way out. She was crushed, despairing. To have got so far . . . and now she was stranded. Not even a cold floor for a final resting place. All she could do was sit hunched on this beam until drifting into sleep, she lost her balance and fell to her death.

Very soon Grayson would die, too, just a few miles away. Daisy tried valiantly to fight back the tears. Sweetman would be on his way to Pitt House by now — she couldn't see her watch, but she sensed it must be close to eleven o'clock. He would be driving northwards, his suitcase collected, ready for his getaway. A getaway that would leave a trail of death behind. She sat with her eyes closed, squeezed tightly to prevent the tears which constantly welled. When she opened them at last, she noticed that the light had subtly changed. It seemed to have become a very little brighter, and she peered across at the window. It had been a chilly day and the sky had remained grey and clouded throughout. Now, though, a moon was shining somewhere in the sky and touching the narrow casement with its silver.

Daisy looked at the window again. It had to be too small to squeeze through, even if she were able to open it. On all fours, she crawled along the beam towards it. The panes of glass were wet. It must have been raining and raining hard, and a sliver of moonlight was glancing off the small drops of water and making them dance. There was no catch to the window but, even if there had been, it was unlikely to work after all these years. She looked again, trying to measure the space in her mind. Just maybe she could fit herself through. It was a long shot but what had she to lose? She crawled backwards to where she'd been kneeling and pulled up her improvised rope. If she ever got out of this place of death, she would need her clothes. Then back to the window, dragging the clothes behind her. Very carefully, she wrapped the cape around her hand and punched at the window. The glass was tough and she had to punch hard several times before the first crack appeared. She kept on punching while the cracks multiplied, until finally she had reduced the glass to shards which fell one by one into the void below.

The night air hit her full in the face and she gulped it down in large breaths. It gave her new strength. A new determination. The living world was out there and within her reach. In the moonlight, she could see a ledge just below the window and beyond that, she thought she could make out a tangle of bushes marching into the distance. She threw her clothes down and heard them land very softly some way below. Hopefully, that meant there was a bush to break her fall — she would have to drop from a considerable height. Climbing down a steep, smooth wall which lacked visible handholds, was an impossibility.

She managed to scrunch into a small ball and started to feed herself through the window — leg, arm, head. There was barely space and her body scraped and stuck against the iron frame. Jagged pieces of glass still lined its edges and they caught at her bare skin. Daisy knew she was bleeding, but she couldn't let it deter her. She was almost there. Her second arm was free now and she reached down for the ledge with both hands, at the same time wrenching the rest of her body through the narrow space. Hanging on to the ledge with both hands, her legs swinging free in the cold night air, she couldn't see what lay immediately below. For all she knew, a marble statue or unforgiving gravestone could lie waiting, but she had to believe she'd be all right.

Closing her eyes, Daisy let go.

CHAPTER THIRTY-FOUR

The breath was once more punched from her body as she plummeted downwards . . . landing in the middle of a large bush. It took some minutes before she could disentangle herself but, once she'd struggled through the flurry of branches to a grass clearing, she was able to take stock. Her neck throbbed, her arms and legs were cut and bruised and her face trickled with blood, but she had stayed in one piece. The moon was riding clear and a few yards away her white starched pinafore shone brightly in its light. Retrieving a handkerchief from its pocket, she wiped away as much of the blood as she could.

It was difficult to dress. Her hands were so cold that they fidgeted and fumbled with buttonholes and studs but, at last, she was ready, and wrapped what was left of the cape around her shoulders — the rain had stopped, but it was still unseasonably cold. She had no idea where she was, other than in a cemetery. An overgrown cemetery at that, and without an evident pathway.

In the crystalline light, Daisy saw that she had been very lucky in her fall. A mass of gravestones surrounded her, scattered at random, as though thrown by a giant hand. Their lichened heads poked through tall grass and wild saplings, the leaves seeming to whisper angrily at her intrusion. And everywhere ink black shadows and a mountain of glistening vegetation. She stood for a moment and listened. Soft rustlings filled the undergrowth, and she took some comfort that other living creatures were near.

Edging her way around the mausoleum walls to what she judged must be the front, she searched the darkness ahead. Surely, there would be a path leading from its door. There was. A meagre strip of gravel, but it had to go somewhere, she reasoned, and hoped fervently it would be to the cemetery entrance. Walking as fast as she dared along the badly pitted ribbon of shingle, she felt hemmed in by the multiplicity of graves, most of them abandoned, their drunken headstones forming a battered army on the march. She tried to block their louring shapes from her mind and focus on the path ahead, but the place was frightening. Every so often, a towering angel or crucifix hidden in shadows, would rise from the dark to terrify. And somewhere in the night, an owl hooted.

Daisy hurried on, skirting fallen branches and the patches of rubble that here and there blocked the path. While the moon floated free, her progress was steady, but then the sky began to haze and, quite suddenly, the moon was lost and the world turned wholly black. It was so dark she could no longer see her hands. Forced into a shuffle, her feet were constantly searching for the path — if she continued to move at this snail's pace, she fretted, her mission was certain to fail. She must find her way to the road, she must get to a telephone.

In frustration, she began to walk too swiftly, blundering ahead in the dark, until out of nowhere she lost the path. Feeling grass beneath her feet, she tried to turn back in the direction she thought she'd come, but the pathway eluded her. She turned again and now she was thoroughly confused. Her foot hung in the air ready for another step, when the moon chose that moment to swim from out of its basket of cloud and Daisy could see again. Down into an abyss. She had been about to walk into an abyss! It was an underground city, a circle of small houses each with its own door and lintel, and dug at least twenty feet deep into the ground. Beside each door was a carved scroll, a roll call of the inhabitants, she imagined. Standing on the grass precipice, she looked across the chasm. One more step would have plunged her downwards onto stone flags. While the moon still shone, she must hurry and find the path again.

It was only feet away, but she could have cast around for ever in the dark without finding it. She followed it as quickly as she could, twisting and turning, in and out of bushes, up and down steps. The path was passing again beneath an avenue of dark trees, this time so dark that not even bright moonlight could penetrate. Plunged once more into blackness, Daisy stumbled and fell amid a heap of rubble. A tomb had broken open and its contents spilled across the path; she had fallen over part of a shattered headstone.

Grasping a chunk of its stone to haul herself upwards, a small piece sheared from the memorial and came away in her hand. She felt it round and smooth with a trace of decoration on one side, and something made her keep hold of it. Her body was hurting just about everywhere, but she dragged herself to her feet, and once more crept forward until she found her way back into the moonlight.

The path was wider here — and must mean she was nearing the entrance. Thank God! Down another flight of steps, beneath another clump of overhanging trees, and she emerged into a semi-circular space. The cemetery was very old, a Victorian burial site, and this had been a turning circle for the horse-drawn carriages. Walking to the barred gate, she read the sign above. *Highgate Cemetery*. So, she had come hardly any distance from the safe house. More importantly, she was only a few miles from where Grayson was waiting with Chandan Patel. A few miles from where he was about to face Sweetman's gun. She must get to him.

The cemetery gate was locked, but that was the least of her problems this night. If she could escape a stone prison, she could get over an iron gate. Dropping down on the other side, she turned up the narrow road to her left. It was a steep hill and her exhausted body made hard work of it but, on reaching the top, the sight of a red telephone box brought her close to tears. She would ask the operator to put her through to Pitt House. Even now, she had time to warn Grayson that Sweetman was on his way.

But when she reached the box, she found its glass shattered and the black Bakelite that had once been a telephone, in pieces on the floor. A stray bomb had done its job. Daisy felt her heart pinched — but she must walk on, find another telephone. A white enamel sign at the side of the road announced that this was Hampstead Lane and must, she reckoned, lead to Hampstead village and a phone box.

Half walking, half running, she had travelled at least a mile before she came to another red kiosk. A woman was talking animatedly into the receiver. Daisy sent up a prayer of thanks — this one was working. She knocked at one of the small panes and the woman turned her head and frowned. Daisy mimed using the phone, but the woman turned her back.

This was too urgent for manners, she decided. When she opened the door to the box, the woman abruptly broke off her conversation.

'Well, really!'

'Please, this is an emergency. I must use the phone.' She hoped her uniform might help her plea. The woman looked her up and down scathingly, and Daisy realised she must seem no better than a tramp.

'Then find another phone box.' The woman turned her back again.

'There isn't one.' A note of panic had crept into Daisy's voice.

'Of course, there is. There's one further down the road. Now let me finish my conversation.'

'How far down the road?' she persisted.

'I have no idea.' The woman slammed the door shut.

Daisy immediately pulled it open, but the woman grabbed the door from inside and held on to it. A tug of war ensued which would have been comic, if it had not been so desperate.

'Please, you must help me.'

'I don't know who you are and I don't want to. Go away.'

'Do you know where Pitt House is?' It might be easier to find the house than another telephone box. 'Is it near?'

'Keep following the road,' the woman snapped. 'Turn right at Sandy Lane, then left. Now go away.'

Daisy went away. She blessed the moonlight. Without it, she would stand little chance of finding Pitt House. The streets were unfamiliar and she had no idea of the building she was looking for. In the blackout, she would soon have become lost. She began to run again, past substantial properties on both sides of the road, glancing briefly at their name boards, in case the woman had told her wrongly. Along the road, she'd said, and turn right — no sign of the house here — then turn left. Nearly dead with fatigue, she was forced to drop down into a walk. On and on, house after house, but never the right one.

She almost missed it. A laurel hedge had grown across the discreet board, its gold lettering faded by the weather. But this was it. This was Pitt House. A long driveway led up to the mansion, winding its way through clumps of trees. If she never saw another tree, Daisy thought, she wouldn't mind. She had no idea what she would find at the end of the drive and walked as quietly as she could, keeping to its darkened edge, but fearful that the crunch of gravel might signal her arrival. She could see the outline of the house now, the roof, the windows, and finally, an impressive front door.

In the shadows of the last clump of trees, she came upon the car. It was unpretentious, slightly shabby, and seemed not to belong here. She stole up to it and felt the bonnet. Still warm. Peering through its window, she saw a battered leather suitcase waiting on the back seat. It was Sweetman's car, it had to be. He was here and she was too late.

Then she heard the voices and ducked back into the shadows. A man was at the entrance to the house, his feet scraping noisily at the gravel. She came out of hiding and stared at his back. She knew the jacket he was wearing. It was Mike Corrigan's. She wasn't too late! The man was waving a pass at the guards and, when they seemed reluctant to let him through, he tried to push past.

She heard one of the guards say, 'Just a minute, sir. We'll have to check. Mr Harte is already here and he'll vouch for you.'

No, her heart was saying. Don't bring him to the door. Please don't. But the guard had gone inside the house.

'I don't need Grayson to vouch for me,' the man was saying in his slightly odd accent. 'Now let me through, old chap.' And it seemed as though he would try to shoulder the remaining guard to one side.

Daisy started forward as though every demon in hell had landed on her shoulders. 'Don't let him through.' Her voice was cracking. Find your voice, she begged herself, shout it loud and clear. 'Don't let him through,' she yelled. 'He's not Mr Corrigan.'

The guard must have heard her because his hand went immediately to his gun. Sweetman heard, too, and spun around, pulling a gun from inside his jacket. For a moment, as he caught sight of her, it looked as though he would drop it in sheer astonishment. But a voice from the door made him turn again, and this time he levelled the weapon.

'What's this about?' Grayson's figure was silhouetted in the doorway. 'Is that you, Mike?' He peered into the darkness, his hand above his eyes.

'Unfortunately not,' Sweetman snarled, and his hand was on the trigger.

The guard was raising his rifle to take aim, but it was too late. Too late, she thought. The stone in her pocket became large, urgent. She fumbled for it and, with all her waning strength, hurled the stone at the back of Sweetman's head. It hit him dead centre, pitching him to the ground and sending the gunshot flying harmlessly into the air. Throwing a mean stone was something else Daisy had learned at Eden House.

CHAPTER THIRTY-FIVE

'How are you feeling?'

Her friend's face leant towards her. What was Connie doing here? Where was here?

'How are you, Daisy?' Connie's voice was a little shaky.

'I'm fine,' she murmured automatically. That's what you always said, wasn't it? She tried to raise her head, but the effort was too great and she slumped back on to stacked pillows.

'You're not to think of getting up,' Connie warned. 'You need to rest.'

'I'm in the Sick Bay?' she hazarded.

Her friend nodded. 'And you're staying here until you're completely recovered.'

Daisy had hardly ever been to the Sick Bay. She knew nurses were sent here immediately they felt at all unwell, not so much as a sniffle was allowed to pass unnoticed on the ward. But she'd managed to survive eighteen months' training without a sniffle, and her only visit to this part of the hospital had been on errands for Sister Elton.

'I'm fine, really I am,' she repeated.

Her neck was still sore and inflamed and she ached from head to toe, but otherwise there didn't seem a great deal wrong. Her mind, though, was cloudy.

'You may think you're okay, but you've been through a tremendous ordeal.' Connie was soothing. 'And you need time to get over it.'

Daisy's mind grappled with the idea of an ordeal and memory kicked in just a little. There had been guns, she recalled, and a dark, gravelled drive.

'Grayson,' she said suddenly.

'He's fit and well. He's been here most of the time you've been sleeping. He's only just left.'

'He's been here, in the Sick Bay?' She sounded incredulous.

'He was given special permission — under the circumstances — but he had to leave and check in at Baker Street. There's a lot of sorting out to do, apparently. He promised to come back later. That's if you want to see him.'

Daisy wasn't sure she did. There was a lot of sorting out for her to do, too, but she was overcome by such heartfelt relief that he was safe and not dead at Sweetman's feet, that she pushed the doubts aside. Instead, she tried to concentrate on remembering. In her mind's eye, she saw the house, Pitt House, and then Sweetman levelling his gun at the figure in the doorway. She felt the stone in her pocket and that last desperate effort, using every ounce of her remaining strength to deflect the gun. But everything else was a blank. How had she got there? How had she come here?

'You blacked out and you've been unconscious ever since,' her friend explained, sensing her confusion. 'But it's so good to see you awake and talking.' She bent over the bed and gave Daisy an enormous hug.

'What time is it, then?' She struggled to see the clock, but once again had to slump back on to her pillows.

'It's four in the afternoon. You've been out for sixteen hours. That wicked man injected you with insulin, and you've been in a delayed coma. I can't believe how you managed to do what you did.'

It seemed there had been trouble and she'd been in the middle of it, but Daisy could remember nothing beyond that one scene. And what was Connie doing here in the middle of the afternoon?

'Shouldn't you be on the ward?'

'More special permission. I've been given an hour off to come and see you. I've been sitting here willing you to wake up, and then you did! Evidently I'm just the medicine the doctor ordered.'

'Evidently.' For the first time, Daisy's face creased into a smile. 'And you say that Grayson was here.' Her tone was wondering.

'For hours.'

She was overcome by a rush of vanity. 'What must I look like?'

'You don't look too special,' Connie said frankly, 'but then you have been through the wars.'

'Give me a mirror.'

'I wouldn't, really I wouldn't.'

'Give it to me this minute, Telford.'

Connie shrugged her shoulders resignedly. 'Okay, but remember you're the heroine of the hour, so it doesn't matter what you look like.'

Daisy took a quick glance in the mirror. No almond cream skin greeted her but a sallow wash, enlivened only by strips of pink sticking plaster dotted at intervals around her face. One cheek sported a very large, mauve bruise.

'How did that happen?' She pointed to the plasters and then to the bruise.

'Don't ask me. That's how you were when you were brought in. Your legs and arms are pretty trashed, too.' Daisy pushed up the sleeves of her nightdress. A neat row of darkening bruises greeted her, interspersed with a latticework of cuts.

The inspection left her silent and brooding. 'Would you like some tea?' Connie asked brightly.

'Thank you, that would be good.' Her reply was automatic, her mind elsewhere. 'Those cuts . . . I climbed through broken glass. I remember now.'

'You're not to worry about them. They're not too deep and they shouldn't leave a scar.'

'And the bruise,' she continued without hearing her friend. 'I fell. That's right, I fell into a grave. I was in a cemetery. The grave had broken open and I tripped on some smashed stone.'

'Think about it later,' Connie advised. 'When you're back on form.'

But Daisy's mind was chasing memories and wouldn't let go. It was all coming back. 'I picked up one of the fragments of stone. It was the one I threw.'

Her companion shook her head. 'You won't give up, will you?'

'What happened to Sweetman?'

'The baddie, you mean? He must be in prison but, other than that, I don't know. You'll have to ask Grayson when he gets back. That's if you're willing to see him. He told me you'd given him the heave-ho.'

Daisy looked down at the starched white sheet and plucked at its trimming. 'I can't have been thinking straight.'

'You can't have,' Connie agreed. 'What made you do it? The last I heard you were both deliriously happy. I know you felt bad about Willa, but why dump Grayson?'

'I can't expect you to understand.' She closed her eyes, as if to shut out thoughts she still found painful. 'I don't really understand it myself.'

'Try me.'

Daisy opened her eyes again and looked uncertainly into Connie's. 'I was overwhelmed . . . bad memories crowding in on me. Such a lot of hurt. Memories of all the people I'd known who had died. I felt as though it must be my fault, that I had to make up for it in some way.'

So many deaths, she thought. A mother she'd never known, Anish and Gerald, Willa, her own small baby, all those years ago on board ship. Her life had seemed nothing more than one long roll call of the departed. No wonder she'd refused to welcome happiness when it offered. It was time she changed the subject.

'More importantly, how are *you*, Connie? What's been happening?'

'Quite a bit and I'm feeling nervous,' the girl confessed. 'It's tomorrow I meet Colin's parents and I do so want them to like me.'

'You've no reason to feel worried. You'll go down a storm.'

'I think it may be an extra special occasion.' Daisy saw her friend's plump cheeks flush bright pink. 'Colin wants me to fix a wedding date and make it soon.'

'And will you? Set the date, I mean.'

'Of course. I want to marry him as soon as possible. I really love him.'

'That's wonderful.' And it was, Daisy thought. She was delighted for her friend, but finding it difficult to keep the fatigue from her voice.

'You need to get more sleep,' Connie said quickly. 'And I need to get back to the ward.'

'How is everything there . . . ?' her voice trailed off. She should be going with Connie, returning to the ward herself. But she was so very tired.

'Everything is fine, but we want you back as soon as possible. Fit and raring to go!'

* * *

Despite her fatigue, Daisy didn't sleep. Her mind refused to rest, so she simply closed her eyes and tried to remember. Talking to Connie she had seen the whole of that last scene unwind in slow motion. The stone hitting Sweetman at the back of the head, the gun firing uselessly into the air. Grayson silhouetted in the doorway, the dark drive she'd followed. But now her mind wandered back even further: along the drive, along the walk she'd taken, the endless walk, and before that . . . a cemetery filled with gothic terror. Tall, white walls floated hazily into a corner of her mind and she recoiled instantly.

She had reached the mausoleum, reached the moment of her imprisonment and her mind closed down. She could not bear to relive those hours of cold desperation and the horrifying risks she had taken to escape. How had her body stood up to such an onslaught? But it had. Somehow, she'd reached Pitt House and done what she had to. Daisy knew what had driven her — love, pure and simple. Love for Grayson and the dread she would lose him forever. But he was safe, and so was she. She could relax.

Or could she? What would she say to him when he returned? What could she say? It was clear he was concerned for her — he'd been here hours, Connie said, watching and waiting. When he came back, he'd want to check she was feeling better, want to thank her for her part in the night's doings, but there would be nothing more, nothing deeper.

She remembered how tight-lipped he'd been when she'd last seen him. How lacking in warmth as they'd stood together by the ruined house in Ellen Street. He'd sent her away with Michael Corrigan, refusing to offer one jot of sympathy for Gerald's brutal death. He had been cold and unforgiving, and Daisy understood why. They had loved each other passionately, and then she'd walked out of his life. Curtly, refusing to talk, refusing to explain. That would be uppermost in his mind. And why would it not?

It wasn't the first time she'd rejected him. Not the first time she'd behaved unreasonably, or so it must seem. For so long, her feelings had been in conflict, missing him when he'd gone back to India, waiting eagerly for his letters to arrive, yet when he'd returned, unable to relax, to enjoy his company. And why was that? He was an attractive man, very attractive; he was interesting and intelligent; and he'd made it plain how much he liked her. But there had been a bar of ice where her heart should be and it had refused to melt, a bar that had *the past* running through its very centre like a seaside stick of rock.

Until the Ritz, when for one glorious night, she'd broken free of her bonds, but guilt, as always, had been waiting in the wings and it proved a short-lived freedom. It was only when Grayson was threatened, when she knew she was about to lose him forever, that her heart had found its truth again. Without a doubt, she loved him. Perhaps she always had, from those very first moments in India. But Gerald had been her husband and she'd not allowed herself to feel more than friendship. Gerald had got in the way of anything deeper and, when a month ago he'd come back from the dead and sent her life haywire, he'd got in the way again. But not any longer. Once the post-mortem was over, she would sever the last link in a chain that for years had held her fast. She would stand by his grave as she had by Willa's, and send him on his journey with as much dignity and respect as she could muster.

* * *

Grayson came bearing flowers, an enormous bouquet of early summer blooms. Passers-by stared at him as he walked from his car, but it was the moment he entered the hospital that he felt most awkward. Here he was, bringing a surfeit of flowers to a woman who'd made clear that she wanted no part of him. But she was a patient, he reasoned, and that's what you did for patients — you brought them flowers.

Cautiously, he put his head around the open door. She was propped up against what seemed a hundred pillows, and her face had still not regained its lovely colour.

'Where on earth did you get those?'

It wasn't the greeting he'd expected but it broke the ice.

'Don't ask. They're strictly off ration.' He walked up to her bedside and deposited the flowers on a nearby table. There was barely room to accommodate them.

'From someone's garden?'

'Something like that, but a very important someone.' He wouldn't tell her that the blooms had been handpicked that morning from the Palace gardens. 'You're the nation's heroine right now, and nothing is too good for you.'

She gave a weak laugh. 'It's not kind to make fun of me when I'm feeling so feeble.'

'I'm not, on my honour.' He took the seat by the bed and looked at her closely. 'You're the David who slew

Goliath, although a very pasty David, it has to be said. How are you feeling, or is that a foolish question?'

'I keep telling everybody I feel fine, and I do. A few cuts and bruises, that's all. I could get out of bed this minute and go back to work.'

'Don't even think of it. David needed to rest after his momentous victory, and so do you.'

'Sweetman wasn't much of a Goliath.'

She slithered down the bed as she spoke. She's tired already, he thought. God knows what she'd had to contend with before she'd appeared on the drive of Pitt House.

'Sweetman is a very dangerous man,' he remonstrated. 'He holds the most extreme views and isn't afraid to act on them.'

'Have you discovered who sent him to England? I imagine he must have supporters back home.'

'He's still being interrogated. But you're right. It looks as though he was sent undercover to sabotage any attempt to bring India into the war on our side. There'll be a group or several groups somewhere in the homeland, rooting for the Germans to win this war, and that's who we need to get to.'

'And his colleague? Do you know who he was?'

'His name was Hari Mishra and from what we've managed to piece together from contacts in India, he seems to have been as much a dupe as a conspirator. He's currently lying in the morgue awaiting a post-mortem.'

'What will happen to him?'

'He'll be cremated as soon as the coroner releases his body. Then his ashes will be scattered at sea.'

'And Sweetman?'

'Once we've finished with him, he'll be handed to the police and charged with Mishra's and Gerald's murders.'

Daisy said nothing and he could see the mention of her husband had disturbed her. He wished he'd kept quiet. 'But for you, it would have been three deaths,' he said as lightly as he could.

'That must mean Michael Corrigan is still alive. I didn't like to ask. I know he's a close friend of yours.'

'He's alive all right, though the car is a complete write-off.' Grayson pulled a wry face. 'He's suffering from concussion and a lot of nasty bruises, but he'll be back on duty in no time.'

Leaning forward, he fixed his eyes on her face. He had something to say and he didn't want to be deflected. 'You're adept at changing the subject, Daisy. I'm not sure how you do it, but you're very good. Before Mike intruded into our conversation, I was trying to say thank you — awkwardly, I know — but thank you for saving my life.'

'There's really no need. Consider it a fair exchange.' She sank deeper into the bedclothes, as though trying to hide from the spectre of her own rescue in Jasirapur.

'But there is. Most definitely. If it hadn't been for you, I'd be lying alongside Mishra in the morgue at this very moment. What an aim you've got. And I thought girls couldn't throw straight. Doesn't that just show me!'

Without warning, she began to cry. The small, clear teardrops gathered and spilled onto her wounded cheeks and she made no attempt to brush them away.

He reached for her hand and drew it from the bedclothes. 'My poor girl. What you must have been through. One day I want a full account of your adventures, but I won't press you to talk right now.' He took out a large, white handkerchief and gently wiped away the tears. 'We've plenty of time for that. At least, I hope so. We *are* speaking now?'

She looked as though she might begin crying again, but instead she gave a very loud sniff. 'I'm sorry,' she murmured brokenly, 'I'm sorry for what I said when we met in the square. I was so stupid.'

He shushed her. 'I was the stupid one, not to realise how devastating these last few weeks have been for you.'

She balled his handkerchief tightly between her hands. 'I felt so guilty about Willa, you see . . . I went to pieces. And that made me unjust. I hope you'll forget what I said.'

'There's nothing to forget.'

Her confession was unexpected but comforting. It didn't mean she was any nearer loving him but, at least, he was no longer the enemy. It could be worth trying his luck with an idea that had been gathering pace.

'There is something I don't want to forget,' he said softly. 'I mentioned a trip to Brighton some weeks ago. Do you recall?'

'I do, but didn't we agree it would have to wait until the war was over? The south coast has been out of bounds to visitors since March, hasn't it?'

He fished around in his pocket for a small, white card. 'It has, but take a look at this,' and he waved the paper in the air. 'A special pass. And as soon as you're on your feet again, we're going — with your agreement, of course. I can requisition a car and I've been saving petrol for just this kind of jaunt.' He wondered if he should make a decisive strike and decided to risk it. 'If you felt able to travel the Saturday after next . . .'

She didn't immediately reject the proposal as he thought she might. Instead, she prevaricated. 'But the hospital . . . if I'm well enough to gallivant to Brighton, I'm well enough to be back on the ward.'

'Not so. You're signed off work for the next two weeks — by no less a personage than Matron herself.'

She pulled herself upright and he saw her cheeks flush and her eyes begin to sparkle. It was the first time she'd looked like the old Daisy for what seemed a long time.

'I don't know what to say.'

'"Yes" is the word you're looking for.'

'Thank you, Grayson.' Her voice still sounded unsure, but her smile was genuine. 'Thank you for thinking of it.'

'It's Connie Telford you need to thank. It was her suggestion. At least, she suggested taking you away for a few days out of this crazy city, and the trip to Brighton slotted in nicely. So are we on?'

'Yes, we're on. Let's go.'

CHAPTER THIRTY-SIX

Brighton, early May 1941

They were lucky with the weather. May had dawned wet and miserable, but for the two days they were by the sea, the sun shone for them. As soon as Daisy was shown to her bedroom, she opened its shutters — to the lapping of water and the glitter of sunlight on waves. The hotel Grayson had booked was situated between the town's two piers and only a roadway separated it from the beach.

The beach, though, was no longer for enjoyment. Thousands of yards of barbed wire had been draped along the seafront and large cubes of concrete — anti-tank traps, Daisy presumed — had been set up at every stairway or ramp. If she craned her neck left and right, she could see searchlight batteries at points along the coast, and a phalanx of anti-aircraft guns. Brighton might not be suffering the terrors of the Blitz, but the outcome of the war was as uncertain here as anywhere else in Britain. And given the town's position, its people must be in constant fear of invasion, since the enemy sat waiting just the other side of the Channel.

They had lunch in the hotel restaurant, a skimpy affair of minced beef with greens and potatoes. The rhubarb pudding and custard that followed was even skimpier and the coffee had certainly never seen an original bean. But neither of them minded. It was sufficient to be young and alive, to breathe the fresh air, and feel the sun warming their skin.

'Shall we try the seafront?' Grayson offered her his arm. 'We won't be able to walk there after six. There's a curfew in place.'

Daisy was more than happy to saunter along the once beautiful promenade. She had never visited the English seaside before and everything she saw was newly fascinating.

'What a pity we can't walk on the beach,' she mourned. 'I'd love to crunch over those pebbles . . . but all that barbed wire.'

'All that barbed wire is keeping us safe. The beach beyond is mined.'

'How on earth do you mine pebbles?' It was a novel idea. 'Has that been mined, too?' She pointed towards a long jetty that marched seawards some way ahead. It was the smaller of the piers, a delicate construction of Victorian ironwork, but now pummelled and war weary.

'It's not looking too wonderful, is it?' he agreed. 'When you went to fetch your jacket, I had a chat with the girl on Reception. She tells me they've removed whole sections of decking from both piers to prevent them being used as a landing stage. Hardly surprising — on a clear day, you can see the German lines across the water.'

'I had no idea. That's truly frightening. In London, you're convinced you're the centre of the world. You think you're suffering for the whole of Britain, but it's not so. Brighton is hurting, too, and plenty of other towns, I guess. It can't be much safer here.'

'A bit, but there's still danger. They brought evacuees down at the beginning of the war, but recently they've had to send them on to the West Country. I don't think the powers that be ever thought bombs would fall here. But they have and, since March, the whole of the south coast has been a defence zone.'

'I wouldn't think the town large enough to be worth the bombers' trouble.'

'It's not a main target, but any Luftwaffe pilot with bombs left after attacking London, drops them here.'

They had stopped by a fortified enclosure and Daisy leaned over the barricade to take a closer look. 'I think that must have been a paddling pool.'

'A children's paddling pool, wired off and no doubt mined. What we've come to!'

Despite his words, Grayson's expression was cheerful. His face had lost the weariness it had worn lately, she noticed, and, standing in the bright sun, hair glinting and his skin slightly tanned, he looked the man she'd first known.

He gave her shoulder a gentle touch. 'Shall we walk back? I'd like to take you to the Pavilion while it's open.'

'I'm amazed the building is still standing.'

'So far, at least. Not one hit.' They struck inland and started along the road running parallel to the seafront. 'It's sparked a rumour that Hitler plans to use the palace as his headquarters when he invades.'

She looked up at him, half expecting him to be laughing. 'It's just a rumour,' he reassured her, 'but they've moved all the artworks to the countryside for safekeeping.'

'We're preserving some treasure, at least. Just look at that.' An enormous mound of scrap metal had been heaped together on the opposite side of the road. 'Those must once have been beautiful railings. Wrought iron as well.'

Grayson shook his head. 'You have to wonder sometimes whether we're destroying as much as the Germans. The old tram tracks have been torn up, too. A real shame.'

They'd arrived at a spot immediately behind their hotel and, from here, it was only a short stroll to the exotic palace they had come to see. Daisy gave a gasp when its minarets first swam into view. It was as though a piece of India had been dropped from the sky into the decorous heart of an English resort.

'Do you like it?'

'I'm not entirely sure.' She was puzzled. 'It's a little . . .'

'On the wild side? It *was* built as a pleasure palace, though there's precious little pleasure in town these days. Even the racecourse has become an internment camp. The Regent would *not* have approved.'

'But it's such an extraordinary place.' Daisy was finding it difficult to drag her eyes away from the rash of cupolas and decorated arches.

'You can look your fill later,' he said in her ear. 'We should go in now. Remember, we're on a hunt.'

'But will they still have the records we want? After all, the building isn't a hospital any longer.'

'True, but I believe the basement offices still house an archive of stuff from the Great War. With a little persuasion, I think we can get whoever's in charge to let us look. But we should see something of the palace first.'

'I'm already dazzled.'

'That's nothing,' Grayson smiled down at her. 'Wait till you get inside.'

And he was right. She was overwhelmed by the building's sheer opulence. They walked slowly from room to room, each more magnificent than the last and, by the time they reached the Music Room, she was wide eyed and stupefied. Sinking down on a bench, Daisy tried to take it in.

As elsewhere, the ceiling here was gilded, supported by pillars covered in gold leaf and decorated with carved dragons and serpents. A lamp, coloured crimson, gold and white, and made to resemble a huge water lily, hung from the centre with gilded dragons clinging to its underside. More dragons embellished the crimson canopies of the four doorways leading out of the room, and still more writhed above the blue and crimson window drapes. Large ottomans, decorated with fluted silk and covered in enormous satin bolsters, lined every wall, with an Axminster carpet of spectacular design spread across the floor: a riot of golden suns, stars, serpents and dragons on a pale blue ground.

She sat entranced by the grandeur and hardly noticed when Grayson found a seat beside her. 'You've been sitting motionless for at least ten minutes,' he said indulgently. 'Perhaps we should make our way to the basement now — try our luck with those records.'

'Do you really believe my mother could have nursed in this marvellous place?'

'I do. I'm not sure how marvellous it would have been then, but I *am* sure she trained the Indian orderlies who nursed the wounded. We should find her name in the records, and then you'll believe it.'

It took a little while. The custodian needed no persuading. Indeed, he was eager for them to look at treasures that most people passed by, but the pile of dusty registers took some time to trawl. Then, Daisy saw the name — Lily Driscoll. Her fingertip hovered over the entry. It seemed as holy to her as any saint's relic, and she stroked her finger back and forth across the faded ink.

'She really was here,' she said in barely a whisper.

'She was,' Grayson agreed.

'And you found her. How very clever of you!'

'I am in the intelligence service,' he teased. 'When I can tear you away from the register, I think we should find somewhere for dinner. I know it's early but there's a curfew to beat.'

'I'd rather like to wash and change first. Can we go back to the hotel?'

'We can. We might even find there's enough hot water for a bath, though I'm not promising.'

Today, there was ample water and Daisy lay back in the tub, relaxed and dreamy. The bruises along her arms and legs were still fading, but the cuts on her face had mended. She hoped her mind had mended, too. She felt right somehow, right in a way that had earlier been missing. She'd enjoyed being with Grayson today. He had found her mother for her and that was priceless. But it was the feeling of being close that she'd loved most, the feeling that now there were no secrets between them, no resentments.

She dressed in the frock she'd worn to the Ritz. It was too elaborate for a simple meal, but she didn't care. It was the only decent thing she had, and she wanted to look her very best. She tied a band of black velvet ribbon around her dark curls and thought she looked well. No dark marks, no drawn cheeks. That was hardly surprising — she must have slept for England this last week. But it was more than that. For the first time in a very long while, she was happy. Truly happy.

They found a small restaurant a few yards past the Palace Pier. The meal would be uninspired, she knew, but it hardly mattered. Her heart was singing and she wondered that nobody could hear it. Grayson looked particularly handsome. He'd found a smart grey suit from somewhere and the crisp white of his shirt made his eyes appear bluer than ever. She found it difficult to stop her glance straying in his direction and lingering a little too long.

The dessert plates were being cleared when he said. 'Shall we go back to the hotel? It won't be long before we have to, and I can't drink another cup of what passes for coffee to save my life. A brandy at the bar will do us good.'

After taking her first sip, Daisy wasn't sure she agreed — the liquid was fiery and burnt her throat — but, after a while, the taste mellowed and she was encouraged to try again.

'Did the agreement ever get signed,' she asked lazily. The hotel bar was snug, a log fire burning in the grate, and her body had eased into its warmth. 'The one Mr Patel came to negotiate?'

'No, it didn't. When Congress heard the news, they were quick to recall their envoy.'

'So, Sweetman was successful in disrupting the talks after all?'

'Only for a while. And he didn't succeed in much else. His plan seems to have been to discredit the Service, to spread rumours that we were behind Patel's murder. That would have ensured there would never be an agreement.'

'But wasn't that what he achieved?'

'I don't believe so. The future stays open and negotiations will go on. His grand project is in tatters. Botched and beaten by a slip of a girl!' Grayson stretched his legs to the fire. 'In any case, since then things have moved on. You won't know, but a new regiment — the Burma regiment — is being formed this Autumn. It will recruit from among Moslems and Sikhs, so Indian participation isn't that crucial. Sweetman is old news.'

'He'll stand trial, though?'

'He will, and be found guilty. And almost certainly executed. His people back in India will do their best to forget him as soon as they can.' Grayson swirled the amber liquid around his glass and watched it on its circular journey. 'But that's all past. I'm more interested in the future.'

'Connie is getting married to her doctor,' she offered. 'She met his parents last week and, apparently, she was approved. It's likely to be a late summer wedding. She tells me you'll be getting an invitation, so make sure you watch your post.'

'Connie's forthcoming nuptials aren't what I had in mind.'

'They're what I have in mind,' Daisy retorted, her forehead puckered. 'I haven't a clue how we're to manage a wedding dress. Parachute silk would do for the underskirt and bodice, but it's sure to be difficult to get hold of. And even if we find some, we'll still need netting for the overskirt.'

He leant towards her. 'I was talking about you and me. What the future holds for us, Daisy.'

She felt suddenly very shy. Grayson was clearly content in her company, and she knew he was relieved they'd renewed their friendship. But lovers? He'd not behaved as a lover today. He'd made no move to take her in his arms, to kiss her in the way he'd kissed her before. No doubt, she had disappointed him too many times, and he was unwilling to take another chance. Daisy couldn't blame him.

'Perhaps we can leave the future to sort itself,' he said gently, when she made no attempt to answer. 'You've been through an awful lot these last few weeks.'

Including losing my husband for a second time, she thought. Two days ago, she had walked from his graveside and thought herself free at last. But the image of his body lying dead in the ruins of Ellen Street kept returning. When she'd seen his face — a face she had once adored — scarred by that single bullet hole, she'd felt genuine sorrow, a yearning for things to have been different. And the feeling still haunted her, a shadow over any future she might have.

Grayson was as good as his word. For the rest of the evening, he made no mention of the terrible events she'd endured or the future that lay ahead. Instead, he talked about the sights they'd seen in Brighton that day, the latest news from Baker Street, how his mother was winning the war single-handedly in Pimlico. Later that evening, he walked her to her bedroom door and she wondered what would happen if, by chance, he asked to come in. How would she react? She need not have wondered. It seemed to be the last thing on his mind.

'It's been a good day,' he said cheerfully. 'I hope you enjoyed it.'

'I did — immensely. Coming here was the best idea you could have had. It's been wonderful to be out of London, and especially wonderful to see my mother's name in those records.'

'I've been tossing up whether we should make tomorrow another Indian day. We don't need to leave town until after lunch and, if the weather holds, you might like to visit the Chattri. We'd have to take a bus, though — I've only just enough fuel to get us back to London.'

He must have seen her blank expression. 'It's a monument a little to the north of Brighton, dedicated to the Indian soldiers who died here. I believe it's a fair walk across the Downs, so if you'd rather not go, just say.'

The thought of walking across the wonderful hills Daisy had glimpsed to the rear of the town was enticing. 'I'd love to go,' she said. 'Let's have an early breakfast and walk.'

He bent his head and gave her a gentle kiss on the cheek, then walked down the corridor to his room. 'Till tomorrow,' he called over his shoulder.

* * *

She found it difficult to sleep that night and she knew why. The past still confused her and she thought that maybe it confused Grayson, too. Or, at least, made him uncertain. When he'd mentioned their future, she was sure he'd had only friendship in mind.

Grayson was special. He always had been. On the surface, honest and decent, a man you could trust with your life. But scratch a little and a different character emerged. Still honourable, still decent, but someone who'd chosen a job that was lived for the most part in the shadows. Her fellow orphans at Eden House would have called him 'soft', yet he was anything but. He'd known a comfortable home, the best schooling that money could buy, and a family eager for him to succeed. But he'd chosen to ignore the prizes he'd been gifted, and follow a very different path.

From the first, Daisy had suspected he was a man who enjoyed hazard and she'd been right. He'd said no to the ceremonial glories of a military career and walked away from a safe life as a sugar planter. Instead, he'd found his niche in the Intelligence Service. It was a murky business and a dangerous one. She had no idea if he was involved in operations abroad, but these past few weeks had shown his safety couldn't be guaranteed, even in England. And the dangers wouldn't end now. There would be other Sweetmans in the future. But that didn't deter her — she loved that part of him, the part that delighted in adventure. She loved every part of him. If only she could shake off the echoes of the past, if only he could see how much she wanted to love him.

CHAPTER THIRTY-SEVEN

Grayson awoke very early to a light filled room. The sun had found chinks in the lopsided blackout curtain and was dancing its narrow beams from wall to wall. Pushing open the window, he breathed in the sharp tang of a full tide. It was a day for walking! You could walk for miles in London and never feel refreshed, but here the clear air of the South Downs beckoned. He wasn't sure about Daisy, wasn't sure she was up to the expedition. She'd left the Sick Bay only recently and he reckoned they would have at least a mile climb from where the bus dropped them. The view alone would be worth the effort, but he didn't want to exhaust her.

She was intensely vulnerable in every way. So far, she hadn't confided much of what had happened to her the night she'd arrived at Pitt House. She'd been imprisoned somewhere and managed to free herself, that much he knew, then walk or stumble her way to the house, but all else remained a mystery and he didn't want to pry. He guessed she wasn't yet ready to revisit those difficult moments.

Not ready either to revisit Gerald's death. The man had been nothing but bad news for her since the day she'd married, and Daisy was sensible enough to know she'd do better without him. But the human heart was unpredictable, and

Grayson suspected her husband's death had affected her in ways she hadn't bargained for. It was bound to have brought back memories of their first days together, when she still hoped for a happy ending, but there would be memories, too, of the deception and danger he'd inflicted on her.

Grayson longed to scoop her up in his arms and make her forget, and there had been several moments yesterday when he'd been sorely tempted. Last night, she'd looked so lovely, wearing the very same dress he'd slipped from her shoulders at the Ritz, that he'd wanted to do the same again. But that was just about the worst thing he could have done. He must be patient, he told himself. He must give her time and hope that finally, she would come to him.

* * *

It was only just past ten when they clambered from the bus at Old London Road and turned into a bridleway marked *Chattri and Windmills*.

'It's an unusual word, chattri,' Daisy remarked. 'Unless it's peculiar to Sussex.'

'Not Sussex. It's a Hindi word. Urdu too. It means umbrella.'

'Why umbrella?'

'The monument is shaped like one, I think, as a symbol of shelter. It offers protection to the memory of the dead.'

'It sounds very spiritual. It must have been designed by an Indian.'

'It was, by an architect from Bombay.'

'He chose a wonderful position for his handiwork.' They paused for a moment, gazing at the landscape that surrounded them.

Hill after hill folded one into another, etched against a cloudless sky, as though cut from cardboard. Only the seagulls, swooping and hovering above, broke their smooth contours. Ahead, a white chalk path meandered its way upwards in an ever steeper curve.

'We should save our breath for the climb,' he warned.

It was going to be a long climb, he could see, but Daisy swinging along beside him, seemed untroubled. He looked down and saw her mouth upturned in pleasure. It was a glorious day to be walking, the sun warming their faces and spreading its glow far and wide over the green downland.

Grayson carried a large basket in one hand, but had refused to tell her just what was in it. He'd managed to persuade or otherwise bribe the kitchen staff to pack a picnic that went beyond the limits of rationing. The chef had even discovered a stray bottle of wine unaccounted for, and Grayson had managed to whisk a couple of glasses from the breakfast table and cadge a corkscrew. He wanted it to be a memorable day, perhaps the first of many.

A large, octagonal structure swam slowly into view. In the last few minutes, Daisy had begun to look a little wan, but she'd done far better than he'd expected and they had almost reached the gleaming white marble without pausing for breath. As always, she was far tougher than her fragile appearance suggested. The memorial sat proudly atop the hill with greensward stretching beneath its feet in every direction. In the distance, slate roofs and red brick spread for miles east and west, but to the south beyond the town, a thin ribbon of blue marked the moment where sea met sky.

'It's quite beautiful,' she breathed, as they finally drew level with the white marble dome and its eight pillars. Walking slowly towards it, she read the inscription carved in both English and Hindi:

To the memory of all Indian soldiers who gave their lives for their King-Emperor in the Great War, this monument, erected on the site of the funeral pyre where the Hindus and Sikhs who died in hospital at Brighton passed through the fire, is in grateful admiration and brotherly affection dedicated.

'How very splendid. And these are their names.' She traced her finger down a roll call of soldiers. 'Did all these die in Brighton?'

'I believe so. They're a small fraction of the Indian soldiers who fought in the Great War, of course. One and half million of them.'

He walked forward to join her and in silence read the names. 'There are so many,' she said.

'Thousands were lost at Loos and Neuve Chapelle and the Somme, too. Such carnage, and only miles away. It was said the boys playing cricket at Brighton College could hear the sound of the Somme guns.'

'My mother might have known some of these men.' Daisy's eyes were heavy with sadness.

'And helped to save many more, don't forget.'

'I wonder . . .'

He said nothing and she began again, 'I wonder . . . if it was one of these men who gave her the brooch in the photograph. You thought it had probably been mass produced in England and sold on a market stall. But what if it was the real thing? After all, it was a copy of a pendant worn by a local goddess — Nandni Mata. Do you remember? What if one of these men gave it to her as a thank you? It might have come from India after all, from Jasirapur even.'

'It's possible,' Grayson conceded. He could see that it was something she wanted to be true. 'We'll never know, but when you look at the photograph again, you can think of this place.'

She turned around in a full circle, her eyes sweeping the landscape, unrolling mile after mile beneath their feet. 'It's the most beautiful setting for a monument, but so isolated.'

'As the inscription says, it was the cremation site for Hindu and Sikh soldiers. The monument is built where the funeral pyre was lit. Then, after cremation, the ashes would have been scattered in the sea.'

'As Hari Mishra's will be.'

'As Hari Mishra's,' he agreed. 'The Moslem soldiers were buried some way away. At a mosque in Surrey, I think.'

Daisy turned back to the list of names, her finger running down the lines, one by one. He didn't know why they were so important to her, and perhaps she didn't either. She was almost at the end when her finger stopped. He saw she had reached the letter 'R'.

'Rana,' she said, her face shadowed. 'Anish's name. This couldn't be his father.'

'There are plenty of Ranas in India. Why did you think of him?'

Daisy breathed a small sigh. 'Anish told me his father had been wounded in France and sent to England to convalesce. I wondered if he came to Brighton.'

'He might have done. The Pavilion hospital was one of the biggest centres for Indian casualties.'

'He died on the Somme, eventually — after he'd been patched up in an English hospital and sent back to France. To his death.'

Something was worrying her, but Grayson couldn't fathom what. Any mention of Anish Rana always produced this strange reaction in her. It wasn't sadness as such. That was too mild an emotion, but rather a kind of angry grief. In some mysterious way, she felt deeply connected to the man.

'You think your mother might have known Rana senior?'

'It's possible, isn't it? If he was sent to Brighton for recuperation and she was training Indian orderlies here. It's possible they came across each other.'

'If you really wanted to find out, you could.'

'How?'

'Go back to India and speak to Rana's family.'

'Back to Jasirapur?' She looked astonished.

'Why not?'

'I don't know if I could.' There was a tremor to her voice. She was scared of the idea, he could see.

He moved a little closer and they stood together looking at the Chattri's smooth, white dome and its fluted marble pillars.

'Perhaps if I travelled with you, you might consider going.'

'But you couldn't. Your work is in London.'

'I reckon I could always swing a visit. There's bound to be plenty of loose ends to tie up, once the war is over.'

'It's always "once the war is over". If it ever is.'

'No pessimism allowed on this fantastic day! Come on, we'll find a comfortable perch and then we'll eat.'

He walked ahead, a little further along the path, and glimpsed a small clump of weathered bushes, the grass beneath them a cropped cushion. 'What do you say?' he called back. 'Will this do?'

Daisy lingered awhile, but then started along the path towards him. With great good fortune, he'd found a rug at the top of his wardrobe and, by the time she reached him, had spread it across the grass and half unpacked the basket.

'So, that's what you've been keeping hidden. It looks delicious.' She plumped down beside him.

'It's meant as a treat. I hope it lives up to its promise.'

'Even if it doesn't, the whole weekend has been a treat.'

'And one you've deserved. Every hour of it.'

'One we've both deserved,' she said. 'Treats are in short supply these days.'

He looked out over the rolling hills and the smooth grassland, to the white-tipped waves in the far distance. 'What do you think life will be like when the war is finally over?' he asked.

'It's anyone's guess.' The corners of her mouth drooped a little.

It *was* anyone's guess how this terrible conflict would end, but you had to believe that right would triumph and life would be good again. 'You're certain to have been made Matron by then.'

Daisy giggled. 'In that case, it's going to be a very long war.'

'I'm afraid it will be, but we'll come through. And you'll be riding high. You've a profession now and there will always be a need for nurses. It's the soldiers that worry me, the men returning from battle. What will they come home to? And the women. How will they feel once the euphoria of peace is over? Right now, they're doing men's work — sweeping the streets, working the buses, staffing the factory floor. Even the ones with small children. But when peace comes? What's the betting, they'll be shooed back into the kitchen, and that will come hard. Hard for the men, too, knowing their wives and sweethearts can do their jobs as well as they.'

She shook her head. 'It's impossible to know how people will feel — we'll be living in a different world. Can we eat now?'

'Sorry, Daisy. You see — I need you to kick me into shape! Stop the dreamy bits from taking over. We certainly can eat. Here—' and he offered her the small plate of sandwiches. 'Ham, I think. Well, more probably Spam.'

She smiled across at him, sandwich in hand. 'Whatever it is, it tastes wonderful.'

'Can't be Spam then. But this *is* a pork pie — shall we share?'

She nodded happily. 'I'm sure it's eating out of doors that makes the food taste so good.'

'It's certainly better than anything we've had so far this weekend.'

'Or it could just be that you bullied the hotel unmercifully to give us the best they had!'

He poured her a glass of wine and they laid propped up on their elbows, nibbling at the few small cakes the chef had packed, and looking out at the scene below them.

'I don't have anything to go for,' she said out of the blue. 'To India, I mean. I never made friends there. Only Jocelyn, and she's living in Assam now. And as for talking to Anish's family, I doubt they'd want to speak to me. Not after what happened to him.'

'They could be persuaded, and it might do you good. You could exorcise some ghosts.'

'I don't need to. The ghosts have gone.'

He was fairly certain they hadn't, but said teasingly, 'Then it must be me that's vanquished them.'

'You're very sure of yourself,' she mocked, plucking one of the long grasses at her side and tickling his nose with it.

He grasped her hand. 'Enough woman! And after my particularly wonderful picnic!'

'Thank you for giving me such a happy memory, Grayson. And for being so patient,' she added, leaning over and kissing him on the cheek.

He'd been determined to keep an iron hold on himself and thought he'd done well, but this was a provocation too far. He reached out and pulled her into his arms. 'Not that patient.'

He hadn't meant to, but in the end he found himself powerless to resist. He kissed her fully on the lips, a long and loving kiss, then silently cursed himself. He'd ruined the day. She would pull away, distressed. But she didn't. Instead, she took his face in her hands and kissed him back.

CHAPTER THIRTY-EIGHT

Their journey back down the hill was slow. They found themselves stopping every few minutes simply to look at each other — it was as though, Daisy thought, neither could quite believe how their picnic had ended. She knew now that Grayson loved her, loved her passionately. His reticence, his apparent indifference, had been a simple desire not to disturb her. But she'd wanted to be disturbed, it seemed. Very much. It was the best of remedies for a conflicted mind and a bruised heart.

Gerald had not been the man she'd thought him, had never been that man. He'd not deserved her help or her sympathy, yet she had given him both. Now he was dead and she must let him go out of her heart and out of her mind. As for Anish, the wound was deeper. But Grayson was right. If she wanted to slay that particular dragon, she must return to India once the war was over. With Grayson by her side, Daisy was sure she could lay to rest the last of her hurt.

They were only yards from the end of the bridleway when they saw the bus disappearing into the distance, but on this golden day nothing bad could happen. When, minutes later, a farmer passed, he offered them a lift in his cart. Sitting side by side on straw bales, they trundled into the centre of Brighton, still smiling, still slightly dazed.

'I wish my mother were here. I'd love to see her face,' Grayson joked, as the cart swung from side to side down the Steine. 'I've a feeling she might be envious of our ride.'

'Really?' From the little she knew of Mrs Harte, Daisy thought it unlikely.

'Yes, really. She's a lot of fun. I hope you'll think so, too.'

She said nothing, the old uncertainty rushing back in force.

'She wants very much to meet you,' he continued. 'She's been nagging me for months to invite you to tea.'

He was trying to make her feel better, Daisy knew, trying to smooth the way for what would be a difficult meeting. If it ever took place.

'I've talked about you. Actually, I've talked a lot about you,' he confessed. 'And it would cheer her enormously to have you visit. She tries to keep busy, but like everyone else the war is getting her down. Her closest friend was killed in last month's raid.'

'I'm sorry.' It was a dutiful murmur.

'So you'll come?'

He was not going to let her fudge. He wanted an answer and he was right. It was time to confront the fears she'd buried deep, fears that were as old as she. They were insidious, eating away at her over the years: the dread of being unworthy, of not knowing who she was, of not being quite good enough. But Grayson loved her and that had to be enough.

The hay wagon drew up outside the front entrance of their hotel, a strange sight even in these strange times. A breeze was blowing from off the sea and Daisy's dark hair tangled in its wake. Battling to secure it beneath a headband, she looked directly into his eyes. 'I'll come,' she said decisively.

He squeezed her hand and helped her down from the cart.

* * *

The bill was paid, the cases collected, and Grayson's parked car stood ready. It was only yesterday morning that Daisy had seen the vehicle waiting for her outside Barts, but since then the world had shifted irrevocably. She was sure now of where she was going and who she wanted with her. Grayson tossed the bags into the boot and held the passenger door open.

'Back to London?' His gaze was warm.

'Back to London,' she repeated.

'But this time, things will be different.' He bent his head to kiss her, uncaring of any passers-by who turned to look.

He didn't start the engine immediately, but laid his arm around her shoulder and pulled her close. 'We belong together,' he said, his face against hers. 'We always have. Since the first moment I saw you on board the *Viceroy*. You were travelling to India to marry another man and, when I learned that, it was a dreadful blow. It didn't stop me wanting you, though.'

She said nothing and he disentangled himself to turn in his seat. Taking both her hands in his, he kissed them finger by finger.

'Do you realise, Daisy, that you were the very first thing in my life that didn't go right for me?'

She reached up, her palm stroking his cheek and coming to rest on his chin. A smile played on her lips.

'Do you realise, Grayson, that you are the very first thing in *my* life that did?'

THE END

THE JOFFE BOOKS STORY

We began in 2014 when Jasper agreed to publish his mum's much-rejected romance novel and it became a bestseller.

Since then we've grown into the largest independent publisher in the UK. We're extremely proud to publish some of the very best writers in the world, including Joy Ellis, Faith Martin, Caro Ramsay, Helen Forrester, Simon Brett and Robert Goddard. Everyone at Joffe Books loves reading and we never forget that it all begins with the magic of an author telling a story.

We are proud to publish talented first-time authors, as well as established writers whose books we love introducing to a new generation of readers.

We won Trade Publisher of the Year at the Independent Publishing Awards in 2023. We have been shortlisted for Independent Publisher of the Year at the British Book Awards for the last four years, and were shortlisted for the Diversity and Inclusivity Award at the 2022 Independent Publishing Awards. In 2023 we were shortlisted for Publisher of the Year at the RNA Industry Awards.

We built this company with your help, and we love to hear from you, so please email us about absolutely anything bookish at: feedback@joffebooks.com.

If you want to receive free books every Friday and hear about all our new releases, join our mailing list: www.joffebooks.com/contact

And when you tell your friends about us, just remember: it's pronounced Joffe as in coffee or toffee!

ALSO BY MERRYN ALLINGHAM

DAISY DRISCOLL SAGAS
Book 1: THE OFFICER'S WIFE
Book 2: THE OFFICER'S NURSE

Printed in Great Britain
by Amazon

62443115R00170